TABL

MW00913999

DEREK

VIOLA

TARAN

ANGELIQUE

DARRION

INTERVIEW

DUKE

ANGELIQUE

RENFRO

DARRION

RENFRO

ANGELIQUE

RENFRO

TARAN

RENFRO

ZANE

TARAN

DARRION

ANGELIQUE

DARRION

EPILOGUE

INTERVIEW

A SNEAK PEEK AT STARFALL: THE LOST APOCALYPSE

CABRINI GREEN VOLUME II:

THE KILLING FIELDS

BY

CHAVOHN NAKIA

&

WARWICK SHACKLEFORD-MASTERS

This is a work of fiction. Names, characters, places,
and incidents are either the product of the author's
imagination
or are used fictitiously, and any resemblance to actual persons,
living or dead, business establishments, events or locales is
entirely coincidental.

Cabrini Green Volume II: The Killing Fields

For more information visit:
www.copyright.gov/

ISBN: 978-0-9890084-9-5

For a sneak peak at all things Cabrini Green visit:

www.chavohnnakia.com

www.facebook.com/nakiamasters

or visit The Non-Blog for news, book signings,

give aways and more at:

starfallseries.com/thenonblog

and follow Nakia & Masters at:

www.twitter.com/nakiamasters

www.twitter.com/chavohnnakia

www.instagram.com/nakiamasters

For my dark and beautiful Chi-Town.
For my family, friends, and all those who believed in me.
They're all for you.

I always knew my sins and the sins of my brothers would come back to haunt me. I now see…Not even the atonement of two lifetimes can undo what we've done...

— Duke DeGrate, *1985.*

PREFACE

Chicago has a long standing history of violence.

From the days of Capone to present day, most cities have a financial district and an affluent district. Like all cities, Cabrini Green was the Windy City's poverty district. Brought on mostly by the tactless failure of the CHA – Chicago Housing Authority.

Inability to enforce policy and procedure, make decisions on design choices and maintenance contracts, forced poor, disadvantaged residents to suffer the blows of managerial ineptitude.

Futher exaserbating matters was the annual budgetary turmoil that left the CHA unable to give the U.S. Department of Housing and Urban Development a clean audit.

The city's Housing Authority became a quagmire and a stark example of how poorly planned policy could wreak havoc on a community's most vulnerable citizens.

Engendered disorder from the unprecedented number of young adults all but pushed out the working class along with the legal monetary means of paying the monthly rent needed to maintain the buildings. Other housing projects such as the Robert Taylor Homes also deteriorated from an equal lack of funding resulting in social unrest and urban war. In Chicago however, Cabrini Green was the most televised.

A plummeting number of residents who aquired honest financial stability left a power vacuum that increased illegal means of survival.

The underworld market of guns, prostitution, and drugs became the order of the day as an economical staple for most of Cabrini's people. Tragic human consequenses followed soon after.

Many became so dependant on this gangland economy often times the lines users stood in to buy their drugs extended from the 4th floor down to the main lobby of the high rises.

Most children in the CHA system found the opportunity for an innocent violent-free upbringing hard to come by. Many of the minds scarred by witnessing destructive acts of violence around them often grew up to repeat the same havoc they feared in their youth.

It became quite trivial for parents to become addicted to hard drugs, allowing the streets to mold and raise their children. But it was during the mid 80's and 90's that Cabrini's innocent would suffer most.

In 1985, nine year old Laketa Crosby was killed while waiting her turn at double dutch. A bullet, meant for a rival gang member, struck Laketa in the head. Her killing marked the 81st homicide in the CHA housing developments since January 1984.

Less than an hour after her death an 18 year old young woman, Jamie Matlock, suffered multiple stab wounds by an unknown assailant.

In 1992 seven year old Dantrell Davis was shot in the head by a warring sniper shooting at a rival gang member. Dantrell was struck down in broad daylight while holding his mother's hand on the way to Jenner Elementary School. His tragic death shocked the nation, prompting the Mayor to close the highrise where the sniper took aim.

In 1997 thirteen year old Shatoya Currie was raped, choked, spray painted with gang signs on her body, and rendered mute. Roach killer was forced down her throat to silence her screams. Shatoya was then taken from the apartment where the assault took place and left for dead in a stairwell. The attack left her blind, mute, and wheelchair bound for life.

Three years later, on the night of New Years Eve, several gang members aimed and fired their weapons in the air to celebrate the new millenium. This brazen show of mayhem was caught on tape by a nearby firestation and shown to the police.

In that same year, plans to demolish the Cabrini Green housing project was announced as part of Hope VI—a new federal program erected to tear down any lawless housing projects across the U.S.

Despite Cabrini's dire conditions, many residents fought against the new redevelopment plans. Those wanting to stay felt their conditions in a familiar area were far better than being relocated to unfamiliar gang territory away from the city's center.

However, their efforts only delayed demolition. Once redevelopment plans resumed, those refusing to move were forced out by eviction and given relocation vouchers.

Demolition lasted for a decade. The last of Cabrini Green was torn down in 2011.

In that same year the CHA publicly announced none of the rowhouses would remain public housing. Instead they would become mixed-income units. This forced many residents to move because the low-income vouchers the CHA provided made newly renovated units unaffordable.

In the spring of 2013, former Cabrini lowrise residents sued the CHA, claiming pledges to return them to their neighborhood, after redevelopment, were not kept. After filing the lawsuit in Federal court, the Cabrini Green Local Advisory Counsil found that only a small portion of renovated homes were set aside for public housing. Any of the remaining residents had been relocated to other areas such as Wentworth Gardens and the Dearborn Homes on the southside.

According to the residents, the CHA promised more than 400 units for public housing, but the construction was never put underway.

Many believed the CHA turned Cabrini Green, the Robert Taylor Homes, and other public housing into hazardous acloves far more debilitating than the slums they were meant to replace. To the poor, the CHA was nothing more than the worst urban policy failure in United States history.

PROLOGUE

Bishop shook his head.

"Are we really doing all of these interviews again?" he asked. "What's the point in shoveling the same shit?"

Renfro shrugged and looked around the bank manager's office. "Look on the upside. We used to have to sift through that shit with our own hands. At least now the department can afford a shovel."

A few simple plants were on the desk. Several paintings of Border Collies hung about the walls. Pictures of the manager's children were next to the telephone. Renfro didn't notice a blonde girl. She was no where in them. Just three boys and who he assumed was Mr. Slidell.

When the door opened, a short balding man in a navy blue suit introduced himself as Mr. Burt Weiser. He took a seat behind the desk.

When he spoke good morning. Renfro couldn't help but notice the effeminate tone in his voice.

Renfro took a seat next to Bishop and set to sorting through the confusion. "I'm sorry, Mr. Weiser, I thought we would be meeting with Mr. Slidell today. Is he not in, or..."

"Oh, he put his two week in about two months ago, I think. His wife just wouldn't abide by his working here any more. Two robberies and then his poor little girl being kidnapped. It was just too much." He scratched his balding head and exhaled. "I always wanted a promotion, but...not under these circumstances. And

I

he's not the only one who jumped ship. After we got hit the first time, nearly half of our clerks quit. It's been even more of a staffing issue since the second robbery. Getting someone to work here now is like asking them to walk in procession at their own funeral."

Renfro nodded. "I understand."

"Would you like his home phone? He told me that if the police had anymore questions, he wouldn't mind cooperating."

"We already have it," Bishop said. "We'll contact him and set up an interview. Thank you."

"You're quite welcome. Well, you can ask away. I'll try to answer with everything I can remember. I don't know if it's because it's been three months or because the trauma just forces the mind to block it out, but some of it's a bit hazy."

Bishop nodded. "We're visual investigators. We like to interview where everything took place. Would you mind giving us a walk through of the lobby?"

Mr. Weiser stood straightaway. "Oh sure, absolutely! Now would be the perfect time. We don't open for another 45 minutes. So, everyone here is bank employees."

The detectives followed him out to the lobby area. Bishop pulled out a notepad and pen then flipped to the first empty page. "What kind of security system do you have here?"

"Well, it's a quite complex one actually. Which is why I was so shocked when we got hit the first time and then again. We just went international six months ago, so we upgraded to a closed circuit surveillance system with an integrated motion detector for the vault. And that's tripped by putting a silent alarm code into the vault's combination lock."

Bishop began taking notes. "Okay. Tell me exactly how the robbery took place. Anything you can remember."

Mr. Weiser told the detectives everything he'd witnessed. He even went into detail about the shots fired and the injury one of the thieves received in the shoulder by his former security guard. As he talked, Renfro looked around the lobby, trying to picture every word as if the robbery were happening in real time. His inward visualization prompted more questions.

"For your security system," he asked, "how is the circuitry set?"

"Hardwired, to my knowledge. Each and every motion sensor is physically connected to the control unit. Every single one. I just don't understand how they waltzed right into the vault like that." Mr. Weiser leaned forward as if he was about to expose something clandestine. "And there was this awful, brutal man. He must have been the leader. He knew Mr. Slidell was about to trip the alarm combination on the vault. He knew! This is the Panther II Electromagnetic Alarm System! We paid nearly $80,000 for it."

"Do you have a third party vendor?"

Mr. Weiser blinked at Bishop, thinking. Then, "Oh yes, Universal Systems Technology, I believe it is."

"Is there a local office here in Northbrook?" Renfro asked.

"No. But there is one in Chicago. Downtown. Not far from the Federal Reserve Bank on LaSalle and Jackson ." He watched the detectives quickly jotting down notes. His brow lifted. "Is there something going on with our vendor that I should be worried about?"

"Well, we're just looking into all possible angles at this point. When it comes to the robbery of a financial institution, there are three main key factors we look for. Why the bank was profiled, the out used for escape, and both of those factors tell us what we really need to know—whether we're dealing with amateurs or professionals."

Mr. Weisner's eyes grew wide. "Which one do you think we got hit with?"

"We're not completely certain," Bishop said. "That depends on finding answers to the first two factors. Let's start with why the bank was profiled. Your institution got hit on a Friday. That is the worst day for banks and it's the best day for bank robbers because it's pay day for most tax paying citizens. But in your case, this Bank and Trust was especially crowded because the branch on the other side of town was closed due to a power outage. That forced nearly every patron, with transactions to make, over to the main branch here as soon as they got off from work. So the amount of cash you had in your vault was nearly triple what it usually is on a Friday evening.

"Also, you just told us you've had a staffing problem. So, you weren't even properly manned to handle a robbery. I'm sure the men who took your vault already knew that. I can't say for certain, but from what you've told us so far, this is probably the work of a group who's been doing this for a while now. We'll keep you posted on anything new we find."

III

Mr. Weisner nodded. "I'd greatly appreciate that."

Both detectives handed him their card. "In case you think of anything else."

"Oh absolutely, thank you."

The detectives neared the doors and the manager followed. "Do you have any suspects yet?"

Bishop nodded. "Two of the men who took your vault are dead, Mr. Weiser. But the men who robbed your bank, we think they're very much alive."

Mr. Weiser blinked. Confused. "I'm sorry, you lost me."

"We think the men who stormed your lobby were just decoys," Renfro said. "The real thieves, you never saw their faces. Which means they're not just hardened crooks here. A skilled robbery organization is probably what we're dealing with."

♛

Angelique motioned to the back wall of her office.

"You can put the boxes in the corner over there."

Old Man Freeman hobbled to the corner and placed them on the bottom shelf of the bookcase. He looked at them quizically as if debating whether or not to peer inside. He was a curious old man, Angelique knew. Always looking about the office. Nosing through her desk drawers. Opening up cabinets and such. Asking about everything he saw.

She didn't mind. Though Anton had warned her of his needy light fingers. As rumor had it, Old Cassius Freeman was quite the thief in his heyday. Yet she had nothing in the new clinic worth stealing except the medications she kept locked in the auto-dispensing cabinet.

In less than a week, the health clinic would be open to every Near North family. Dr. James felt grateful the clinic sat on Halsted, the most northern border of the projects. Mr. Freeman must have also known the location for safety mattered to her. More often than not, the closer you were north, the easier it became to get to safety. Everyone in Chicago knew the safety streets and if you lived on the wealthy northside, you didn't cross them. Ever. Usually, the further south you were the worse things got.

Nonetheless, Angelique was excited like a child with her first toy. But Dr. James warred with her nerves.

So far, the Scott Joplin Gratis program was a success. Every investor interested in Derek Porter's political career had kept their word. With the money flowing in for supplies and medications, treatments and follow ups would go smoother than she thought possible. But there was the recent problem with security. The rape had left her feeling uneasy and quite nervous in Cabrini most days.

Hiring some of Derek's men from Executive Protection did ease some of the worry. But his men did not know the highrises like she did. Nor did they know snipers walked the rooftops of every building until the first morning they arrived. Now she had to fire them.

Darrion DeGrate had ordered her to. Ordered! Like she was some underling on his pay roll. There was no arguing the matter. Turkell, Casper and Taran would stay close. They were nearly brothers to Darrion. He trusted them with her life. In truth she was an outsider from Northbrook and Cabrini was a jungle. Angelique had barely learned it's trees, let alone the animals that lurked in them.

"What's this?" Old Man Freeman asked.

Dr. James blinked up from her errant thoughts. "What?"

He was holding a small white zip bag. "Is this a make-up bag or somethiing?"

"No. It's a clean kit."

"What's that?"

"It's a bag of supplies for hypes. A few alcohol pads. Bleach kit. Cotton balls. Two condoms. A clean spoon. A small sterile water vial, and a lighter. Some come with hypodermic needles. Some don't."

"Well you just feeding the beast ain't you? Why give 'em shoes to dance with the devil?"

Dr. James leaned back in her chair and exhaled.

"What would you have me do, Mr. Freeman? Do you know how many uncapped hypos I see lying on the ground around here? I can't count how many I've crunched under my shoes. And I'm grateful for the ones I do step on because if they're not crushed, someone's finding it and putting it in their arm. They're going to keep spiking a vein regardless. If we can't stop the dope that's floating in here, at least we can try to stop them from spreading infectious diseases and having babies they're too strung out to take care of."

Mr. Freeman looked at the kit in his hand and walked to the window. He was quiet for a long moment before he spoke.

"It wasn't always like this, Doc. Back in the day, when Duke and his father ran the Housing Authority, Cabrini Green was a treasure. When you said you lived here, you said it with a smile. But, see, Duke made sure people took care of the buildings and if you didn't pay the rent on time, you got evicted. You had to go. And that didn't happen too often because it was the parents...the adults that had these units. It wasn't none of this teenage mess running around here with apartments in they own names.

"Back then, if a young girl had a baby, she lived with her mother and father. The young girl didn't get the welfare check if she was underage. Her parents got the check, so she had no choice but to stay up under their roof and abide by their rules. But then, the welfare law up and changed. Now, if you got a baby, even if you're under age, you get your own check for that child. Then, around that time, Duke's father had passed. He had had it with this place. He couldn't take it no more. He left. Then Luke Garrett took over. And he set it up to where, if you were getting your own check then you could get your own apartment. So then, you got all these young girls with these babies who got their own money, now they can get their own place. Now they parents can't tell them shit. Cause they grown. They got all the answers.

"Now, you got these young boys running in and out of their apartment, all hours of the night. Smoking, drinking, whatever they like. And these girls think...well, he laying with me, he must love me. Then they end up having more babies. Some of the fathers, they take care of their own. Some don't. Cause they ain't got time for this young girl and all these babies pulling on her. Not when they got other young honeys around the way. And it's about to get even worse, Doc. Now, the government is gonna increase welfare for these mothers having more babies, but the fathers can't be in the home. And Social Services is coming by to make sure the daddy is gone and complying with the rules. So you got the government enforcing broken homes."

Mr. Freeman exhaled and turned from the window. A ray of midday sun broke through a cluster of winter clouds then. A slight downcast glow lightened his dark, leathered skin. His bleak expression brightened just then. Almost nearing a look of optimism. "But it's still some good left here though. There's uh...Ms. Lillian White, she runs uh...the Community Outreach Program. And there's Jesse Davis. He coach little league baseball and teaches tumbling and such. And Coach Nokes over at Near North High, he runs Track and Field. They the best in the state. Ask Darrion about it, he'll tell you. We ain't all lost, Doc. Not yet."

Dr. James flinched when Hal appeared in the doorway. Private security made her nervous. It was different with Darrion and Turkell. They were more relaxed, yet ready.

Though Hal was confident and well composed as the lead of his four man team, he seemed more on edge than what she was used to. Dr. James assumed it had to do with the obvious. A white team of security guards in a hazardous black neighborhood would unnerve most assigned to the task. Even the comfort of knowing some whites worked in Cabrini Green as legitimate business owners didn't ease their apprehension. Business owners got to go home before night hours hit—and that was if they had to come to their establishments at all to check on things. Most caucasians, who were smart enough, sent their assistant managers to keep tabs on day to day operations while they worked from home and relaxed in their condominiums.

"There's a kid at the door," Hal said.

"A kid?" she asked. "Who's kid?"

"Don't know. He's by himself. Do I let him in?"

"Is he armed?"

Hal shook his head. "We patted him down. He's clean."

She nodded. "Let him in, I'll be right there."

Dr. James reached in her desk drawer, pulled out her gun holster, and slipped it on. A thought to how paranoid she had become ran through her mind. But going anywhere near a glass door made her vulnerable to sniper fire from an adjacent building. A risk she wasn't willing to take.

Mr. Freeman's hastened limp followed close behind as she walked to the front lobby and set eyes on a small boy at the door. She gave a nod to one of the guards who promptly let him in.

Unless her eyes were being cheated the youngling couldn't have been older than seven or eight, plus one. Dark blue jeans. A red ball top winter knitted cap covered his head. Blue and red striped mittens warmed both hands and the dark blue coat nearly swallowed his tiny frame.

Huge brown eyes blinked up at her but he said nothing. Dr. James knew this one was waiting for her to speak. Children often did that. Maybe it was the white coat that meant they were going to get a shot or a mouthful of bad tasting medicine. Maybe they were just afraid of unfamiliars.

She used her small simple voice, "Hi, are you okay?"

He shook his head. "My friend needs help."

"Okay, what's wrong with your friend?"

"She won't wake up."

"Do you know where she is?"

He nodded.

"Okay, can you take me to her?"

Another nod.

She gave a quick glance to the guards. "What's your name, sweeheart?"

"Sammy."

"Sammy, these men are going to come with us, okay?"

He nodded. Dr. James walked back to her office and Mr. Freeman followed close behind. "Do you recognize that boy?"

"Mmm-hmm," he said. "That's one of Capricia's little boys."

"Capricia," she said to herself. That name didn't ring a bell. "Is she a resident?"

Old Man Freeman nodded.

"I'm going to go with them to see about this. Would you mind watching the clinic for me?"

"Oh, no, I don't mind none."

"I shouldn't be gone long." She pulled a set of keys from her pocket. "These are the keys to every door in the clinic."

"I know," he said. "This was my daughter's day care center, remember?"

"Right, I'm sorry." Dr. James felt dim witted for forgetting. He had donated the building to help with the gratis program. Though his daughter was long dead, he often talked about her as if she still lived. For that, Dr. James thought it was only right to name it the Freeman Health Clinic. She decided not to tell him.

Just the look on his face alone during opening day would prove priceless and well worth the surprise.

"That's okay," he said.

She thanked him, handed him the keys and walked back to the front lobby. A pair of wide eyes still looked up at her expectantly.

"Sammy, I'm going to follow you. This is Hal. He's my head of security and these men are going to follow too. Is that okay?"

Sammy nodded and led the way.

♛

Her face was destroyed. Hideous and gruesome. One eye was swollen shut and the other was encrusted with some white thick powdery substance. At first glance, the little girl was not dead, but she was dying fast. Wheezing blood out of a broken nose.

Angelique was horror-struck.

But Dr. James was medically absorbed.

She couldn't have been more than seven or eight years old. Her attacker must have outweighed her by at least one hundred pounds. Obvious signs of sexual assault stained her legs. Some blackhearted pedophile had dumped her here. Left her lying at the bottom of a stairwell for the rats to find.

She barely looked alive. Her clothes had been striped from her and the sick twist took the time to leave his tell. Graffiti marked every inch of her that wasn't covered in blood.

Dr. James suppressed the urge to cover her nose when the hard gust of wind blew the raw, dank smell of poison and urine to her nostrils.

When the wind died down she just stood there until the broken body disappeared and all that remained were red angles and curves of what used to be a little girl.

Someone's little girl.

Surely she had a mother or father.

Dr. James pulled off her medical coat and laid it over her then looked about the stairwell. Wondering how to hoist her tiny frame up the stairs without making agony of injuries that had probably settled to throbbing — or breaking bones that were only cracked.

Hal cursed. It was safe to assume he had never seen such a gut-wrenching sight. He was no more used to it than she was.

Dr. James had almost forgotten Sammy. But he was in fact standing there. Waiting for her to do something. To save his friend.

"Do you live far from here?" she asked.

"No." He pointed up the stairs. "Just up there."

"Okay," she said, exhaling a puff of cold vapor. "Do you have a long skateboard, maybe?"

Sammy shook his head.

"Um...a few cardboard boxes and some tape?"

He shook his head.

"An ironing board?"

He nodded and was up the stairs in a flash. Dr. James gave a nod to Hal. "Go with him. And bring back a blanket if you can."

Hal made up the stairs and gave orders to another guard who quickly rushed down the stairs and took his place.

Dr. James knelt down by her side. It seemed wrong forcing what came out of her mouth next. But it was a doctor's ethics to speak comfort. Even if it was a flat out lie. "You're going to be okay, sweetheart. Just hold on."

Sammy didn't take long. Less than a minute later they returned with the ironing board and a quilt. Dr. James laid the quilt over the little girl then took the ironing board and laid it on the ground. "Okay," she said to the guards. "I'm going to need some help. One of you slide your hands under her torso very, very gently. The other hold her legs and I'm going to hold her neck and shoulders to stabilize her spine. Sammy, you're going to take the ironing board and slide it under her when we roll her to me. Everyone with me?"

They all gave a nod.

"Okay, let's move."

♛

"Who does this to a child?" Dr. James said to herself.

She had carried her with one of the guards back to the clinic and put her on the examination table, ironing board and all, then started an IV and put her on a saline drip to replace some of the

X

fluids she'd lost. But Dr. James knew a bag of sodium chloride was far from enough to treat her.

A closer look at her body revealed more than cuts and abrasions turning to bruises. Her pelvis looked deformed. Not misshapen. But it was as if her hips protruded a little more outward than a child's should. From an anatomical standpoint Dr. James knew the obvious.

Both hips were dislocated.

Worse over, her right ankle was obviously fractured.

Waiting for an ambulance would only cause the joints to swell until putting her hips back in place stood next to impossible without putting her out.

Then again, if she put them back in now, she would have had to put the little girl to sleep. But the swelling and the pain afterwards would be much less. With any dislocation the faster the reduction, the lesser the healing time and joint damage.

Dr. James cursed.

"What's wrong?" Mr. Freeman asked.

"Both hips are dislocated. I'm going to need some help."

"I don't know nothing about fixing nothing like that."

"You're not going to...I am. What I'm going to need is for you to apply some reverse pressure to her shoulders while I push her hips back into place. I'm going to have to put her out first."

She went to Ophelia and told the little girl everything that she was about to do.

To their surprise, she began to cry.

She wasn't unconscious. Just scared.

That was a good thing. At least she was alert enough to know what was being said and her brain function was good enough to pull a response. Even if it was a frightened, terrified one.

Dr. James moved quickly.

She pulled the propofol out of the locked dispensery, then administered a pediatric dose and waited for her to sleep. It didn't take long. Seconds later, little Ophelia was unconscious.

A quick glance to her vital signs on the monitor — satisfied that they were holding steady — and Dr. James went to work.

She directed Mr. Freeman to put a hand on both of Ophelia's shoulders. Then she started with the right hip. Feeling with her fingers for the exact direction of the dislocation. Then she felt down the little girl's leg, making sure her femur and tib-fib didn't bear any obvious fractures before she proceeded. From the quick inspection, nothing else seemed broken.

"Okay, Mr. Freeman, here we go. Apply pressure on the count of three." Dr. James lifted Ophelia's leg and counted. Then as Mr. Freeman pushed down, she pushed inward toward's the little girl's pelvis and gave a hard shove upward. A slight popping sound and Ophelia's hip slipped back into place. Dr. James quickly moved to her other side of the ironing board, gave another three count to Mr. Freeman and did the same to the left hip. She bent both legs, making sure the motility was fluid, then spent the next five minutes monitoring vital signs and cleaning up her pile of used accouterments and paraphernalia.

Once she had gotten some of the blood suctioned out of the little girl's mouth, she charged Mr. Freeman with watching vital signs. Again, he quickly voiced his inexperience.

"I don't know what to watch for," he said. "I ain't never seen nothing like this. Except on TV and when I go for my doctor visits. And even then I don't pay attention. I just listen for the nurse to tell me if my blood pressure's good or bad."

"It's not hard to monitor vitals on a child. Just watch for the numbers to remain steady." Dr. James reached for a dry erase pen in the drawer near the sink, went to the white board on the wall by the door, and wrote as fast as she talked. "It's the same blood pressure for an adult. If she drops below 108 over 70 let me know. If she goes above 125 over 80 let me know. If her pulse drops below 70 let me know. And if her oxygen saturations drop below 90 percent, definitely let me know."

Old Man Freeman looked at the numbers on the board then glanced over at the monitor. He nodded as if it all clicked and made sense. "Got it, Doc."

"Thank you. I'm going to my office to call an ambulance and the police. I'll be right back."

He gave a glance to all of the blood and old semen crusted on Ophelia's legs. "You ain't gonna clean her up no more than that?"

"If I do, it'll just wash away evidence. She's going to need a rape kit done."

"You don't keep those here?"

No but I should.

Dr. James shook her head.

"Maybe you should," he suggested.

"Maybe you're right."

Old Cassius looked at the little girl once more. Lying there unconscious and said, "Is she gonna make it?"

That paused her at the door. His question drew bleak answers. If the girl did live she would be scarred for the rest of her life. People would laugh at her. Whisper as she walked by...limped by. That was if she could even stand at all.

Initial surgeries to repair her face was just the beginning. There would be orthopedic surgeries to correct the fractures that were even considered to be operable and the breaks that weren't would be left to heal as is. Then plastic surgery to repair what was left of her face. Not to mention numerous surgeries to repair any nerve and tissue damage. All of that would be just so she could function. But would she make it? In life?

Succeed? Blossom? Thrive? Have children?

Angelique hoped she would. But Dr. James knew better. Her life was over the second she met the wrong monster in the wrong breezeway.

She glanced at the battered body on the examination table. From the doorway, she looked to still be unconscious. Dr. James hoped she couldn't hear them speaking about her marred future.

"I don't know," she said in a near whisper. "I honestly don't know. But...Probably not." She checked her watch. It had been thirty minutes since they'd made it back to the clinic. She had had Mr. Freeman call Anton. Perhaps she hadn't heard the phone ring.

"Ant still hasn't called back yet."

Mr. Freeman shook his head.

She exhaled frustration. "I don't want to send the cops his way without giving the Disciples a heads up but...he's not giving me much choice here. In her condition, she needs a CAT-Scan of her head and x-rays. I can't wait much longer."

"You know Calvin's number?"

She shook her head.

Mr. Freeman gave it to her and, with that, she walked out of the treatment room and went to her office. As soon as she picked up the phone, the sound of the lobby front door opening paused her from dialing the number. "Hal?" she said.

Within seconds, he appeared in the doorway. "I have somebody named Ant here? He says you tried to call him?"

She nodded. "He's okay, you can send him back."

Moments later, Anton Smith walked into Dr. James' office.

Just to look at him reminded her of the last time they were in the same room together.

Like Ophelia, Angelique had been beaten. Raped by men she assumed to be Zane's hoods. Left for dead in an abandoned apartment. One of them threatened if Darrion didn't pull out of Cabrini they would kill her. Anton had rescued her after Sammy called on him for help. Angelique knew if Zane found out that Anton had helped her, any loyal ties he had to the Disciples would end. That would bring jeopardy and turmoil to him and his family. Now it dawned on her why the little boy showed up at the clinic for Ophelia. Just as he had found her, he found Angelique unconscious while riding his bike through the lowrises. Unfortunately Sammy seemed to be all too well learned at finding bloody victims in the projects. Anton as well.

Ant pulled off his gloves and unzipped his Bulls jacket. "What's going on? Is everything okay?"

"No, everything's not okay. I have a little girl in the back. Her face is smashed in. I'm pretty sure some someone raped her."

Anton cursed. "Who is it?"

"Her name's Ophelia, according to Sammy." She watched the recognition wash over his face. "You know her?"

Anton nodded. "Yeah. That's Pernell's niece."

"Is he a Disciple?"

Another nod.

"Does he know she's missing?"

"Don't know. He works the night shift at Jewels."

"The grocery store?"

"Yeah. If he got off at seven in the morning or sometime around then, he's probably sleep, unless he stayed to work overtime or something."

"Does he usually do that?"

Anton Smith shook his head. "Don't know."

"Well, I need to get ahold of someone she's kin to. Preferably before I send her to the hospital."

"Jesus Christ." He smoothed a hand over his head. Then, "Is she okay?"

"No, she's not okay. And she can't be moved in anything but an ambulance." Dr. James paused. Thinking of the best way to say what came out of her mouth next. There seemed to be no way to soften the blow, so she told him straight. "I'm calling for emergency response. And I'm calling the police."

Anton shook his head. "Doc, I really don't think you sh—"

"Because of what you did for me that night, knowing what you risked to do what you did, I'm obligated to give you fair warning before I pick up that phone. And I know that goes against the code. But this is a little girl here, Ant. It's wrong."

"I know that! And the Disciples will mete it out themselves! That's what we do! That's how it's done! No matter what happens, no matter how drastic, if it happened with us, we keep it between us! You want to call an ambulance, fine. Hopefully they won't get shot at. But you don't involve the police. Period. That's our law."

"Your law is shit when it fails to protect the innocent!"

She picked up the phone.

Anton reached over a stack of medical files and put a hand to the receiver. Blocking her from making the call. "You better think about what you're doing before you dial that number, Doc. You do this, and the repercussions will make what happened to you in the Lows feel like a massage."

Anton's caution meant nothing at this point. Every thought in her head went to the crippled little girl lying on bloody sheets. Every thought trumped his need to keep a rapist at large and unchecked with no retribution. Still, she sensed a hint of a warning in his voice and she didn't like it.

"Are you threatening me?"

"I don't have to. Zane already made that move. Now, put down the phone."

That came out as a cheap shot. One hell of a desperate-Hail-Mary-at the 50 yard line with a nanosecond left on the clock. But she took it.

"Take your hand away."

"Don't do this, Doc. Please."

"They left her in a stairwell, Ant. They tossed her down the stairs like a used up dishrag and left her to die. But not before they pulled her legs so far apart, both hips dislocated while they raped her. Even with surgical intervention, she'll probably never have a life that's worth shit! There is no telling how many hours she laid there, in pain, bleeding out in the cold and in the dark! And you expect me to just sit smiling by, so you and your boys can stick to some fucking G-code? Zane won't give a shit about finding out who did it. He won't care!" She paused then and for the briefest moment, Darrion came to mind. He hated Zane even more than she did. "But I know somebody who will. Now, move your hand!"

When his hand didn't budge, Dr. James smacked it away and lifted the phone from the receiver. Anton cursed, turned away, put his hands on his head in frustration. He must have known his plea would be useless. So why did he even bother? She owed him fair warning and Dr. James made it a point to pay what she owed. Other than that, he had nothing else coming. She pressed the phone to her med-coat.

"You're a look out, right?"

Anton exhaled again. "Sometimes, yeah."

"This is Cabrini, I thought that was always. Zane would be stupid not to have you watching me."

Anton said nothing at first. Then, "Pretty much."

"Well, I'm giving you one hell of an advanced notice. Go make sure you're looking out. The cops are coming. And you're in deep shit with Zane if somebody gets arrested on your watch. So you better run."

Dr. James put the phone to her ear and dialed 911.

Anton cursed and dashed out the door.

"911 what's your emergency?"

"Yes, I'd like to report the sexual assault of a little girl and I need an ambulance at the new health clinic on Halsted."

"Halsted where, ma'am?"

"Cabrini Green."

INTERVIEW

Capricia Mossgrove fidgeted nervously in her chair.

Zella Rice could tell the stocky young mother of two did not like the camera.

Capricia was a stylish woman.

Dangling gold earrings, glossed lips, and a dash of fuchsia-tinted hair accented her short styled crop. She was quiet for a brief moment before she answered the question. It must have been a touchy matter for her, the subject of children.

"There were a lot of reasons why the percentage of high school graduates was low in the Near North. There's a reason they weren't prepared for pre-college courses and prepatory schools and all that. We had more important lessons to teach our kids. Like how to dodge bullets and what streets to walk on. Which people to stay away from on your own block or in your own building. How to dodge the police... 'Cause even if you weren't guilty they were questioning you about who was. You know? We were teaching our kids how to survive. Back in the mid-80's and on up 'til now. It's still bad in Cabrini. I was just one of the more fortunate mothers to make it out. And to make it out without burying any of my kids in the process was a blessing. Believe me. I know plenty of mothers and grandmothers who were not so fortunate."

"How did you make it out?"

"I went back to school. Worked part time at Mark Graff & Associates and got my education and became a nurse. Now, I work at Chicago Memorial. It's nice. I'm making almost thirty dollars an hour. When I got my first paycheck, I cried. I had never seen so much money before. Not with my name on it. Everything has changed. Where I live. What school my babies go to. We all gave excellent insurance. Life is good. Real good. I used to work at Scott Joplin for a little while too."

"Yes that's right. You know Dr. James. I understand you two are very close."

Capricia nodded. "That's my sister right there. At first, I thought she was just like the Mayor. Just another stuck up rich woman from the Northside who was all about votes. And really didn't care about our problems. But as it turned out, she cared. More than I thought she did. And she showed it. Many times over."

"How?"

"She was very hands on. Stopping by all of the apartments and surveyed all of the damage. Her and Darrion did. They got the electricity and the pipes working again. She started the Tenants Association to raise money for a housing lawyer to go after the Chicago Housing Authority. And I'll never forget the time she pulled up to Cabrini with 20 limosines and took all the kids to the opera. It was the best night of my life while I was living in the projects. I saw a whole new life that I never knew existed. My oldest saw it too. It wasn't just some Italians blowing your ear drums out in a language you couldn't even understand. It was a children's opera. Something new that the performing arts school was doing. Sammy was about 10 I think. And he wanted to do theater, but there were no opportunities for him in the Near North other than the school's drama class. But there was no inspiration for him to pursue it beyond that. That night changed all of that. He had stars in his eyes the whole time." She went quiet, smiling. Then her eyes lowered to the floor and the smile faded. "That night ended in bloodshed. Poor Duke. But that's another story in itself right there. But it was nice though. While it lasted."

"We'll come back to that shooting later. That's definitely something we want to touch basis on. But for now, since you just told me what your best memory was, tell me, what was the most trying time for you in Cabrini."

"The time Angie got kidnapped."

Zella nodded, remembering. "That is hard to forget. Those were definitely the shots heard around the world."

"It was just awful."

"Some say it happened because the doctor was interfering with the drug lord's criminal enterprise. Others say it had to do with Darrion DeGrate's return to Cabrini and his family's history with the Harris family ignited a domino effect that ultimately fell back on Dr. James. What happened? What started it all?"

Capricia's eyes changed then. Her gaze dropped from Zella and fell on nothing. As if she had slipped into a blank gaze filled with a distant grief. When she spoke, the words came almost sad. Detached from the happiness her voice carried only seconds ago.

"A little girl...a little girl named Ophelia."

RENFRO

Renfro and Bishop walked the open field where the thieves had been found. Both men listened while Sheriff Walls talked.

Though Renfro didn't like gab in his ear while trying to think, it seemed only polite. Bishop thumbed through the very pictures taken when the three culprits were discovered by Walls and Deputy Carls. So, if it weren't for them working the case as far as they had, there would have been no photographic evidence at all.

"We found them lying right here," Sheriff Walls said. "Just never made any goddamn sense. When they woke, they couldn't remember a damn thing. Nothing. No names, no faces, except for the men they were with right before the robbery took place. But the other two were gone. So, I think it's pretty obvious they got set up. The other two must have put 'em out, took the money and torched the van, then split."

"Who found the van?" Bishop asked.

"A couple of bums walking the area spotted it first. They heard the explosion. But it was one of the residents in an apartment about a mile from here who made the call. Said she could see the smoke from her living room window."

Renfro crouched low to get a better look at the grass and soil. His eyes skimmed over where the thieves had fallen as if every blade had it's own story to tell. Five men had stormed the bank. Only three were left behind to remember absolutely nothing. Sheriff Walls had nothing surprising. It didn't take much thinking to realize those men were set up to fail. A closer look and Renfro spotted a brownish tinge to otherwise green land.

"Bishop."

His partner stepped closer. "Did you find something?"

"Maybe." Renfro pointed to the discolored blades. "I could be wrong. But that doesn't look like sun burnt grass."

Bishop agreed. "Especially in the middle of winter."

"I'd even go as far as to say that looks like blood to me."

"I'd go as far as agreeing with you."

Renfro shook his head. Not believing it. "I think this heist went bad in the blink of an eye."

"Knife play, gun play?"

Renfro pulled a small flash light from the inside pocket of his suit jacket and skimmed over the grass. He paused the light when he spotted more old brown speckles. Searching further, he spotted a wide dark stain. Then he knew.

"Son of a bitch," Bishop whispered.

"To look at the spray pattern here, and this old puddle of blood, gun play would definitely be my educated guess."

Bishop thumbed through the photos until he found the image matching the blood stain and pointed with his pen. "That looks like either old clots or decayed brains there."

Both the Sheriff and the Deputy stepped closer for a better look.

"I'll be damned," Walls said.

Renfro waved the light over more grassland until he spotted a second old, dried, dark pool of blood. "Looks like we found our fifth man, right here."

Bishop looked at Sheriff Walls and said, "There goes your theory, Sheriff." He flipped through the photos until he found a match to the second stain and skimmed over the grass. "What are the odds, they left the shells behind? I wonder."

"Slim to none," Renfro answered. "And even if they did, it won't matter. They'd know to dump the weapons. If this crew is as good as I think they are."

"We might be able to pull a print or two from the brass. Run 'em for a match."

"I think our real crew is too good for any priors. Yet."

"If they're as good as we think they are, you're probably right."

"As good as you think?" Deputy Carls asked, staring down at the old dried blood. He looked at Renfro. "How good do you think they are?"

"Good enough to use a mock crew to do their dirty work for them," Bishop answered.

"I'm guessing," Renfro added with a nod to the bloody grass, "when their set-up crew found out they were finger-puppets, they didn't like it."

"Mock crew?" Carls looked as if he had never heard such a thing. "Care to elaborate, detective?"

Renfro shook his head. "No. Not really."

Bishop let out a chuckle and went back to the photos.

Northbrook's Sheriff did not look pleased with his answer. Walls' dark thick eyebrows tented with irritation to an angry "V" and his fat jowls tensed with resentment. He pulled up the belt holding his round belly as if the jesture of crossness would intimidate him. Renfro couldn't have cared less. Detectives elaborating on their investigations always seemed to lead to more leaks than the Titanic. Until the informers from within the department were flushed out, Renfro and Bishop were taking no chances. It didn't matter if they were onto a most wanted kingpin or a little old lady's missing shoe. Discussing their cases with anyone Renfro didn't know or trust could jeopardize any investigation before they even came close to an arrest worthy of the man hours. He wouldn't abide the risk.

"I think now would be a good time to test that new technology the lieutenant was boasting about in that task force meeting."

Bishop looked skeptical. "You don't think that really works do you?"

"It's 1985. All of this DNA mess is new to me. I don't know. Only one way to find out though." He gave a glance to their sedan parked in the distance. "Do we have any black tops in the car?"

"Yeah, I think we do. But you know what forensics is going to say."

"Unsuitable reference sample, yeah I know. But it's better than nothing. We don't have a body and a fresh puddle here. Filling up tubes is not an option. So they'll have to take whatever we can get. They got all new administration last week, so forensics is probably cracking down on favors under the table. If they decide to kick it back to us, we'll just send it to the crime lab instead."

"How many jars do we want?"

"Enough for the grass and if you can, bring the largest one we've got to collect the soil here."

"Alright." Bishop jogged across the field to the sedan.

"I'd say the odds of finding the bodies are slim to none."

"My wife's a psychic," Walls said. "Since this case is now linked to the gang task force, maybe you could employ her services."

Renfro squinted at a fleck of something that looked to be more than a clump of coagulation. He pulled a ball-point pen from his jacket and nudged it. It seemed hard. Rigid. A few taps at it gave a dull clicking sound.

It took less than a mintue for Bishop to return with the collection jars.

"I brought the kit, three smalls and one wide mouth." He adjusted his bifocals and stared down at what Renfro seemed to be engrossed with. "What is that?"

"Bone."

Bishop bent at the waist to get a closer look. "Are you sure?"

"I know what bone sounds like when you give it a tap." He reached up for the kit and grabbed the wide mouth. "It's bone. I'd bet my life on it." Renfro pulled a pair of gloves from the kit, slipped them on, and grabbed a set of tweezers then carefully picked up the shard from the ground and held it up for closer inspection under the flashlight.

One good look was all it took. Bishop nodded in agreement.

"That is definitely bone."

"Bone from what?" the Sheriff asked.

"Skull, I'd bet."

Renfro carefully placed it into the jar and screwed on the lid. Then he handed it to Bishop, took the three smaller jars and began filling them with bloodied grass and tainted soil.

"So we got three robbers with no memory," Bishop reiterated, "two bodies, which would make our five-man puppet crew, and a torched van."

Renfro nodded.

"So if I'm the real thief and I just robbed the crew who thought they were, what's my out?" Bishop gave a glance to the nearest four way stop. It sat adjacent to the open field with no intersecting streets in sight. "Where's the nearest on ramp to the freeway, Sheriff?"

"Off of Wakeegee," Walls answered. "About ten minutes from here."

"If I had two bodies on me, from a robbery I just commited, I wouldn't take ten mintues to get to a freeway." Bishop glanced down at his partner. "Would you?"

Renfro shook his head. "Nope."

"I think we got more brain here!" Deputy Carls said, staring down at a dark patch of grass not five paces from his boots.

"What's the description of the height of the robbers?" Bishop asked the Sheriff.

"The men that were captured were uh," Walls looked skyward thinking. Then said, "They were 5'9", 5'10", and 5'11", if memory serves. So that leaves a height description of 6'0" even and 6'2" for the two bodies missing."

"So I'm the shooter." Bishop aimed his gun to the height of a six-foot man and checked his stance. Making sure he stood six feet away from the first cranium stain. "Assuming he's a right handed shooter." He rechecked the distance from the ground to the gun. "I pull the trigger." Ejecting a bullet from the chamber, he watched it hit the grass two paces to his right. Bishop holstered his Glock, pulled a pocket light from his suit jacket and began skimming the grass for his bullet. He found it, scooped it up, slipped it between his teeth and kept looking for the casing. Carls joined him. Sweeping his own flash light from side to side. His light paused on a dull tinge of metal.

"You gotta be kidding me," Carls said, leaning down over the casing. He pulled a pin from his coat pocket, lifted the brass from the ground, and held it up for Renfro, Bishop, and the Sheriff to see.

Bishop carefully took the pen from the Deputy and shined a light on the brass. A slight shade of trace markings resembling a finger print were visible. "We got a print." Bishop held the pen upright, cautious not to drop the casing and kept his eyes on the ground. "So the shooter was right here." He pointed to the first puddle. "He put down the first man, there." Then he pointed to the second head stain. "And the next man here."

Carls cursed and shook his head. "Here's the second casing." He pulled another pen from his coat and retrieved it from the grass. "You got any more jars with you?"

Bishop nodded. "Hold onto it for now." He glanced from where Carls found the second casing to where the second body left its violent remains. "Two bodies, and no time. So, then what? Where did they drag them to? They had to carry 'em out out somehow." He looked about the field. "There are no drag marks. I'm not seeing a blood trail. If they dragged the bodies from here to the lot, there'd be a trail."

"Maybe they had body bags," Carls guessed.

Bishop shook his head. "No, this happened quick. However it went down, it went real bad real fast. And with a skull blown wide open, let alone two skulls blown wide open, you can't stop a leak that bad that quick. Those boys had to rock and roll, put 'em down in a flash, snatch up the bodies and get ghost. They had no time for premeditated extraction. If they did we'd have five bodies missing, instead of two." He skimmed the grass moreover, took a few more steps and added, "I see no tire tracks here. If they loaded up the bodies into a getaway car, there'd be tracks from here to the lot." His flash light froze on a few more specks of blood. Then he searched for more. Sweeping the light from side to side, further outward, and found nothing. "It stops here. We got no more blood after this spot. It all stops right here. So where did they go?"

Carls stared at the grounds where Bishop stood. "Another van maybe?"

Was he slow?

Irritated, the detective shook his head. "Again, there'd be some kind of impression marks. From a spin-out, or just the weight of the vehicle itself and the bodies in it." He went quiet then. Looking east-bound. Then west. North. South. Nothing seemed to spark a theory or notion. Suddenly, Renfro watched a flash of awareness wash over his dark features. Detective Brian Bishop pointed skyward. "No tire tracks because they weren't on the ground," he said. "They were airborn."

Renfro stood and looked skyward then at Bishop. "O'Hare is less than ten minutes from here. And it's only thirty-four miles to Midway. No way they got cleared for the airspace."

"Unless they know somebody in Air Traffic Control who got 'em cleared for it."

"Or they landed somewhere else so they didn't have to."

Bishop looked at Walls and Carls. "You got any private airports around here?"

"Several," Carls answered. "There's Northbrook Aviation about five miles west of here. There's Brunner. Mill Rose Farm, but that's a restricted landing area. There's Koppie over in Gilberts. And there's Sky Soaring over in Union."

Renfro shook his head. "They wouldn't take that long to land."

"There's Executive Charters," the Sheriff chimed in. "But that's owned by Alderman Porter."

Bishop and Renfro froze. Without so much as a blink, they gave each other a knowing look.

Their inkling was not lost on the Sheriff.

"What?" he asked.

Renfro's brow lifted. "Nothing."

Walls' eyes narrowed. Not believing them. But Bishop changed tact before the wary look begged questions. He looked at Carls and said, "So you interviewed the bank manager?"

"That's right," the deputy answered.

"And what did he say about the security guard that was shot? Did he make it?"

"We wanted to interview him," Renfro cut in, "but he's nowhere to be found."

"Well, I don't know how serious his injuries were. And all the bank manager said was he took one dead in his chest and it was his second time in a robbery. And that must have been enough to spook the guy because he never came back. Him or the new hire."

Bishop pulled a notepad and pen from his jacket pocket. "What was his name?"

"Uh...De...DeShawn." He gave a firm nod. Sure of his answer. "Yup. That was it. DeShawn Martin."

"And the other guard?"

"I can't think of it off hand." Carls glanced at his superior.

"I'm drawing a blank here," Walls said. "I'll have to pull the reports and give you a call on that one."

"It was something with an 'R' or a 'T' or something."

"And what hospital was Martin sent to?"

"I believe it was Vanguard Weiss Memorial."

Bishop scribbled down the information and flipped the notepad closed. "So your wife's psychic, huh?"

"Yes, sir," the sheriff said with a nod. "Best there is in all of Northbrook."

"Uh huh...Well, did you ever think of putting her on to finding them?"

"She only does missing persons cases if the person is officially reported as missing."

"There was a kid who went missing about nine years back," Renfro said. "Walking from school. Never made it home. So the Missing Persons Unit decided to employ this psychic detective to investigate by means of postcognition and dowsing. Supposedly, through the spirit of the victim, she worked that case." Renfro shook his head in disgust. "She never came even remotely close to finding that kid. You know where they found him? Three month's later, his body washed up on a beach in Gary, Illinois."

Sheriff Walls regarded him with indifference. As if he couldn't have cared less. So long as the 'she' was not his wife. Men did that. Renfro knew. Dismissing the faults in their own. Ignoring the smell of bullshit even if it was smeared right on their upper lip. It wasn't rudeness or blindness. It was just the standard denial of human nature. "And you know what?" he went on. "So far, these so-called psychics haven't proven shit. Not one of them has ever said, *'I see where the body's buried. And I'll take you there.'*"

"Maybe if you talk to her," Walls said, "you'll see things a bit differently. Perhaps if you ask a few questions, she'll change your mind."

Renfro shook his head — done with the matter — turned, and walked back towards his car.

Bishop hmmphed and pushed up his glasses. "If I talk to your wife or her cracked crystal ball, the only question I'm asking is this...Where's Haffa and what's tomorrow lottery numbers? And I'll bet if every next breath on the planet depended on it, she couldn't give me an answer."

Renfro watched the Sheriff and the deputy get in their Crown Vic and disappear up the road. By then, Bishop had carefully secured the jars in the kit and placed them on the floor of the back seat. He joined Renfro in the blocked off section of the parking lot where the getaway van had been torched.

Any remnants of the vehicle's frame and residues had been removed weeks ago. Nothing remained now, save a scorched surface of cement.

As the January wind blew cold, the faint smell of charred metal wafted up to his nostrils.

"What are you thinking?" Bishop asked him.

"We don't know how much they cashed out on that take. But we do know it won't last for long. If DeGrate is anything like his father, he won't abide living off his family's money. I mean, if that were the case, why take scores at all?" Renfro looked up to the noon-day sky and watched a whisp of clouds blot out the sun. With a dark cast looming down, it looked as if the world took on an ill-omened tone too imminent to ignore. "It's not about the money."

"The rush?" Bishop guessed.

"Worse," Renfro said. "Vanity. They do it because they're good. And they do it because they don't want to do much else."

Bishop shrugged. "Makes sense."

"So what do we know about master theives?"

"They usually have day jobs. Keep up with normal appearances. Most have ordinary daily routines to thrwart suspicion."

"Yeah, but their day jobs and their overall lifestyles have to coincide with their true trade or their scores are amateur at best. So let's find out what our boys are up to. Who they're employed under. Fresh off of a robbery like this, they couldn't spend the money right away. They're too smart for that. Trying to trace unusual spending patterns, from a DeGrate is pointless, and that's why the Sheriff couldn't make a monetary trace and hit a dead end, because the family is already rich. "

"What about the rest of his crew? Maybe they indulged for the holidays. Or plan to in the near future."

"A little recon work and we'll know soon enough."

"What about their mock crew?"

"We need to pay them a visit and do all three of those interviews again. I know Club Fed up in Marion is full so, until they have room, our puppets are being held in County. Whatever they can remember, maybe we'll catch something Walls didn't."

Bishop shrugged. "You never know."

"All three of them have priors and they were all out on parole. So, they'll be going away for a long time behind this one." Renfro thought on the security guard again. Tracking him down wouldn't be that difficult. They could just get the address from the bank manager or the hospital. He doubted the man saw anymore than the frightened patrons, but a few questions might give way to something. "We should interview the hospital staff that treated our unsung hero," he said. "I doubt they know anymore about his whereabouts than we do, but..."

Renfro's pager went off. He looked down and checked the number. 7281 — The extension to his desk phone at the police station.

Both men headed back to the sedan. Renfro slid in behind the steering wheel.

"What's the page?" Bishop asked.

"Back at the station."

"Are we headed back there? Because we still have to drop these samples off at the lab."

Renfro shook his head and slipped the key in the ignition. "We'll head back to the Sheriff's department and use the phone. Then We'll check out that private airport and take a look around Executive Charters. We'll see if we can get ahold of the flight manifest."

He made the drive to the Cook County Sheriff's Police department in less than 45 minutes. Both men walked into the building and headed for the Sheriff's office.

Renfro rapped lightly on the door seal. Walls looked up from a pile of paperwork. "Sheriff, I don't mean to bother you again. Can I use your phone to return a page?"

Walls nodded, picked up the multiline phone and sat it on the corner of his desk. "Sure."

Renfro dialed the number to his office desk.

"Renfro's desk," someone answered.

"This is Renfro. I got a page."

"Oh right, this is Travis. Someone called for you and left a number...uh, you got a pen?"

"Go ahead."

"The number is 773-728-2953."

"Who?"

"He didn't leave a name, but he said it was urgent."

"Okay, appreciated."

Renfro hung up and dialed the number. Someone answered on the third ring.

"Hello, detective."

The voice didn't sound familiar. "Who am I speaking with?"

"A man who can give you what no one else can."

"And that would be?"

"Your mole, detective."

"Okay...I'm listening."

"Turn on the news."

Renfro put the phone to his shoulder and covered the receiver with a hand. "Do you have a break room with a television or one near by?"

Sheriff Walls nodded and pointed out the door. "Right this way."

"How do you put this line on hold?"

Walls reached across the desk and hit the hold button on the multiline phone. "Just hang up and you can pick it up in the break room if you need."

Renfro and Bishop followed the Sheriff to the break room. Walls handed Renfro the remote and he turned it to Fox News. Listening to the reporter, he didn't blink for nearly a minute straight.

> "...in what appears to be a hostage situation in the Cabrini Green highrise building on North Hudson. So far there is no word on Doctor James' condition and the police have made no attempts to enter the building. Most residents who were outside of the building before the incident have been kept from entering. From what we can tell, no shots have been fired and no arrests have been made. Just a few months ago, Dr. James erected the Scott Joplin Gratis Medical Program with the aim of providing medical care for the sick and elderly who could not afford medical insurance. The good doctor is engaged to Councilman Porter. And while some argue that her efforts were no more than a political ploy for votes, no one can argue many of the positive changes since her arrival. Her gratis program proved to be quite a succesful campaign for the underprivileged, until now..."

"Who is this?"

"Zane Harris. And I'm about to hand you the bust of your shitty career."

"In exchange for?"

"A guarantee that I walk out alive and so does my family. And once I give you a name, my grandmother is in witness protection immediately after. She don't spend more than one night in this city."

"I can get her immunity in exchange for the mole."

"You and I both know immunity in the streets is bullshit. That's not gonna cut it."

Renfro hit the mute button on the remote, silencing the television.

"Is the doctor still alive?"

"She is. For now. Guaranteed witness protection for my grandma. Not out of state. Out of the fucking country. Canada or some damn where."

"I can't guarantee that without talking to my superiors."

"Then I suggest you talk to your superiors. Let 'em know you got a mole for pull. They'll bite. Or you better hope they do."

"They're going to need proof that you can deliver that."

"Look, if you want to increase the chances of getting that name, you better make sure you get to me before DeGrate does. Because if he tries me, I'm gonna kill him. And negotiating with a body on me, won't exactly work in my favor, so if he comes at me, the deal's off. And if they raid any of the buildings before my G-Moms is set, deal's off. Cause I'm not going down without a fight. Getting your traitor is incentive enough, so make it happen. No deal, no mole. You take your time, detective."

Zane hung up.

Walls cursed at the news coverage of the highrise building. Sky footage showed every façade completely surrounded by police. "Is that really happening right now?"

Renfro thanked the Sheriff for his time and looked at his partner. "Let's go. Looks like we got business in Cabrini."

DUKE

Salvatore D'Amico extended his hand in greeting.

Duke DeGrate shook it and gave a nod.

"I appreciate you taking the time to meet with me Mr. DeGrate." He handed Duke a hard hat. "If you please. OSHA regulations, I'm sure you understand. Violations are always a concern." Duke obliged and placed the hard hat on is head. A smell of new plastic came to his nostrils. D'Amico motioned to follow him towards the construction site. "Right this way."

Duke gave a nod to Viola before he followed D'Amico. "This won't take long."

She nodded in response. Leaning back in the rear seat of the black sedan, she propped elbow on the window sill. Her smooth chin rested on a hand as she looked about the undeveloped property. Even through the darkness of the her sunglasses, Duke could see she was bored and ready to leave. But he had promised he would make it up to her.

Two hours ago, their lovemaking had been interrupted by a phone call from Dutch. Tony Bragga, who made a name for himself as Salvatore D'Amico's right hand man, delivered the message of a meeting in Rockwell. It came off an odd request for a man like D'Amico.

Rockwell was no place for an impromptu meet. A CTA, street level brown line for transportation, private schools, and the north branch of the Chicago River was all it boasted. It was no Little Italy. Just a place stuck in regression. An industrialist's paradise. Perhaps the made man chose a place that would make both men feel equally out of their element.

When Duke's convoy pulled up to the curb of D'Amico's construction sight, he found it hard to miss the potential consumer's district Rockwell could become.

For a Saturday, the workforces were in full action. Bull dozers, cement trucks, workers carrying shoulders of timber. A buzz saw buzzing off in the distance. Rarely was city labor approved on a weekend.

Quite the emergent land indeed.

"I have to admit, I'm surprised to see construction like this on a Sunday."

"Well, business is booming, Mr. DeGrate. With the economy improving and financing becoming more available, Chicago is a developer's delight."

"The Department of Buildings granted you After Hours Variance?"

D'Amico nodded. "Until 2:00 a.m. Monday through Saturday. 7:00 p.m. on Sundays. Holidays as well."

Duke was impressed. He wondered how the entrepreneur charmed Mayor Burns into looking the other way on that one. He looked around at all of the workers. "Contractors?"

D'Amico smiled and shook his head as if to say he would never stoop so low. "Union. Always."

Of the International Construction Laborer's Union's nine North American regions, Salvatore spear headed the Great Lakes region. Most who knew him, from Minnesota to Ohio, considered him to be a good man to be acquainted with.

"New housing?"

"Multi-million dollar mixed-use development. Set to be completed in three phases. The first phase is a pedestrian-friendly neighborhood with 900 luxury apartment units, and 3,000 condominiums as well as 600,000 square feet of office space. The second phase will be an upscale hotel, 1,200 rooms along with 150,000 additional square feet of retail included. The third phase, I'm sure you will find very interesting. The Federal Bureau of Investigation is opening a new field office building right here in Rockwell. Total, this 50 acre neighborhood will have more than 2 million square feet of office space, retail space, and restaurants. This project is projected to be complete sometime within the next two to three years."

As the sound of buzz saws and bull dozers mingled with Duke's thoughts, his mind drifted toward the possiblity of a new endeavor. When D'Amico had had Bragga arrange the meet, he honestly could not fathom what his boss had to offer that would sway a dividing of his Class A shares. Especially considering that a member of D'Amico's mob had tried to kill his entire family in Galena just months before. Though, Duke felt his brow arch with thoughts of new commerce, he still found it difficult to ignore the warning from just prudence. If D'Amico could secure a building contract for the FBI, his reach stretched further than Duke imagined — which further envoked his cautions. "Sounds like a new paradigm on the frontier of expansion," he said.

"Construction for this development has already created more than 1,200 jobs to stimulate the economy. Within the next few years, it's bound to employ triple that amount. When this project is complete, all of these new stores will offer consumers a variety of merchandise, fresh produce, boutique shopping, and posh living. All of these new stores will need employees to work them. I'd say a new paradigm in proprietorship is more like it. And it's my understanding that Mr. Porter is going to need more than a few speeches — all be it well spoken ones — to stay in the good graces of the people if he plans to succeed in the world of policy makers." D'Amico turned to Duke with an earnest look in his eyes. "Your candidate needs more than just votes. He needs to keep the voters glad they dropped a ballot in the box with his name checked. Any runner for office can promise more employment opportunities. He could be the first Mayoral candidate ever, out the gate before election day, with a guarantee of employment already in progress. In the eyes of the people, that's not just a man who says that he can, Mr. DeGrate. That's a man who already did it before the first vote was even cast."

Duke took a moment to look over the grounds of the construction site. Using the time to think. It was a magnanimous outcome. But all great triumphs have the forebearers of surrender and sacrifice. "Your offer?" he finally asked.

"The split?"

Duke nodded.

"Of the twenty-five percent you plan to purchase from the church, forty-sixty. That's fifteen percent of the church's interest in the company, which leaves me with ten percent. Which means you still keep majority shares and the highest controlling interest.

Of the nine seats on the board of directors, you'll own four instead of six. Those two will go to me. But that leaves three seats owned by the company, so with you holding one more seat over their heads, you still come out on top."

Duke thought on his proposal. When he opened his mouth to speak, a dull pain raced through his left arm. A low groan was all he would allow to manage.

His discomfort was not lost on D'Amico. "Are you alright?"

Duke nodded, rolling his shoulder to ease the ache.

"It's a fine offer. Unfortuantely I must decline."

D'Amico did not seem to let his answer upset him.

Duke didn't see anger on the man's Sicilian features, yet the offense in his blue eyes was ever apparent. "May I ask why? If it's the percentage split, we can always renegotiate so that we're both—"

"No," Duke interrupted, "you're proposal is very tempting. It's a well thought through and very lucrative offer. Though as intriguing as it is, I think we both know that if I'm in business with you, I won't just be in business…with you." Duke paused, thinking of the right way to word his aversion for Zosa. Then, "I have a pebble in my shoe, Mr. D'Amico. Hindering any steps forward that I've been trying to make. Regrettably, that pebble now hinders your steps as well."

"And…if this pebble were removed?" D'Amico asked. "Would you find those steps a little easier to take?"

"Your enforcer came after my family."

D'Amico was silent for a moment before he spoke again. As if silence seemed the safest decision to make.

"Zosa is a very ambitious man," he finally said. "He made that move without my knowledge. I hope you know that, Mr. DeGrate."

"If I didn't, Mr. D'Amico, we wouldn't be having this conversation. Even after the attack, I wanted no more violence. I chose to look the other way then. I choose the same now. That decision is because no one close to me was taken from me. I can not and I will not ask you to settle anyone's account on my account. That's not the kind of man I am. But if some misfortune should transpire on anyone close to me, I have a very motivated son who won't take that lightly. And inspite of everything I would do to stop it, that would take our families to a place we hate. A place we know is pure dread. It's a place we have worked all our lives to avoid."

"I heard your son already made that clear to Zosa." D'Amico let a slight grin come to his mouth. "I'm sure Tommy will never look at fine dining the same way again."

Duke was taken aback by that remark. But he recovered quickly. D'Amico didn't seem to notice. It was not unlike Darrion to send a warning. Though Duke made it clear he wanted no retaliation, he should have known what his son would do. They would have to have a talk about that and soon. But now, Duke felt obligated to defend his son. Even if Darrion's behavior was out of line. "Anything done to keep the peace was worth doing," he said.

D'Amico held up a finger. "Ah! But among men like you and I, that would be an end of our means. We would have had a sit down and the whole indiscretion would have been meted out and everyone would have walked away with something gained. We're peacemakers you and I. Zosa, he's not the yielding kind. And his methods are way past bedtime." He looked up at the January sky. Then out on his construction crew and motioned a hand over all his Sicilian blue eyes could see. "This, all of this, is a means. A means Zosa can not see. He doesn't care about the work it takes to build something and the alliances it takes to keep it."

Duke looked out on the property, and just when he started to see part of D'Amico's point, what the mogul truly meant struck him. "Zosa is a threat to you as well. Isn't he?"

"He's young. And ambitious."

"He's got the backing of a lot of motivated soldiers. If he wants you removed, it won't take long before he sets out to do so."

"Death is simple. Life is complicated. My demise is not what worries me. What worries me is what he's striving to turn my family towards."

"Gambling?"

"Drugs." D'Amico let out a breath. "I kept him close when he was young. Tried to teach him how to build wealth at an early age. In the hopes that when he got to be my age and he'd look back on his life, he'd have more achievements than regrets. Just didn't turn out that way."

Duke shook his head. "It's a tragedy when a promising protégé becomes a prodigal liability. I'm sorry for your troubles. But they are *your* troubles. And any decision you make, has nothing to do with me."

"Yes, but your circumstance has everything to do with me, Mr. DeGrate. I do feel some responsibility for my enforcer's actions. That being said, I think removing that pebble from your shoe and mine would make it easier for us both to take steps towards one another. This type of thing, sends a message. We have a rule that no one challenges. It keeps respect. It keeps the order. *No one man is above the Family.* Zosa has misremembered that. Ringing that bell of remembrance is what I do best."

Salvatore D'Amico fixed a steady, piercing gaze on Duke then and said, "May his demise bring you peace."

♛

Duke stared at the stone water fountain as the driver pulled into the circular driveway. He had had it installed last Tuesday and still wondered if black marble was the right choice for Cupid and His Broken Arrow. It certainly gave a different perspective on karma. Quite the sculpture and it told a cautionary tale. In a dark twist of fate, someone's aim was better than Cupid's. Love's most fabled instigator had suffered an arrow through his own shoulder. As a result, the fat little shit had traded full cheeks of hope for a round face pinched in resentment and his stubby little fingers had snapped his own arrow in two over a knee. Three winged young females floated frozen about his face, leaning in for a kiss. With one look at that statue no one, who came to the DeGrate's home, would wonder why Cupid cursed his own aim.

Viola hated the damned thing. She scowled at it the day it came out of the crate on the front lawn. She stepped outside cursed, rolled her eyes, and said, "For that nasty bit of fate, Cupid should blame his dick, not his bow."

Duke knew not to let her remark pull him into an argument about his former mistress. So he smartly kept his mouth shut.

She had her say. He still had his statue. End of.

After politely sitting in the car while he met with D'Amico, his wife decided now was a good time to run a few errands. He asked her to remain in the sedan and allow the guards to escort her. But his wife refused, demanding to drive herself. So, Duke gave instructions for his private security to follow her to the grocery store and anywhere else she chose to go. He knew Viola hated a designated train following her in traffic. However, that did little to discourage taking measures to keep her safe.

Duke walked in through the front door and stood at the window, watching her leave as two armed guards in a black four door tailed close behind the red Jeep. He stepped away from the curtains and crossed the living room to an unusual silence.

By now Legend would be at his legs. Sniffing him from shin to shoes. As if his presence would bring home some new smell different than the day before. Even Luna would muster the strength to limp into the room. Even if she didn't have the vigor to run toward him anymore, she'd inch forward until he met her halfway.

It didn't take long for Duke to grow tired of the quiet. He made his way to the den where Luna could sometimes be found on her favored rug, deep in sleep. Sometimes her pain pills kept the sounds of cars approaching and doors going ajar from reaching the pit bull's ears. He looked about the room, spotting everything in it's place.

A high thin wimpering sound drew his gaze to the kitchen. Perhaps Luna's injuries had flared up again. Though the wolf attack happened in November, her wounds were still healing and her pain pills were only to be given twice daily. One tramadol at 7:00 a.m. and another twelve hours later at 7:00 p.m. — and only as needed per the veterinarian.

Duke walked toward the kitchen and checked his watch. Luna's medication wasn't due for another six hours and fifteen minutes. Hopefully she could hold out until then. Another pill right now would harm more than help.

Duke pushed the oak door open and froze.

Stark as night terror, with inconceivable dread, his eyes locking on the bloody end of his ailing pit.

Cuts came to his vision from all over her late frame. Deep gouges high and low and hacked across her back. Something long and sharp had plowed into her flesh where her hindlimbs met her underbelly and cleaved her clear up to the breastbone. Her entrails lay spilled out in a pool of dark blood. Duke did not know how long she laid there dying, but her death had not been quick. His eyes took in the red that stained the lower cabinets and marble tile flooring. It looked as if the blood came rushing out in a black, spewing surge.

The sight of her mutilated body shocked him speechless.

Legend left her side and put bloody paws to Duke's thighs. The white pit looked up in his eyes and whined then went back to Luna's side.

A spell of vertigo spun the world then. As Duke tried to blink it away, a shooting pain lanced down his arm and a sharp aching came to his chest. His knees went out from under him then. Helpless to stop it, he toppled sideways to the floor. When his mouth opened all that came out was a spittle of vomit. Legend leaned a bloody, wet nose to his cheek and pushed against his slack face. As if the gentle nudging would be all his master needed to rise to his feet.

But no more strength came to him. This time, Duke knew his failing heart would not forgive.

His eyes began to close and all that filled the mogul's fading vision was Legend pacing around the pool of blood he and Luna lay in. Whimpering. Whining. Calling to the pitch of a wolf's rallying cry.

DARRION

Darrion stood there with the phone to his ear.

He was listening. But the words wouldn't register.

His eyes pulled from the darkness of the hotel room as Anton's voice blared through the receiver. "Hello?!"

Darrion blinked out of his stunned daze. "I'm here."

"I tried to tell her not to go to the police, KD. I swear to God, I tried to talk her out of it."

"Where is she now?"

"At Zane's place. He's got Lefty, Q-Ball and his evil ass grandma watching her."

"Is she alright?"

"She's unconscious. Or at least she was when I left. That was hours ago and they knocked her out when they took her from the clinic."

"Where are you now?"

"At my place. Zane sent me to keep watch for the police. He thinks they might try to break through the welding on the back door." He paused and heaved a deep breath. "It's crazy in Cabrini right now. If you saw this shit...I swear it's gotta be at least fifty or sixty squad cars out there, man. This shit is bananas."

Darrion stared at the bloody corpse on the bed. It was amazing how one blow, one devastation could make all others cease to matter in the blink of an eye. Or the ring of a phone.

Kincaid had took to murding black women. Leaving evidence of how much he enjoyed his work all over her mutilated body. It was planned to be a simple swift kill. Darrion, Taran, and T-Bone were supposed to slip into Kincaid's hotel room, snuff him out, and be gone before his body hit the floor. What they had found instead was no hillbilly, only a dead — assumed to be hooker — slashed and left to rot on red soaked sheets.

For making their bank robbery his own day of retribution, he deserved his demise. For killing two men involved in the robbery, two men that probably had Aryan ties — he deserved his demise. For harassing Viola, for threatening his family, that inbred piece of shit deserved to die screaming twice.

But for the second time, Kincaid slipped away. Except now, he became an insignificant target. All Darrion could think of was Angelique, getting to her, and all the things Zeno would soon be doing to her if he hadn't already.

He knew they needed to get out of there before the wrong person saw them leave. T-Bone must have been thinking the same because he leaned his head out into the hallway and gave a quick glance left and right.

"I'm going to hang up," Darrion said. "When I call back, you answer."

"Alright," Anton said.

He hung up.

"What was that about?" Taran asked.

"Zane kidnapped Angelique. He's holding her hostage at his place."

"What?!"

"Oh shit," T-Bone said. "Has he lost his fucking mind, man?"

"We gotta go, now," Darrion said.

"Who was that on the phone?" Taran asked.

"Ant. And if I know Chicago PD, all the avenues are flooded with squad cars."

Darrion handed the phone back to Taran and went to the door.

T-Bone looked out to the hallway again and motioned it was clear. They left the room and slipped out the back entrance unseen, then made their way down the stairs to the rear parking lot.

The men rushed to the car. Darrion slid behind the steering wheel and started the Buick. The engine turned over with a sputter then came alive with a low rumble. A thick smell of exhaust fumes came through the vents. He wondered if T-Bone's lemon would make it to Cabrini without a backfire or transmission failure.

Lunch leaned forward from the back seat. "Tell me he's dead."

"No," T-Bone said. He leaned his passenger seat forward and let Taran slide in the back seat. "But the body he left hacked all to hell is."

Lunch cursed. "Who'd he kill?"

"Don't know her. Somebody's money maker. I've never seen her before. Not from City Lights."

"He wasn't there?"

"No," Taran said. "And finding him is on the back burner right now. We got a bigger problem. Zane's got the Doc. He's holding her hostage in Head Quarters."

Lunch cursed again and smoothed a hand over his blonde head. "How did that happen?"

"According to Ant," Darrion said, "they took her from the clinic." He hit the gas, the tires spun out then the Buick lurched forward. He steered the wide body out of the lot and sped off down the street.

"What about the guards that were supposed to be watching her?"

"My guess? Dead if God is good."

"And if he's not?"

"Alive and wishing they were dead."

"So we're going to Cabrini." Lunch nodded. "And how are we going to Cabrini? By now, it's all over the news and the projects are flooded with cops."

"We'll get in. We're just going to need a little help from some recently acquired allies of Xavier Pope."

Lunch thought about it. Then his brows lifted as if it suddenly clicked. "The new senior regents, MG, Freddie Machete and Guesser."

Darrion nodded. "If Zane's men and the fiends can slip in and out undetected, so can we."

"Where are the newly promoted?"

"They were recently relocated," Taran said. "in light of their new advancements. So they're no longer in Cabrini."

"They don't answer to Zane anymore," Darrion added. "Which means, he might be a little salty about that. So if they wanted to live to enjoy their elevations, a new address was necessary. Now they have to answer to Pope's number two and if we want inside Cabrini we should have no problem squeezing that information from any one of them."

♛

It was common knowledge among those who knew him, Ceasar Black was an avid French cuisine man. Any time during the year, if one needed to exchange a word or two, they could find the Disciple King's Under at his restaurant, The Black Boar.

In Streeterville, on a Sunday, just before 1800 hours, Darrion knew the restaurant wouldn't be open until 1900. Ceasar only catered to affluent, nighttime patrons.

Driving T-Bones contraption wouldn't do. So Darrion sped back to the Waldorf Towers, parked around the corner from his high-rise building, and called Anton back to get all of the information he could, then the men changed vehicles. His red Mercedes would draw less eyes on Ceasar's side of town.

What he learned from Ant turned his skin to gooseflesh. Apparently, the rape of a little girl had sparked Zane's act of capture. Now the little girl was missing and it was safe to assume he was holding Angelique hostage until the little girl was found and disposed of. Which further led Darrion to believe the blackhearted deed was all to protect his twist of a brother, Zeno.

All he could do was find a way in as soon as possible and get Angie out before Zane got deperate enough to end all evidence of the rape by any means necessary.

Twenty minutes later, the men were standing in the main room of the Under's establishment. MG, Machete, and Guesser stood waiting as well.

They were told, by a man Darrion assumed was the assistant manager, Mr. Black would be with them shortly. Business kept him in a meeting with his chefs a bit longer than expected. With that, the well taylored suit disappeared into the back room.

Darrion looked about the place. Taking in every inch of architectural style. Beaux-Arts classicism up close and personal. Gothic revival owned the walls. If the man was trying to make a statement towards vertical-style modernisms, he'd done so, and boldly.

Then again, Ceasar had to blend well with the ritz.

Bound on the west by the Magnificent Mile, Streeterville held some of the city's tallest skyscrapters as well as upscale stores, medical facilities, universities, high-rises, and hotels. Inspite of his illicit ties, Xavier's Under had gone through great pains to distance himself from the kind of dark element he had been raised in. But that was why they had come. Ceasar didn't like noise and he especially didn't like noise that made headlines. For that reason, Darrion knew Black would do whatever was necessary to end the doctor's peril as swiftly as possible.

Moments later, the King Disciple's number two walked into the great dining room, followed by one of his maître d's and spoke in greeting then took a seat at the center table. As always Black was swathed in a well tailored suit. Dark eyes genial yet stern. Flat features and sharp cheekbones owned his face. At a glance he looked to be nearing his mid thirties. Not one grey hair had set in. He seemed to be handling the stresses of street boss well. So far.

Darrion never cared much for the man. Neither did Turkell, Taran, or Casper. But he could not help but respect him. Ceasar Black hadn't become the second in command by accident. In order for any man to rise in the ranks of the underworld, he had to trade away part of his humanity. That much both men had in common at one time or another. He waited until the server poured his tea and disappeared back into the kitchen before he spoke.

"Quite the predicament, gentlemen," he began. Then he looked at Darrion. "I'm sorry about your doctor. Zane and his cronies have been a bomb waiting to go off for quite some time. It's awful circumstance that she was there when it did. Anything you need, if I can I will. Just let me know."

"Appreciated," Darrion said. "And actually we do need something."

"Ask away."

"Restraint from the Disciples when we go in to get her. And we have to go in because the cops can't do shit. If anything they're a worthy distraction. But that won't hold if they send in the National Guard. And they're threatening to."

"How do you know that?"

"A little bird flew over and told me."

The street boss nodded. "Alright. Fair enough. I'll make sure you have little resistance on the way in. Anything else?"

"Just so you know, we thought about negotiating, but Zane is through talking."

"Zane is brutal," Taran added. "But Zeno is a fucking twist. If we don't get to her before he does, he will gut her like trout and try not to spill any on his shoes."

"I know Zane. I know him better than his own soldiers. Better than Pope. I can get to him without killing any of the Disciples still loyal to you and Pope. But if the cops make a move on him before I do, I can't guarantee that."

"You're connected to the Alderman," Black said. "You can make one phone call and that'll change."

"Right now, the Alderman is probably in a gridlock with the Mayor and the Chief of police. And on top of that, he's got every eye in the city watching. He's going to do what's best for the residents, Chicago PD and his fiance, while keeping his image with the press in tact. Any requests to go against that will fall on deaf ears. I'd play that card if I could, but even if I could, the moment the Harris brothers even think I took it to the police...Well...let's just face it, Ceasar, I'm not going to the police. That's not even my style."

"I second that," Taran chimed in.

"And I third it," T-Bone said as he walked toward the bar and shut the glass door behind him.

"Would you mind flipping the sign to closed please?" Ceasar asked T-Bone.

He reached for the sign and did it.

"Thank you."

Turkell nodded. "No problem."

Darrion looked at the new senior regents. "We're not getting in without a way in. I know Zane's been supplying his clientele despite the recent interference from the media over the past couple of months. He's getting his merchandise in somehow. I know his trade's taken a more furtive route through the projects. I know he's gone underground. And I know because that's what I would do. We need to know where it is."

Guesser slightly shook his head. "I feel for your situation. I do. But giving that up is going to hurt a lot of people if it gets back to the Councilman. Not just Zane."

When Darrion began to object, Turkell cut in and said, "Look, first of all, we don't snitch. And if anything the Councilman can just stay the hell out of the way. Second, we don't care about Zane's product. We don't care about his profits. But we do care about how far he's willing to go to protect it. Especially when it blows back on the Alderman's fiancé."

"Okay," Guesser said. "I can make a call and have a few Renegades slip you in under Zane's nose. They can't stand his ass no way."

"That's not gonna work. Taking a doctor hostage, that shit grips the public. News choppers are already circling the projects. The media is swarming like locusts. I go anywhere near that building, he'll know I'm coming. I need a way in that the cops don't know about, so I can find her before he kills her."

"Zane is a brutal, coldblooded nigga, no doubt. But I don't think he'd do something that ruthless."

"He would to stop the threat of a rape charge."

"What?"

"One of his men attacked a little girl. When Zane found out the good doctor called the police, he took her hostage. Last I heard, the girl's nowhere to be found and Zeno's looking for her."

Guesser cursed.

Even Ceasar's brow lifted. "When did this happen?"

"Just this morning."

"It's not just a the doctor we're after," Taran cut in. "There's a little girl who's being hunted by a psycopath. We can't just shoot our way in like we did the first time. All that'll do is alert Zane we're coming. He'll just send resistance to stop us. That means a higher body count than any of us want and that gets us no closer to finding the little girl."

"No victim, no crime," Darrion added. "Zane is a calculating tyrant. But Zeno is another monster all together. He'd murder everything moving if his brother told him to. And I'm guessing the little girl is hid somewhere safe. For now. But that won't last long. Not with Zane's soldiers combing the projects looking for her. And if they come up empty handed, Zane is going to do whatever is necessary to make the doctor tell him where she is. If she won't, he'll kill her to make sure no witness of the crime exists. We need to stop him before that happens."

Guesser gave Darrion a searching look. It didn't surprise him in the least. Any former underling of Zane's had a right to be apprehensive. Going from coordinator to senior regent was one thing. Going from coordinator to rat was quite another. Guesser still had ties and loyalties to Cabrini. Those strings don't just get cut because the man changed his zip code. Darrion understood his reluctance. "I know you're not a rat," he said. "And I'm not asking you to be. Zane doesn't have to know the intel came from you."

"I don't have a problem with you, DeGrate," Guesser said. "And this whole situation is horrific, man. But if I give up that tunnel, Zane won't be the only one paying for it. And that nigga's blow back is vicious. You not the only one with people in Cabrini that you care about. I got peoples too. And I don't know you like that to be putting their lives on the line."

"You do know me," Ceasar cut in. "And you're going to tell him whatever he needs to know to go in there and bring Zane to heel. Because you no longer answer to Harris. Zane and Zeno's rogue days are numbered in Cabrini." He paused when his maitre d' brought a silver tray, uncovered a holder of sugar cubes, placed a silver spoon next to the saucer and disappeared back into the kitchen. Ceasar dropped two cubes into the steaming cup and slowly stirred the sugar. "What's your favorite meal?" he asked Guesser. "And I don't mean something you eat everytime you go to a restaurant somewhere. What's the one thing you haven't had in years? Your deathrow meal?"

"Filet mignon," Guesser answered.

Ceasar Black hmmphed. "Medium rare?"

"Absolutely."

"Not so much the delicacy it used to be. A bit derogated in the world of cuisine these days if you ask me. But okay." He took a sip of the tea, crossed a leg over a knee, then leaned back in his chair and fixed his eyes on the young man. "All of the finer things in life come with a price. And how do you think you'll be enjoying those finer things in your near future? You don't get filet mignon without slaughtering the cow. You want to come up, old ties have to be severed. This stunt they pulled, it doesn't just hurt. It cripples. When you got the eyes of the nation watching, it's over for you. Ain't no coming back from that.

"You're a senior regent now. The Harris brothers, they chose their path. You chose yours. It's time to own your place, youngblood. Spaceships don't come equipped with rear view mirrors. Start thinking ahead. Our future endeavors go beyond Cabrini. Besides, when the Harris' fifteen minutes of fame are up, everything in the projects will be just like it used to be before they dug that tunnel. Except your affiliations won't be linked to below tier duties. From now on, you'll be eating that filet mignon with much cleaner hands than you used to." Ceaser gave him a nod that half gestured in Darrion's direction. The young senior regent understood the non-verbal command.

"It runs under St. Dominic's," Guesser said.

"The church?" Lunch asked.

Guesser nodded.

"From Locust to Hudson Ave. Right to Head Quarters."

Darrion mentally mapped the distance. "That's a four minute hike from A to B."

"That sounds about right.

"Guards?"

"You know it."

"How many?"

"Six. Four by the church entrance. Two at the other end."

"Four-man shifts?"

"Yup."

"How many hours?"

"Twenty-four on, twenty-four off."

"How are they communicating?

"Same as ususal. Bricks."

"Brick phones or brick walkie-talkies?"

"The latter."

"Zane don't trust 'em with phones," MG cut in. "Beepers and bricks only."

"What kind of heat are they packing?"

"The kind of heat you hold with two hands," Guesser said.

Darrion expected that answer. Zane would have been a fool not to. He was a madcap, but far from a slow one.

"Watch your back down there, man," MG added. "Zane's got that tunnel boobie trapped. If they even so much as smell you coming, they'll set it off before you get anywhere near it."

"Good looking out. I'll be sure to misremember the location should the good Alderman ask me abou it."

Guesser nodded and said, "What about Zeno?"

"I don't think the Harris brothers will be a worry for anybody after today."

"I hope you're right," Guesser said. "Because if not, the repercussions from this one might just come back on us all."

"We're going to do everything we can to make sure that doesn't happen."

"Alright then, man. Good luck."

Both men bumped fists and gave a one-armed hug.

Then Ceasar politely dismissed Guesser and MG from the impromptu meeting, giving them instructions to take the back exit through the kitchen. After both men left the dining area of the restaurant, Ceasar motioned Darrion to the empty chair across from him and asked him to take a seat.

Darrion did so and noticed Freddie Machete giving Taran a terse look almost bordering on a scowl. That brought the last time they were in the same room to memory.

To Darrion's knowledge, Machete was the only one of Fang's marital arts students that seemed to take to every training session as an opportunity to prove something. On more than one occasion, he took to challenging Taran. Anyone who trained in kungfu knew, Taran was not the most skilled compared to any of Fang's Chinese protégés, but by far he had the fastest hands of any American student.

Machete always thought otherwise. Any effort to challenge Taran was thwarted by Fang's enforcement of respect in his temple. According to his rules one could never challenge another, unless a proven offense had been committed.

So came the looks.

Freddie knew, he couldn't challenge Taran unless something had been done against him and indisputable evidence was brought to Fang.

As always Taran refused to meet his villanous stare. He instead looked at Ceasar Black. Waiting for him to say whatever he felt Guesser and MG did not need to hear.

"I know a thing to two about old, buried bones," Ceasar began. "More than a thing or two, matter of fact. Let me ask you something. In your situation, with this animosity towards the Harris brothers, have you ever considered making peace with your enemies? More money gets made that way."

"If I partner up to make money," Darrion answered, "it wouldn't be with a Harris. Period. They were once in line with my father's vision, but that time is over. And as far as adversaries go, yeah, you're right. My father would say, '*If you want to kill an enemy, make him an ally.*' But when an ally becomes an enemy, and he sends that first bullet flying past your head, all that wisenheimer shit just goes right out the window. And there's nothing wrong with using foes to prosper. Ginding those bones to make bread is worth it, if others get fed. Instead of just you."

Ceasar Black calmly nodded at his answer and said, "You're young, DeGrate. Your father was a hot head like you back in the day. You'll calm down soon enough."

Darrion arched an eyebrow. "Oh, you think I'm reacting to Zane out of anger?"

"I think...no correction...I *know* you've already made up in your mind how this day is going to end. In spite of whatever I say to you. Maybe that disregard is karma in some way. Back when I lived in the Wild Hundreds, there was no talking me down. A lot of people met there demise for me to be me. Back then, I had a very short temper. Highly flammable. Today, that wick is much thicker. Not as easy to strike a match to. I have a long fuse with a slow burn. But it's lit to a block of C-4. And when it goes off, anything and everthing close to you is getting Picassoed."

"I'm calm, Ceasar. Quite so."

"Wrath feels that way. It always does, young prince. When you learn how to let it in. When you know how to use it. It smiles that lie everytime."

♕

We're headed over there now?" Lunch asked as his seat belt clicked.

Darrion shook his head and slipped the key in the ignition. "We need to arm up first. We'll stop by the club and load up in the vault. Then Cabrini."

Just as the engine came to life the car phone rang. He pulled the Mercedes into traffic and answered before the second ring.

"Hello?"

"I take it you watched the news?" Viola said.

"I know, we'll be there in less than an hour. Zane's not going to hurt her. We're not going to let that happen."

"Good. Because your father needs her alive now more than ever."

Darrion put the stick in neutral, hit the brakes in the middle of the street, and paused. "What's wrong?"

"Devin and Fang found him down in the kitchen. Your father had another heart attack. This is it, Darrion. They stabilized him at Scott Joplin and he's awake. But I don't know how long his heart's going to last. He can't wait until after Devin's birthday. He has to have it now."

"Then get another surgeon!"

"That's what the attending said! And all he came back with was some resident from a cardiothoracic surgical training program to assist and they're still searching for an attending to lead. So, I'm telling you the same thing I told him. I don't want another damned surgeon! I want the best surgeon Derek selected for your father! And I don't care what you have to do to find her. You cut through whoever you have to and get her out of there alive. Because if she dies, so does Duke and this family does not work without him!"

Darrion exhaled and spoke as calmly as he could. "We're going to find her, Mama. Don't worry. Just stay at the hospital and try to keep him calm. Tell him we're handling it and everything's going to fine."

"Please, please be careful, son. You have to know this is a trap, Darrion. Zane's always been resentful of you. And that's not your fault. He's just using Angie as a poker chip to get what he wants. And that's you in the ground."

"If things go my way it'll be the other way around."

"He would have to be stupid not to know you're coming."

"He doesn't know how I'm coming. That's an advantange we plan to keep. Nothing's going to happen to me. Don't worry. Tell Pop I'll call him as soon as it's over."

He could hear his mother curse under her breath. She wasn't looking forward to Zane's ire anymore than he was. A long pause drew out between them. Then she said, "Okay. I love you."

"I love you too."

Viola hung up.

"Duke's at the hospital?" Lunch asked.

"Yeah." Darrion put the stick in first gear and resumed driving.

"Is he alright?" Taran asked.

"No. He's not."

"Do you want one of us to stay with him?"

"No. I need ya'll with me. Fang, Devin, and Viola are at the hospital. So, if he needs anything they'll take care of it."

Lunch cursed and sat back in his seat. "This day is not happening."

Turkell Scarbone looked out of the back windshield, then calmly turned back around in the back seat and said, "This is probably not the best time to tell you we're being followed."

Darrion and Taran looked up at the rear view mirror.

"Two cars back," Turkell added. "Black, four door sedan. They pulled out when we left Ceasar's."

"How the hell did we catch a tail?" Taran spat.

Now I have to out run this asshole, Darrion thought.

His jaw clenched as he worked the clutch. Slamming the stick shift in to third, then fourth gear.

Darrion whiped the Mercedes through traffic. All four tires screeched as he weaved through cars. Switching lanes. The black sedan followed suit. Trying to keep up.

As the engine roared, he shook his head. "It never rains it just fucking pours." He gave one last glance at the rear view mirror then slammed the stick into fifth gear. "Alright, motherfucker. Let's see who's better."

VIOLA

Viola DeGrate drove to Scott Joplin Cook County Hospital and went straight to the ER waiting room.

She set eyes on Tu Fang, Devin, and DaVita. They were seated in the chairs closest to the double doors.

Though Fang rarely showed emotion, Viola could see the grave concern in his eyes. Her youngest seemed nothing shy of devastated.

Her daughter looked to be in pieces.

As she neared them, Viola did not bother with security. It would be the same answer given the last time Duke had been rushed to the trauma room. They wouldn't let anyone, not even family, see him until the doctor deemed him ready for visitors.

DaVita stood. Her voice faltered through sobs. "Mom, I don't know how he is, they won't tell us anything."

"I know."

"Is Luna really dead?" she asked, blotting her eyes with a tissue.

Viola nodded.

"Devin said she was...murdered. Butchered to death."

DaVita looked as if a wave of surreal dread and disbelief passed through her like a shockwave.

"I wasn't there to see it," Viola said. "But Devin said he found them both down in the kitchen. Then he called Fang and an ambulance."

"They've been working on him back there for nearly forty-five mintues," DaVita added, "and they haven't said a word about his condition or how serious it is."

"They'll tell us something soon," Devin said.

Viola looked at her son—keenly aware of how vulnerable he was. Though he kept a postive voice to ease his sister's worry, one word of fatal news about his father and Devin would have have been devastated for the rest of his life.

DaVita stood inertly as if half in a disconnected daze and Viola hugged her secondborn. "He's going to make it through, sweetheart. Don't worry."

"There was so much blood," Devin said. "God, it was everywhere. I just can't believe there was so much blood. Who would do something like that to us?"

"I don't know, son," Viola lied.

"Is it the same people who came after us at the cabin?"

"No."

"How do you know?" DaVita asked.

"Because the men who want Derek to fail, like to get their point across by more clandestine means. What happened to Luna, was too sloppy. Whoever did that, doesn't mind getting their hands dirty."

"Who?"

"We'll worry about that when your father's better." Viola gave her children an assuring smile. "This family is going to be alright. There's nothing we can't pull through."

Even as she said the words, Viola knew it was a lie. Everything had set them far from alright. She had trusted her firstborn when he promised that sick twist wouldn't hurt them. She believed Darrion's sureness. He would find him. Those were his words to her. Taran, Turkell, and Casper would find that bastard and put him in the ground.

Duke had been defenseless and alone. Fang had been in Chinatown, tending his temple. That Viola knew. If her husband held any true fears about a monster in his own home, Fang would have been by his side. Yet somehow, in the midst of the entire family's predisposition and fears, they had gotten careless.

"Ms. DeGrate."

Viola looked to the sound of her namesake and saw a man she assumed was the attending standing by the trauma room doors. He looked young. Not resident young. But young enough to surmise he had no more than ten years experience in emergeny medicine. Dark hair. Blue eyes. Olive skin devoid of a single solitary age line. Christ.

"I'm Mrs. DeGrate, his wife."

"Oh, I'm sorry," he said with a quick glance to DaVita. " You two look very much alike. I just need your signature on his registration. You can take care of that later after we — "

"How is he?" Abruptly interrupting seemed to be the quickest way to learn Duke's condition. Even if it came off as rude. "When I called, I was told it was possibly another heart attack and they were looking into an attending for surgery."

"He's stable for now. And somewhat awake. Your husband told us he has a history of heart disease and he's suffered two heart attacks in the past."

"That's correct."

"Fortunately, this was not one of those. It wasn't a third."

Devin breathed a sigh of relief.

"Then what was it?" DaVita asked.

"An angina attack. It can sometimes feel like a heart attack because it's pretty close to one. Which is also due to poor blood flow through the vessels."

Viola listened as he explained what she already knew. Duke would have to be kept in the hospital on a continuous nitroglycerin drip. News of his failing heart was received with the same worry and sadness that always came.

When the doctor gave permission for one family member at a time to visit Duke, Viola insisted Tu Fang was family and assured him Duke would vouch so. He nodded, held the trauma door open, and introduced himself as Dr. Patel.

Viola followed him to Duke's bedside.

At the sight of him, she knew this time was much worse. He didn't simply look weak. He looked drained. Leaden. She had never seen her husband look so vulerable.

She sat her purse down in a chair and kissed his forehead. Duke's lids parted briefly then closed and he drifted back into sleep.

"He also told me he's scheduled for bypass surgery," Dr. Patel said.

"Yes."

"When?"

"He was hoping to wait until after the 25th."

"Why after the 25th, if you don't mind me asking?"

"It's our youngest's eighteenth birthday."

"Okay. That's understandable. But, he can't wait that long."

"I know. Even his surgeon was insisting."

"Who's his surgeon?"

"Dr. James."

Dr. Patel's expression completely changed from staid and serious to an odd wariness Viola did not expect. His blue eyes narrowed as he spoke. "I'm sorry. I hope she comes out of it alright."

"Thank you."

"I hope the military doesn't have to move in. If they do it's gonna get real ugly real quick."

Viola's eyes grew wide with dread. "What?"

"Oh God," Dr. Patel said, blinking surprise at her. "You haven't been watching the news?"

♛

Fang, Viola and her two youngest children stood watching the news footage on the lobby television in stunned silence. Threats to call in the National Guard had been confirmed. Orders to evacuate all surrounding buildings had been given. No word of Dr. James' safety had yet been verified.

Viola's initial thought went to Derek. If he had not arrived at Cabrini, surely he was on the way. Which also meant Wendelll, Roth, and Prescott would soon be there as well. She supposed it was a good thing Duke was in and out of consciousness. Another blow could very well kill him.

Without doubt, her firstborn already knew Cabrini was under military threat. As of late, nothing moved in those projects, lest Darrion heard of it. A pang of forewarning rose in her chest and her breath caught then. As a mother, Viola had learned to analyze the consequences of every action and inaction around herself as well as her family and every adversary.

Of all of her children, Darrion always had the worst of enemies.

Even as a boy, Viola knew his tenacities and confidence would always earn him foes. Growing up in those highrises left little room for cowardice. Both Duke and Dutch had raised him to be loyal, steadfast, a shrewd thinker, and ruthless when he had to be. Under their tutelage, Darrion was a fast study. By the time he was a teenager, the only place he'd called home became an aclove of corruption and death. Many looked to Duke and Darrion for change.

For that reason, Viola vowed to get them out of Cabrini before the men she loved became revered for all the wrong reasons. What she did to ensure their future would haunt her to the grave and beyond. But it was done. Or so she had thought until recently. With all of the years that passed since that night, Viola took comfort in the solace of kept secrets. Now it became apparent why Zane went mad. She had made an agreement with him. For the past decade that agreement had held well for the both of them. Her private accord with a Harris went sour the day the good doctor decided to intrude on his enteprise. If she new Zane like she knew his grandmother, he would relish nothing more than spilling the truth before he killed Darrion. Viola had been a fool in thinking giving Cabrini to Zane would shadow the hatred he felt towards Duke for allegedly killing his father.

"There has to be a phone I can use," she said.

"Are you going to call Darrion?" DaVita asked.

Viola nodded.

"I already spoke to him earlier, but I probably won't reach him again. I already know where he is." She crossed the lobby to the security desk and used the LAN line telephone to call her son. He didn't answer.

That came as no surprise. Which meant trying to call Turkell, Taran, or Casper was pointless. More than likely Darrion was already at Cabrini or on his way there. Which meant they were with him.

Viola turned back toward the television and set eyes on Karolai Reynolds embracing DaVita in a hug. In all the years she had known her, if there were someone to be considered a close enough friend, Karolai fit the integrity.

In seeing her, Viola felt the comfort of meeting an old friend. After all, it was Karolai who introduced her to Duke more than thirty years ago. She was Viola's short height. Lean, with smooth skin, brown eyes, wide cheekbones from a distant line of Cherokee, and thick dark hair that flounced about her shoulders in soft, relaxed curls.

Viola went to her friend and embraced her. When Karolai suggested they step out for fresh air, she didn't object. Standing in the ER waiting room wouldn't cure Duke or free Angelique from Zane's lunacy any faster than her despair or worries. So, the twosome left the lobby for strong Chicago winds and the cold chill of winter.

A glance to the clear night sky brought nothing but the feeling of disdain. Though it was beautiful, despite the weather, such an atmosphere of stars seemed to mock her pain.

"Twenty years ago," Viola said, "no one would have gotten anywhere near Duke. Christ, what happened to us, Kay? How did we get so complacent?"

"Because you had every right to be," Karolai said. "You and Duke earned your right to live the dream. You earned your peace."

Viola looked at her dear friend. By the lingering look of dark reflection written all over Karolai's face, she knew there was more coming. "But?" she asked.

"But…You know how this game is played, Vi. This is what it is to live the life. I knew, even back then, when we all walked away from Cabrini, a day like this would come. To say 'I'm out. I'm finished. I'm through.' We can walk away, but the truth is, especially if we done harmed a lot of people out there, it ain't no such thing as 'I'm through.'"

Viola felt her eyes burn as they welled with tears. Karolai's words stung. But no DeGrate ever kept company with kowtows. No matter what, Kay always told her the truth. Even if it grated. Even if it left her raw about it.

"And we harmed a lot of people," Kay went on. "You, me, Duke, Dutch, Zander, Pope. Troy. Casper. All of us."

"I did what I had to do for my family. I don't live with regret. But I can't let my son pay for what we were."

Viola turned and walked back to the ER double doors.

Kay followed.

"What are you going to do?"

"Call an old friend. And an old foe. This shit with Zander ends tonight."

ZANE

Zane Harris watched more squad cars flood the avenues.

A sound of a propellers pulled his gaze up to the sky. Several news helicopters circled overhead. One thing stood true of Cabrini, in the highrise towers, the view from the fifteenth floor of his living room window left no inch of the lot or the cross streets hidden from sight. Every badge on the ground stood massing in groups. Intent on setting whatever plan they had in motion.

It was time for Zane to do the same.

But, first things first.

Zane walked over to his hostage and stood there for a moment. Watching her chest rise a fall with slow, deep breaths. Head half slumped to the side. Long, dark hair draped over one limp shoulder like a slack cape. She'd been out for hours now. Lefty and Q-Ball had tied her to one of the oak armchairs. Zane wondered how hard Lefty had hit her. If she didn't come round soon, he'd have to make her wake—and no one liked being slapped out of their sleep.

For now, his grandmother stood watch. Keeping a close eye on the doctor. Muriel pressed the oxygen mask to her face and sucked in a deep breath of O2. Since her heart valve replacement surgery, she seemed better. More alert. More energetic than before. But the doctor had said following surgery, she would need contintuous oxygen for the next few weeks.

It almost seemed mocking.

Just before the truce between his King Disciples and the Almighty Renegade Disciples, the doctor had offered to do his grandmother's surgery for free.

Zane took well to the offer.

Though she agreed to pay all of the expenses before and after the operation, he suspected that kindness was a deep regret for the bitch now.

One thing the doctor had to learn about Cabrini was that all good deeds given don't get one in return.

Zane made it clear to DeGrate, she was to do her thing and leave. No staying past a certain time at night. No unwelcomed or unnotified venturing into territory that wasn't cleared for outsiders and though he never discussed the code with DeGrate, Zane assumed he knew rule number one: Never, ever take it to the police.

She crossed the line when she took a private situation and made it public.

Rape? Of a little girl?

Zane refused to believe it was Zeno.

Yes, his brother had a need. A thing that drove him to hunt things. Prey on the weaker souls. That darkness, the pills couldn't touch. Zane and their grandmother understood that bottomless place Zeno lived in. Zane tried to control it. He tried to pick just the right ones for Zeno to feed to the darkness.

But no matter how many he chose, there would never be that last one he would ever choose. There would never be never more. No day would ever be the last day.

Zane had made peace with knowing his younger brother bore the burden of a hole that would never be filled. So there would always be more preys. Eventhough the doctor was more like a gift for Zeno, her pain was her choice. She wanted Cabrini and she got her. In all of her stark, terrifying splendor.

There was nothing his brother hated more than a woman who thought she could do or say anything without punishment. Zane knew if he didn't give his blessing for Zeno to take her, he would have done so at his wanting—and when the want took over, often times Zeno would lose himself to the darkness and then he would kill. A dead doctor in Zane's projects would have been the end of everything he worked so hard to build. Now, sacrifices had to be made.

Now, she was a necessary lamb.

His brother had a weakness for women who needed to be broken. Still, Zane just couldn't force himself to believe that Zeno could ever do such a thing to a little girl.

Zeno did not hate children. He just unloved them in a disregarding way. As if they weren't even there at all. They were just trivial bodies, existing along side him.

He never regarded them as threats that needed to be taken. But the doctor thought otherwise.

Zane knew, if he had to, he could bring himself to do the unthinkable. To protect his brother, he could silence a child. But the doctor had hidden her well and the old man was nowhere in sight. Which led him to think Freeman had to do with the girl's disappearance. It wouldn't take long to find that cripple.

For all his brother's faults, Zeno could find Moses in a burning bush if Zane gave the order to.

His pager went off.

Zane checked the numbers: 412*47*94.

During police raids, beeper code was mandatory and it was always the same. When a page went out, the first three numbers meant the room number, the middle two where the phone alphabet for the building the page came from and the last two meant the phone alphabet of who sent it.

Room 412; Head Quarters; Zeno Harris.

Grandmother Harris went to her bedroom, then sat back down on the couch and looked at their hostage. Watching the unconscious doctor seemed to pique her interest.

"Grandma," Zane said, "I'm going to the fourth floor to meet with Zeno. Page me when she wakes up."

"You got a piece on you?"

Zane never walked Cabrini unarmed. She knew. But Zane understood her asking was just a grandmother's worry.

"Two," he answered.

Muriel reached between the couch pillows and pulled out a Glock 9. She cocked it and handed it to him. "Take three. And stick close to your brother."

Zane Harris nodded. "Yes, ma'am."

He left he apartment and took the stairs to the fourth floor, passing several abandoned apartments with missing doors along the way. Just as he'd ordered, every one of them had a sniper posted with muzzles bored through holes in the boarded up windows. At his word, every cop within range would be shot dead.

They were smartly parked back far enough to keep out of pistol range. But they would have to leave the projects all together to dodge a well aimed rifle scope.

Zane sent out information to his snipers via pager. No walkie talkies. No brick phones except for the soldiers manning the tunnel. Every Disciple in the highrises was to be on alert at all times. Zane knew every cop on the ground had their bricks set to channel 4. Every word communicated between them on the ground, he'd hear of it.

Zane entered apartment 412, adjusted the channel on his brick to 4 and sat it on the only table in the empty room. He went to the window, and removed the cardboard. Revealing the lot below and a near, but distant view of what looked like every squad car in the city. A glance to the sky revealed the night. Soon, his plan would be put into motion.

Killing the two officers last year was done for two reasons. To seal a truce between the Kings and the Vice Stones and to keep the police jackets as a future cloaking device. When they moved to raid Head Quarters, Zane and Zeno would slip out of the tunnel, undetected and disappear into the streets of Chicago. They would have to lay low for a while. But with the Vice Stones, they could take over new territory outside of the projects, expand their business, and buy out their connect with the Chinese from the Kings.

For now, as it stood, the only reason the Red Dragons in Chinatown supplied the Kings was because the Dragon Head, Johnny Eng, had a good repore with him. In spite of Sampson breaking off from the King Disciples and starting up the Almighty Renegade Disciples, his revolt didn't change Zane's arrangement for pure China White cocaine. His connect didn't do business with Pope or Sampson. He only cared about supplying the one gangster who knew how to move product.

If Zane had the connect, he had the power. He had to learn, with accepting that power, sometimes things had to change direction. But that didn't mean his power would wane or diminish — it would just shift.

While he knew that proved to be a difficult road ahead, side-winding a DeGrate in the meanwhile was something a Harris did well.

To perfection in fact.

Giving up Cabrini was a decision not difficult to accept. After DeGrate half-assed returned to the projects, and became Pope's bitch to do so, Zane knew Pope would stop at nothing to muscle the Harris organization out and kill him and Zeno.

But he had plans for Xavier Pope.

I have plans for your daughter as well, motherfucker.

Zane felt the air shift. Then the soft ruffle of denim at his back and the sound of footsteps broke his thoughts of the future.

He didn't have to turn to see who entered.

He knew Zeno was there.

Zane kept his gaze out the window. "They find the little girl yet?"

"No," Zeno answered. "Freeman."

Zane popped the collar of his leather jacket. "Good. Let's see how long it takes for those old bones to break."

RENFRO

DeGrate got away!" detective Travis spat.

Renfro inwardly cursed and pressed a finger to his opposite ear. Drowning out car engines and the chatter of the officers behind him. "How did that happen?"

"We tried to stay on him. He took off and it practically turned into a high speed chase! Son of a bitch ran us off the road into the barrier drums! There's water every fucking where!"

"You alright? Do you need me to send an emergency unit your way? Fire department? Are you trapped in the vehicle? What do you need?"

"I'm fine."

"Is there another officer with you?"

"Yeah, Keel. I got a scrape on my forehead and I think he's a little bruised up, but we're not injured. Car's totaled though."

"Alright, hang tight. I'm gonna send a tow and a few more officers your way for backup. When you get a chance, go to the hospital and get yourself checked out."

"Okay, Renfro. Thanks."

"You got it."

Renfro hung up and cursed out loud.

"What?" Bishop asked.

"So much for the tail on DeGrate."

Renfro had hoped keeping tabs on him would give plenty of foresight on his whereabouts. Should he try to head towards Cabrini, Renfro would know of it first. If what Zane offered was true, the last thing he needed was the discovery of a mole compromised by civilian intrusion. As of now, the effort to thwart it had failed. All he could do was wait for him and put a stop to whatever he had planned to go after Harris.

"If they couldn't catch him," Bishop said, "he's probably on his way here."

Renfro nodded. "Yup."

"Then we better—"

"Yup." No need to let him finish that sentence.

"Cause when he gets here he's gonna—"

"Yup."

Renfro made his way through the crowd of uniformed officers and headed towards his lieutenant, Sandavor Delgado. He gave the superior a quick update on DeGrate. Delgado assigned two officers for backup to Travis and Keel. Renfro called for tow assistance at their location.

"What do you and Bishop have on Cabrini that we can use to infiltrate those highrises?"

Renfro shook his head. "Right now, no more than you."

"We know the layout," Bishop chimed in. "We know which gangs control which buildings. We know who the regents are. The lieutenants and all that. But as far as how to actually get inside, as far as Head Quarters is concerned, the Mayor screwed us all on that one. She didn't take down the welded door when she left, so all of the other buildings in the projects followed suit. So there is no back way in. We have to come at them from the front."

"And if they see us coming anywhere near them, the sniper's will have a heyday."

"What we can do is pull together some marked maps that we have back at the department. There in Renfro's desk. We'll get them, bring them back here and brief everyone on the layout of the buildings and we can figure out an extraction plan for the doctor and the best way to seize as many weapons as we can. And in the meantime, keep any residents coming home from work out of the buildings for now. The less people we have in the buildings, the less units the soldiers have to disappear into when we do make that move. Cause they're going to run into any apartment they think they can hide in. Usually it's a girlfriend or an old person who's too afraid not to let them in. So we need to keep them where we can see them and work on evacuating the rest of the residents as soon as possible."

"What's the ETA for the National Guard?" Renfro asked Delgado.

"Thirty minutes. You two should hurry up and get those maps. Because you'll also probably be briefing the commanding officer of those troops once they get here."

Renfro and Bishop walked back to their vehicle.

"Do you still have your brother-in-law's truck? We're gonna need it."

Brian Bishop shook his head. "I got a better idea."

"You got a van or something?"

"Nope."

"What?"

"Susie. She's finished."

Renfro froze.

Two years ago, it was just an idea.

In 1983, Bishop went to a Macintosh pre-launch summit in Elgin, Illinois. Still reeling from the buzz of new technology, one month later, he attended a police conference in Justice. Most of the conference focused on a lack of proper surveillance equipment and a lack of vehicles to properly use and transport them. From his admiration of operating systems, military equipment, and his love of reconnissance, came the ludicrous idea to somehow combine all three. When he first mentioned it Renfro thought it was too far fetched and without a proper budget, it would never happen. Delgado thought it was an excellent idea, but warned him a painstaking road of crowdfunding lay ahead.

On a cop's salary, Renfro thought he would never get the money to pull it off. But Bishop was a meticulous underdog. If you told him he couldn't do something, you just fucked up and told him he could. A few cashed-in favors from his uncle, J.D.'s junk yard, fundraisers, carwashes, and money from his own savings got it going. Then after writing countless letters, he received a small $5,000.00 grant from the government and Renfro was amazed at how far Bishop could stretch it.

An acronym in name, the Surveillance Unit for Search & Seizure, Intelligence, and Enforcement came from his brain. S.U.S.I.E. was his baby.

Instead of heading back to the police department, Bishop drove them to a private lot in Justice, Illinois that Renfro had never been to before. He was surprised such a place actually existed that close to city limits. While there were a good amount of suburbs near Chicago, short term parking options for over-sized vehicles were few and far between. According to his partner, Justice Truck and Storage was owned by a friend of his uncle. Not only did it boast 24 hour gate access, there was also an on-sight residential manager and secured video surveillance. As a favor, Bishop was cut a deal on the monthly parking fee.

They pulled up to the main gate and Bishop announced himself via intercom. Seconds later the gate rose and Bishop drove around towards the far back end of the lot. As they passed the last row of cars, S.U.S.I.E. came into view.

At the sight of her, Renfro was locked in an openmouthed daze. Moments later he was given a full tour of the renovated tour bus.

Burnished, steel enforced siding. High beam head lights. Working emergency lights perched high on her rooftop. Dual slide out rooms, a conference room, bathroom, and a 20-kilowatt generator. She even boasted a 10 to 12 personnel workstation fitted with chairs and refurbished computers — with department systems and software already installed. But the cherry on top was three holding cells for detainees and a weapons cage.

Gleaming in black, the acronym S.U.S.I.E. gleamed in large silver lettering along her siding next to a massive Chicago PD badge.

Renfro was speechless. As Bishop talked, all he could do was blink in wonder of it all.

He was standing inside a mobile precinct.

♛

As S.U.S.I.E. pulled onto Larrabee, just south of Oak Street, a mass of officers parted like the Red Sea. As if a shockwave of astonishment passed over them like a plague, looks of disbelief washed over all of their faces. They stood there. Eyes wide. Staring. Mouths agape as this mass of a steel enforced behemoth rolled to a stop.

As her door swung open, Renfro stepped out to gasps and wolf-whistles.

"What the hell is that?!" Chief Reynolds asked.

"This, ladies and gentlemen, is our new field post," Renfro answered. "The Surveillance Unit for Search & Seizure, Intelligence, and Enforcement has been designed by Brian Bishop specifically for what we're up against. And today, we are armed better than our adversaries. Today," he went on, motioning a hand to the silver lettering on her black siding, "Susie, is at our disposal." He glanced at his superiors and motioned them forward. "Chief, Lieutenant, Deputy, I'd say now's a fine time for a grand tour."

Reynolds and Deputy Chief Riles stepped aboard the mobile unit. Several officers, including Campbell and Sanchez, joined the curiosity and boarded the bus right behind them.

Lieutenant Delgado motioned Renfro and Bishop aside. They walked behind the bus, out of sight from the crowd quickly gathering nearby. Renfro assumed the spot was chosen by Delgado to keep their conversation stifled by the engine.

"What's up, Lieutenant?" Bishop asked.

"My UC tells me there's another way into the projects."

"Where?"

"A tunnel. Can you believe that shit? The fact that Zane actually had the audacity to build an underground channel to run his enterprise doesn't surprise me. But the fact that a two-bit thug got the pull for the resources to do it, I'm shook. More than somewhat."

"Where's the tunnel?"

"Supposedly, the only way to access it is through an adjacent structure and —"

"Hey," Chief Reynolds interrupted. "Are we going to get a tour here, or what? People are starting to touch shit they shouldn't be touching and they're probably going to break shit that'll cost somebody's pension to fix."

"Whatever they break, I guarantee it's low assessment."

"Exactly," the Chief agreed. "And they still won't be able to afford it. Now's a good time for me."

♛

Well," Bishop began, "she's from humble donations mostly. But everything in her is ours." As he walked the main aisle, Renfro, Chief Reynolds, Lieutenant Delgado, Deputy Chief Riles, and Officers Cambell and Sanchez walked behind him. "All the swivel chairs have been refinished with black telfon spray. All of the windows are bullet proof. Body work is steel enforced. Enough to stop a .357 Magnum at close range. Behind you there are three holding cells with bolted bars for shackles and a gun cage for our armament needs. Between the two is a main wall for mapping of whatever area we're targeting. To the right of the holding cages you'll see a hanging fold out table secured to the wall. To the left of the gun cage you'll see a door to the restroom and wall mounts for our gear. Duty belt, night sticks, flash lights, smoke bombs, extra cuffs, etcetera... And if you turn back around and look this way, you'll see all of the computer stations are wall mounted as well."

Chief Reynolds was the first one to speak. "What kind of programs to they run?"

"Everything we need and use back at the department. Records management system. IT general. Enforcement database. Now that were apart of the task force, I was hoping to have a systems guy out here sometime next week to install the NCIC database. That could cull from the local, state, and federal files on some of the gang members in the projects. Though most of them are so low-level they probably won't even show up on their radar, but still..."

"Are these brand new?" Deputy Chief Riles asked, pointing to the computers.

"Refurbished, but they work."

"What about the windshield there," Delgado asked.

"Bulletproof also. And there's a grill guard for close encounters."

His lieutenant looked around the cavernous space. Taking in all of its features. "Close encounters, you make it sound like were going to war."

"We're in Cabrini, sir. We sure as hell aren't going to a peace rally."

"No shit," the Chief agreed.

"I don't think anyone's made contact with Zeno or gotten any word from the doctor," Campbell said. "But if we plan on getting her out safe, it won't be with peace talks. The Disciples aren't the yielding kind."

"We don't know that for sure," the Chief said. "The Councilman will be here soon and he's prepared to make a statement both on behalf of the police department and the doctor."

"And you think that's actually going to work?"

"You don't?"

Campbell shook his head. "I grew up Cabrini. I know the Harris family. I know them well."

"And?" Chief Reynolds asked.

"And they won't go down without a fight, Sir."

"You three know these highrises better than most of the badges out there," Delgado said, looking at Renfro, Bishop, and Campbell. "What do you suggest?"

"We let the Alderman give his speech," Bishop said. "We let the reporters have their field day on whatever they think they know about what we plan to do. It'll provide a worthy distraction. And when you give the word, Renfro and I will go in. Not to arrest Zane and Zeno. We'll never get that close. But while all of his best soldiers are guarding Head Quarters, we can hit Bankroll, Hudson Mob, Camp Ball, 2 Bill, and any surrounding area to round up as many weapons and Disciples as we can. If we weaken his outer defense, all he'll have are the men next to him."

"And it won't be enough against the entire force when we move in to arrest his ass," Renfro added. "We take his weapons, we take his power. And if you give us the right men, and put out enough disinformation, we can do it right under his nose."

"Who do you need?"

Renfro looked passed him at the two uniformed officers. "Campbell and Sanchez will be a good start."

Just last year, Renfro and Bishop had arrived at Cabrini in the middle of a turf battle. Zane's Disciples were warring in a takeover and muscled the King Cobras out of the last building they held claim to in the Reds. The Cobras lost. Defeated, they had been pushed across Division Street to the Whites. Unfortunately Campbell and Sanchez were pinned down by a trash dumpster. Bishop launched smoke bombs at the shooters while Renfro had raced to get the two officers out alive as well as retrieve the bodies of two other officers who had already been shot and killed by sniper fire.

The Chief glanced at officer Sanchez. "I'm not familiar with you. What division?"

"Patrol," Sanchez answered. "Gang Crimes-North Unit."

"She's a rookie, but she's worked Cabrini before," Renfro said. "Campbell knows the layout. All the cover spots. How to work the breezeways once we're inside."

"You think four will be enough?"

Renfro shook his head. "I'd rather have four who know where the hell they're going than twenty or thirty officers running around like rats in a maze. In these projects, getting lost will get you killed."

"Well I don't think four is enough and I'm not willing to risk it without backup. So, you, Bishop, Campbell, and Sanchez will lead in. I'll send in ten more to back you. Splitting partners is never a good idea in the projects so you and Bishop can stick together, Campbell and Sanchez will do the same. And with the ten extra I'm giving you, that'll be five more officers each. And since you know the layout, now's a good time to bring us all up to speed."

"I'd like to sit in on this as well, if you gentlemen don't mind?"

It was an unfamiliar voice. A woman's voice.

Renfro turned around and followed all eyes to the door.

Dressed in a bland gray pants suit, her badge flashed on the hip of her belt clasp. Tall for a female, with short blond hair, a slim crooked nose, and far apart eyes, she looked like a woman not to be trifled with. Renfro hadn't heard her walk in.

Two more suits stood behind her. Both men. They looked to be near her in age. Late thirties to mid-forties was his guess. Every superior had a right hand man in the field. It didn't take much to conclude these men were her right and her left.

"Detective Renfro," Chief Reynolds said, "detective Bishop, this is Special Agent Pamela Stahl, FBI. Agent Tim Cowen, DEA. And Agent Will Lomax, ATF. I figured since you two were recently brought onto her task force, now would be the perfect time to meet."

Stahl shook hands with Renfro and Bishop.

"I'm sorry we haven't met before," she said. "I was away at a training conference in Sacramento."

"It's a pleasure."

"I hear the pleasure's all mine. Your chief tells me you and your partner had the highest number of arrests in your unit last year."

Renfro nodded. "That's right."

"Susie's going to help us arrest a hell of a lot more," Bishop added.

Stahl looked around and overhead at the cavernous vehicle. "I have to admit, I've never seen anything like this."

"Nor has anyone," the Chief said.

"And you think this is going to be enough to reign in the Harris brothers and all of his soldiers?" she asked Renfro.

"I do."

"How can you be so sure?"

Renfro said nothing at first. He knew the answer to that would compromise the advantage of having a close bite on an informer. But to hold back now would damage more than benefit. He told the truth.

"Zane called me. He wants to give up his mole."

Chief Reynolds eyes went wide with disbelief. "What? When?"

"Just over an hour ago."

"And you didn't think that was valuable information to share with the rest of us?"

"No. I didn't."

"And why is that?"

"Because for all I know his mole could be in this fucking room."

Several voices raised in protest. Chief Reynolds had to nearly shout over them just to silence the objections. "Alright! Everybody calm down! No one's accusing anybody of anything."

"We're after his supplier," Stahl cut in.

"We're after his mole," Renfro said, "his guns and his whole fucking crew. And tonight, we're going to get everything we came for."

"You have to get into Cabrini first," Agent Cowen cut in.

"Without being sniped the second they see a badge in their rifle scope," Agent Lomax added.

"Yeah," Renfro agreed. "Good thing we did some digging around and there's another way in."

Special Agent Stahl fixed a hard, steady gaze on Renfro and Bishop, folded her arms on her chest and said, "Impress me."

"Alright," Renfro began. He reached into the desk drawer and pulled out a map of Cabrini, then pulled down the folding table and rolled it out for all of them to see. He led with his finger as he talked. "These are the Reds. They're called the Reds because all of these buildings are built with red brick interiors." He moved his finger across Division Street. "These are the Whites. They're all called the Whites because they're made of solid concrete. Ironically, both are divided by Division Street..."

VIOLA

Viola dialed Patricia's number and hung up before it rang.

After a few more seconds of deliberating, she caved, and called her again.

"Porter and Associates."

"It's Viola."

There was a long pause then. Viola expected that. She stared off into traffic and paced the sidewalk for a few seconds, waiting for Patricia to say something. When she didn't Viola gave her a little push.

"I'll wait for the shock to wear off."

"Go on," Patricia finally said. "I'm listening."

"Am I hearing sirens? Where are you?"

"I'm here in my office. Watching it one the news. It's the television. Of course the media's being held back by the police. Which means I'll be held back by the police if I go down there. So, I'm more productive here. Derek just got there."

"Does he plan to make a statement?"

"Within the hour." Patrica went silent. Then, "Christ I can barely think straight. How the hell did this happen? I thought she was protected! How did Darrion let them get their hands on her?!"

The answer to that you and I would both like to know, Viola thought. But voicing that concern to Ms. Porter would show cracks in the confidence she had in her firstborn. That she refused to do. Any worries toward Darrion's reliabilities were not for Patricia to know. So she chose to stick to the more impending worry at hand.

"Your son is in trouble," Viola said. "Your future daughter-in-law is *very much* in trouble. But you may not be aware that my son is in trouble as well and that effects all of us. That stand-off in Cabrini isn't about the doctor who knows too much. This isn't about her interfering with Zane's organization. He wants my son's head on a plate. He always has. And he knows that by holding Angie hostage, Darrion will go after her and Zane will kill him. That can't happen. Not because of me. Not because of what we did."

"We didn't have anything to do with what happened to Angie. That is old, dead and buried. This is about his criminal empire set to burn. She got in his way. He wants her gone."

"It may be buried to you because it's easy for you block it out from the ocean view of your high rise luxury condo. But from Muriel's shit view in the projects, it's far from repressed. She hasn't forgotten a damn thing. This is about revenge not money."

"What does she know?"

"Muriel doesn't really know anything. Just that Zander died and Duke was never held as a suspect or charged with the murder. Neither was Xavier. They both broke away clean. But she knows you hand a heavy hand in the media and she knows I turned my back on Zander and I left him for Duke."

"Then she has nothing, Viola. If we put you infront of a camera and call her out, all that's going to do is hint to an admission of guilt when you've done nothing to feel guilty about."

"This isn't about guilt. This is about paternity. This is about the hatred a mother who lost her only son. And now she is trying to make sure the same shit happens to me."

"You think Zane's going to kill Darrion. How?"

"He's going to find a way inside Cabrini no outsider knows about."

"That's impossible. Both CPD and soon the National Guard will have that place on lock down. Nobody can get in or out."

"Darrion knows those projects better than anyone. Cabrini is in his DNA. And if he's going after her, if he wants a way in, he's going to find a way in, believe me. So outfoxing a bunch of cops to do it...it ain't rocket science."

"And once he gets in, then what? He's has to get past all of Zane's soldiers if he wants to get her back safe."

"Exactly," Viola agreed. "And we both know how that ends. Darrion is going to play right into his hands and he'll wind up dead before he gets anywhere near her. Duke will never survive that. It'll break him. It'll break my family. That can't happen."

"How do you plan to stop him?"

"I need a way in with the media. To communicate with Muriel. Try to end this before it gets to that. Right now, the stand-off is so firm, no one can get in there to negotiate except by phone. And that's if they even have one. I heard through the grapevine you know someone who has ties to Fox 32. I need you to get me on camera. If I send a message to Muriel, she'll send one back."

"And what if she doesn't?" Patricia asked. "We have to think about the possibility that you're right. If this isn't about money, what can you offer her? The truth? Are you really going to out what we did? On national television? That wouldn't just hurt you, it would destroy everything I've worked for!"

In spite of everything that was happening, Patricia only stood to think of herself of course. Even with what her son must have been feeling. Nothing carried more importantance than protecting the great Ms. Porter's perfect repute. Viola scowled and said, "Don't worry. You're name won't be mentioned. She'll only know my part in it, so you're protected. Okay? Are you breathing a little easier now, Ms. Innocent?"

"I know this is hard for you, Viola. But think about just how right you really are about her. If Muriel is that hell bent on revenge, she's not going to talk to you. At all. The pain is too deep. If you want a voice of negotiation, it's going to have to be Duke. And Muriel's not going to want to deal with him either. He's going to have to talk to Zane."

It suddenly hit Viola that Patricia didn't know about Duke's health. She had no idea he was near death. "That's not an option. Duke's...he's not in a position to deal with that right now, so Zane's gonna have to deal with me."

"I know you don't want Duke anywhere near there because of the church and how it might attract negative attention to the family, but there's no other way. In their world, they don't negotiate with women, Viola. Zane won't deal with you. It has to be Duke."

"That's not going to happen."

"Why not?"

"Because he's in the hospital. It's his heart."

She heard Patricia gasp.

It took all of her not to roll her eyes and say something rude. Listening to her husband's former mistress have a moment of unwelcomed concern was something she did not want to deal with.

"Is he alright?" she asked.

Viola went cold. "If your future daughter-in-law doesn't make it out safe, he won't be. So let's keep focused on the good doctor. I can take care of my husband. That's not why I called you."

"Okay. I'll call Riva and we'll get in touch with Fox. They're probably already down there anyway. It shouldn't be hard to get you in front of a camera." She paused and let out a breath. "Have you thought about how you want to do this and what you want to say?"

"You're the crisis manager. You tell me."

There was a pause for a long moment. Then, Patricia was talking so fast, Viola wanted to reach through the phone and slap her just to shut her up.

"I'll call Riva and have her meet us at Cabrini then I'll talk to Pat Travers, he's a DA at the Cook County State's Attorney Office and if I bend his ear before anyone else can, I'll know what he's thinking and what to tell Colin. He's a defense attorney for my firm. Then I'll make a call to Chief Reynolds, to let him know you're coming. He owes me a favor. In return for letting Riva get a personal interview with Reynolds, he'll get a negotiation from Zane through you. You'll tell Reynolds that you have former ties to the Harris family that might be beneficial to negotiating a surrender. If we can pull this off, he's not going to let you anywhere near the barricades, but you'll be close enough to let Zane know you're there and with the Chief standing beside you, he'll know you mean what you say. As far as what you're going to say when the cameras are on you, you're a mother. So you want to plead like one. Don't turn it on yourself or Darrion. That'll seem selfish and it'll bleed alterior motive. There's deep hatred between the DeGrates and the Harris' so don't even mention your family. Keep it on the public. Keep it on the innocent children who may be affected by the gunfire. Offer to provide the best defense attorney money can buy and to give your full financial support for his trial once he's arrested — if he let's Angie go unharmed and he turns himself in. I can handle the attorney, Riva will handle the media, and you can handle the sit down with Muriel when it's all over, if she'll agree to one. How's that sound?"

Viola just stood there, blinking in disbelief. "You wanna run all that by me again?"

♛

"Hi, Mrs. V."

Viola ended the call with Patricia and turned to see Anton Smith coming down the hall. She couldn't hide the surprise of seeing him with a dust mop in his hands and an employee badge clasped to his environmental services shirt.

"Hi, Anton. What are you doing here?"

"Oh, my grandma had foot surgery. She's still recovering. They're getting her diabetes under control. So, until then, she's right down the hall. Room 403."

"You work here?"

Ant nodded. "Yes, ma'am. I actually had to leave Cabrini and clock in for a few hours to cover half of somebody's shift. Even with all that madness going on." He slipped a hand in his pocket and his eyes fell to the floor. Somehow he found it difficult to meet Viola's gaze. "I'm sorry about the doctor. I hope she's alright."

Viola gave him a searching look. She didn't know where his loyalites lied and they certainly didn't lie with the family or Dr. James. Still, something told her, he was no unswerving soldier of Zane Harris' either.

Last she had laid eyes on him in Cabini he was a tramatized boy with teeth too big for his mouth and a voice too small for his age. He looked much older at the Christmas party last year. Then again, she imagined like most young men in public housing, Anton Smith had to mature much sooner than a young man should ever have to.

Finding Angie battered and bleeding, after Zane's men had had their way with her, set proof to that. Anton had called Viola and waited for her to arrive and get the doctor out safely. Surely that night left a stark impression of intimidations and violence. Viola could not imagine all of the terrors he faced day in and day out in that hell he called home.

"Me too," she finally said. They were both silent longer than Viola was comfortable with. Everytime she was near Anton, she was reminded of his older brother, Amari. Darrion's closest childhood friend. It left him all but gutted when he died. Anton was just nine years old then. Viola could have taken him in. But by then, he was an uncle to a sickly baby boy. Ida Smith was already in too deep with Zane for protection and Tanisha was lost to the needle. With Casper Jr. already adopted to the family after the death of his father and Turkell's need for a home, as a mother, Viola did what she had to do to save her own. She severed all ties to Cabrini and left Anton behind. So did Duke. So did Darrion. Deep down she knew, for Anton, the sting of that abandonment would never fade. "When Amari passed," she said quietly, "I was always sorry I couldn't do more for you."

Anton shrugged. "It's okay. I know you had a lot on you to deal with."

It was too much like him to say such a sweet thing. But his forgiveness didn't make it right. "Darrion feels the same way. He handles guilt worse than anyone I've ever met."

"KD? Feel guilty?"

God, he actually looked shocked. Viola wanted to shrink into the wall then and disappear from that affable, forgiving face. Anton really didn't know how much it hurt Darrion. Leaving them all behind.

"Naw," he said, shaking his head. "It probably hurt real bad when Amari died and everything. But he didn't feel no guilt behind it. He didn't kill him."

Viola cocked an eyebrow at him. "But he never went after who did."

Anton looked away at nothing. His eyes settled on the quiet of a dim-lit, empty hallway. Viola found it so unwittingly truthful. How silence said more than words could.

"When your brother was killed, I begged my son not to retaliate. Doing nothing, hurt him more than you know. But his restraint, kept the peace. And my son had to understand that nothing would come from killing Zane other than more violence. More killing. More war. And more pain for the innocent who had no choice but to endure it. Darrion chose mercy, for me. For his father. But that doesn't mean he didn't care. It doesn't mean he never wanted revenge."

Anton looked at Viola. Something changed in his eyes then. She watched the innocence fade to a knowing tell.

To a gaze that bordered on guile.

"Not that you'd stick around to stand in his way if he ever had the chance to take it."

Anton adjusted his grip on the dust mop. Still silent.

"Working the late shift, hmm?" she added. "How convenient."

Viola let that sit for a moment. He wanted retribution for Amari's death. It must have been hard for him. Living under the reign of the man he believed killed his brother. Maybe, after so many years of pain and loss, he deserved that reprisal. What could Viola say to that? Her thoughts went to Angelique then. She hoped the doctor lived to save the only man she ever loved. Duke was her world. Without him, they were all lost.

"Do you think Zane will hurt her?"

He looked at her then. All she saw was honety in his eyes.

Anton slowly shook his head. "I don't know."

"What happened?"

"A little girl got hurt. And the Doc, she was going to call the police." Viola's regard took on new dread then. Of all the ever changing laws among the gangs, rule number one was steadfast. Silence and secrecy. No matter what, you don't tell. You don't rat. You don't flip. Rule number one was worth killing for. "I tried to talk her out of it," he went on. "But she wouldn't listen. Said because it was a kid, all bets were off. I had to warn 'em so, I did. But I didn't think Zane would...I didn't think he would go this far."

Oh but he would, and he did, Viola thought to herself.

Gut instinct and old street logic wouldn't allow her to put anything past a Harris. Zane was capable of murder, Zeno was capable of masochism, and their grandmother Muriel was capable of smiling malice throught it all. Reveling in watching her grandchildren become the things she'd made them to be.

Part of that bitter, seething hatred Viola felt blame for. Being Zander's woman had pulled her into a world that faded from promises and purpose to betrayals and the darkest reign. By then, she had already fallen in love with Duke. By then, she had pulled away and closed her heart to a man who was more enthralled with becoming a brutal gangster than a leader made of respect and admiration.

Even now, Muriel did not forgive.

She would never let it go, until Viola felt the pain of losing a son to a bloody end.

She was not a religious woman. Even now, she was not raised to believe calling on God would save a soul, if that higher power was only called on when things went wrong. But Duke needed someone to speak on his behalf with the church.

It was time to reach out to Pastor Troy.

"I need a private phone," she said.

"You don't want to use your brick phone?"

She looked down at the oblong bulge in her purse. "I hate this damned thing. I practically need a shoulder strap just to carry it."

Anton nodded. "Okay."

Viola looked down the empty hall and glanced at the lobby area. Both were emtpy, but she couldn't risk the chance of someone walking by and hearing her conversation.

"Is there an empty room on this floor somewhere?"

Anton stood there, thinking.

"One you just cleaned and turned over. That's not assigned to a patient?"

He snapped his fingers. "Yeah, there is one as a matter of fact. Follow me."

DEREK

Derek Porter came to a halt as several police officers blocked his path. Ordering him to stay back for his own safety.

As he stood there, looking at the mass of officers, he actually took the time to count more than eighty squad cars and those were just the cars he could see.

All of the intersections leading from Locust to Hudson Avenue, Oak Street, and Sedgwick were blocked off. Effectively keeping everyone back from the Head Quarters building.

Derek didn't know much about the highrises and the lowrises. But from the times of his youth, when he came to visit Duke and Darrion, none of the buildings had names associated with the gangs that claimed them.

Over time, that changed.

Now, every building was territory to the King Disciples, King Cobras, Black Dragons, Vice Stones, the Deuce-One Boys and several other gangs he couldn't remember.

Derek felt a wave of futility come over him. This was his ward. As Alderman of the Near North it was his place to know these things. Perhaps if he had known more about the gangs, he wouldn't have even considered Angie's proposal to do gratis work in Cabrini.

He had told her it was madness.

Prescott had swiftly agreed.

Garrett swiftly disagreed.

In the way of political advantage, at the time, it seemed like the only sway. Not just for every black resident in Cabrini, but for Archbishop Cordenay, who had personally assured him every effort to put an end to the housing project's lawlessness would be rewarded. Derek knew by reward, his eminence meant every available class A share of O'Meravingi would not be denied him.

Which also meant he could use those shares to wager every influential backer in the state. At the time, Angie's idea appeared to be the surest way to get it done. Gaining the populace in the polls happened at a blinding pace. Overnight, Derek seemed to be the most promising hopeful for the new Mayor of 1985 despite running against the Italian hopeful, Caruso. It all seemed to be unfolding like a dream.

Until it became a nightmare much too real to ever wake.

Until Angie was taken hostage by a sociopath.

Warring with his emotions only brought him to one thought: Where the hell was Darrion? His absence came as no surprise. Missing in action the night Angie was attacked and robbed, Darrion was pre-occupied with bedding the one nympho who threatened his entire Mayoral campaign.

Without Darrion, there was no guarantee anyone would be infiltrating that building on the Alderman's orders alone. He knew Chicago's acting Mayor, Jane Burns would be making the ultimate calls.

As of now, he was simply being held back like one of the bystanding residents. That would not do.

Derek stepped toward one of the officers and began to protest his exclusion. Wendell threw a hand up to stop him. "There's nothing you can do but wait until they can strike up some kind of negotiation on Angie's behalf, Derek."

"You don't know a Harris like I do. They don't care about negotiation and they don't bargain!" He slapped Wendell's hand away and walked up to the first officer he locked eyes on. His name tag read Moorehouse. Thinly framed, with dark skin and wide eyes enlarged behind thick glasses, he looked a few pounds short of adolescence. Just by the fresh color of his uniform, it was plain to see he was green out of the Academy. Derek knew a harsh word or two would break him. "I'd like to know what you plan to do to get her out of there unharmed and if you don't have that answer, I need to speak with the leading officer who does. Preferably Chief Reynolds if he's here."

It must have been Porter's tone that did it. With a sudden recognition of who he was the officer pushed up his bifocals and swallowed. "Alderman, right now we plan to gather enough officers to infiltrate the building in force once the snipers have been removed from the rooftops. Then we'll plan to find which unit they're keeping the doctor in and bring her out safely."

"And how do you plan to remove snipers that you can't even see? From this far back they have a better shot at you than the other way around."

"Sir, as Mayor Burns ordered, the National Guard are on their way. They have aerial advantage with helicopters and sharp shooters and hopefully, they can cause the Disciples to abandon their posts with warning shots."

"And if that doesn't work?"

"Sir, worse case scenario, if the snipers fire back, they'll have to take them out. That's not what we want on national television. And to my knowledge, all attempts to contact them have failed. These gang members don't have phones registered in their names. I don't think they even have home phones. But, even if we can't negotiate, we have to infiltrate that building. And if taking out those snipers is the only way, then…we're going to have to take that course of action."

"What's the ETA?"

With a glance past the Alderman's shoulder, officer Moorehouse, gave a nod to the road behind him. "They're here, sir."

Derek turned and froze as a massive motorcade of armored Jeeps and several artillery tanks rolled into view. Three Army helicopters hovered in flank overhead in the distance.

He fought the dual emotions of humiliation and relief. To think the slums had come to this. In all of his years as a Chicagoan, not once did he ever think the Army National Guard would have to be called into his ward just to take back a neighborhood that sat less than a mile from every affluent disctrict in the city. In spite of all efforts to change things, Cabrini was a parasite latched onto the face of what was once a beautiful city. If it cost his career, Derek would see to its end.

As of now, there was no telling what the Disciple leader was doing to his fiancé. For that terrifying reason, Derek didn't care if it took a massacre to get her out of there.

As the armada's formation drew nearer, the world seemed to slow. Behind him, the swarm of the media flew to his back. Camera flashes. Followed by a flood of reporters. All of them harping over one another. Shouts of control from the officers mixed into the media frenzy until it all drowned to an inaudible cluster of hyped statements, unconfirmed details, rumored tactics and threats of arrests from restraining officers.

As the first armored Jeep rolled to a stop, a soldier Derek assumed was in command, stepped out and approached him. Tall to height of 6'3", the man towered over him. Russet skin. Broad chested. Thick in the neck. Well armed for conflict and equally clad in battle dress uniform. Two birds gleamed on his thick shoulders.

"Colonel McGregor reporting, sir. I need to speak with whoever is in charge here."

"I am," Derek asserted. "Alderman Porter of the 42nd Ward." He motioned to the roof of the Head Quarters building. "Atop of that highrise are snipers armed with long range rifle scopes and they're damn good shots. What we have is a hostage situation involving doctor Angelique James. She's being held captive for reasons unknown at this time. The King Disciples are the dominant gang. They claim territory in that building and several adjacent highrises throughout the projects. All of the street soldiers are armed and most of them are violent offenders. Your resources are going to be needed because getting her out safely is top priority."

"That's where you're wrong, Alderman. Loss of life and damage to the structure of that property and protection of the civilian population is our top priority and that dictates our purpose of attack."

Without warning glass exploded, cutting their conversation. Everyone scattered like seeds in a panic.

Before Derek could register the shock, he was thrown to the ground by McGregor. He fought the urge to yell out as a sharp pain raced up his left arm.

Several officers threw open the doors to their squad cars. Using them for cover. Drawing their weapons as they scanned the building for shooters.

It was like looking for a grain of sand in a pool of tar. All they could see were boarded up abandoned units from that far away. Without binoculars, spotting a muzzle through a hole in whatever the snipers used to cover the windows was impossible.

More shots rang out. Followed by exploding glass.

Derek watched as the windshields of several squad cars smashed and shattered from gunfire. More glass came showering down to the concrete.

A young soldier exited the armored Jeep and took aim behind the safety of the vehicle's door. "Sir," he called out, "I think they're shooting at us from the roof!"

McGregor gave him a turse no-shit-look. "Then shoot back!"

He gave a nod to his commanding officer. "Yes, Sir."

Derek watched the young troop and several armed soldiers move forward, take aim and unleash a barrage of bullets at the snipers. Uniformed officers moved to pull civilians behind and under their cars. News crews scrambled under the cover of their vans.

From the distant view, much to the Alderman's horror, one sniper fell from the roof to his death.

Terror-filled screams signaled the hoodlum's bloody end.

"Your presence is a threat," Derek shouted at the Colonel over the gunfire. "But you won't be for much longer. If you want to move, you have to do it now!"

Another troop took aim at a top floor window, fired, and seconds later, another Disciple fell seventeen floors to the unforgiving concrete below.

Derek thought he heard a woman scream then. Still pinned to the ground, he glanced toward shouts of hysteria and locked eyes on Roth Garrett. He didn't think a man could scream that…damseled and distressed. Wendell and Prescott were on the ground near him. Face down. Arms covering their heads as if that would slow the thunderous sound of assault rifles.

Gun smoke burned Derek's nostrils. Shells hit the ground like gold rain. Mags dropped. Troops reloaded and in a flash, everything became chaos screams, and the rancid, thick smell of gunpowder and hot metal.

ZANE

Zane Harris ignored the sound of gunfire and wiped the blood spray from his leather coat with a bandana.

This was getting messy.

Ever the all-seeing hawk his brother was, Zeno had found the old man trying to slip unnoticed through a crowd gathered in the breezeway. Much to Zane's surprise, Freeman didn't put up much of a fight when he was dragged to the ninth floor.

He had to admit, for an old man, he knew how to take a punch. But less than a minute into the beating, Lefty landed the blow that broke his nose. Without warning red sprayed Zane's jacket. Armani leather was not cheap. That pissed him off. Lefty landed another one to his stomach. Knocking the wind from his lungs. The old man let out a painful groan and keeled over, but he didn't fall. Two soldiers held him up by his arms when his knees buckled from the pain.

He could hold out a little longer. Another hour. One more throw to the jaw. Maybe two. If Zane chose to keep it with fists. Only a few minutes had passed since his capture and they hadn't even gotten to the knives yet.

"You're making this a lot harder than it has to be old man," he said. "Tell us where the little girl is and we'll let you go. You don't, and we graduate from blows to blades."

"You gonna reap what you sow," Freeman rasped. "Every single last one of you." He coughed unhealthily and spat blood to the concrete floor. "For all the years you hurt your own people." He paused, gasping for air. His head went slack against his shoulder. "Them chickens done come home to roost. Every cop down there gon' see to that. Them same soldiers gathered around you like you the Messiah, gon' run from you like you the plague before it's all over with."

Zane hmmphed and smiled a crooked smile.

He gave a nod to Lefty and the loyal Disciple hit him again. Freeman let out another wail of agony. Again both legs gave but the men held him steady.

A door opened in the hallway.

Zane turned and saw a small boy standing in the doorway of an apartment. Looking at them.

Maybe it was the sound of pain that drew him to the hallway. Maybe it was the gunfire. Maybe both. But, in some way it seemed the kid felt entitled to watch because he lived there.

"Go back inside!" Zane yelled. "Shut the fucking door and stay in there!"

At the bite of his tone, the boy flinched, drew back and shut the door. Zane turned back to Freeman. "We're gonna pay the Doc a little visit. See if she shares your point of view about my immediate future. But if I were you, I'd be more worried about yours."

DEREK

Derek watched the Colonel's orders being set into motion as the helicopters set course for the building.

Thomas Prescott, David Wendell and Roth Garrett had managed to follow their Alderman to safety behind an armored tank.

Prescott was the first to voice his distress.

"They just opened fire on a building in full view of the public with news vans everywhere, Derek! There's bodies all over the ground on live television!"

"As soon as we can," Garrett cut in, "we have got to get you in front of a camera. You have to address the people of this city and let them know the situation is under control before this causes a panic."

"No one's going to panic," Prescott said, heaving labored breaths. One look at him and Derek knew he lied more for his own reassurance than anyone else. Prescott nearly looked a breath away from hyperventilating. "No one's panicking here!"

"Bullshit!" Wendell spat, eyes wide. "Cause I'm one of 'em!"

"We're all fine," Garrett said. "Nobody's hit." He looked at Derek. Every bit of ire the Alderman felt must have been ever apparent on his face because Garrett took measure to assure him. "Angie's going to be fine, Derek. They're trained soldiers. They don't shoot aimlessly at civilians. And they certainly wouldn't shoot blindly at a hostage. We're going to get her back."

Derek couldn't think of a single word in response. All he could think of was the possiblity of Angie being hurt. She could have just been killed by one of those bullets for all he knew.

Was she close to a window?

Had she been shot?

Surely she heard the gunfire.

Was she even alive?

In that moment, Derek never felt so useless in his life. To press that boot even further on his neck, Darrion was still nowhere in sight.

Just when his worry began to boil to helpless rage, as if numinously summoned by some incantation, Derek looked past Wendell and spotted Darrion, Taran, T-Bone, and Lunch nearing the blockade. He pushed Wendell aside and set off toward them.

"We'll get her back," Darrion said.

Derek punched him.

Darrion went down so hard and fast, Taran did a double take at the sight of him hitting the pavement. "Whoa!"

Turkell cursed and moved at Derek, but Taran threw up a hand to stop him.

Darrion spat blood, stood and checked his lip.

Lunch and Wendell held Derek back with all the strength they could muster. But the Alderman still managed a free hand to jab a finger in Darrion's chest.

"This is all you fault!" Derek screamed. "I asked you to do one thing! I never should have trusted you! I should have pulled her out when I had the chance. If anything happens to her behind this bullshit between you and Zane, I swear to God I'll kill you before he gets the chance to do me the fucking favor!"

Darrion didn't say a word. He spat more blood, checked his jaw, then turned and walked away.

♛

Less than five minutes had passed and Derek could feel his knuckles beginning to swell. He sat on the front fender of his sedan and looked at all of the military vehicles and police cars. News helicopters circled over head to get a closer view of the military choppers and he could spot at least six news crews on the ground from where he sat. All of them had regrouped since the shoot out and resumed filming. It hadn't occured to him whether or not his brawl with Darrion had been caught on tape. If so, he was cooked.

This night was the worst of his life.

It all went so wrong.

Trusting Darrion to guard her in Cabrini. Listening to Angelique. He never should have allowed it. There were other ways to obtain the black vote. Ways that wouldn't cost the life of the woman he owed everything to.

Guilt bore through him like acid.

Four dead guards on his hands. All of them with families of their own who would grieve them in the media as well as for years to come. Executive Protection had life insurance policies on all of its employees. But no private security company liked dead guards on record.

As long as Angelique came out of it alive, any consequences paled in comparison. But he could do nothing to bring her out safely. Police had already warded him away from the building. Blocking with traffic cones and road barriers. But, from what he could see, the entire task force and every uniformed officer that could fit were inside a massive crime squad bus. Pouring over maps. Brainstorming over every possible way inside the building. If Zane was the twist Darrion said he was, they'd never get anywhere near Angelique before the fucking lunatic killed her.

Derek knew the well aimed words of a strong speech would be his only hope of getting throught to her captive. Hopefully, the effort would be profound enough to make an impact on her safety.

Derek looked up when a pair of headlights beamed into view and saw a familiar Jeep Cherokee pull to a stop near a small, rundown police trailer.

Viola DeGrate.

In no mood to deal with Darrion's mother, Derek stood and walked away.

VIOLA

Viola got out of the Jeep and walked the short distance to the police trailer. By the time she made it to her firstborn, Derek Porter was walking way from his sedan. His loyal trail of subordinates following close behind.

Whatever had transpired, Darrion looked heated. Taran, Turkell, and Casper seemed equally upset. She could guess their argument had been about the good doctor's predicament and there was no telling what both men had said to one another.

"Are you alright?" she asked Darrion.

He nodded and stared off at the mass of police officers and troops. Watching them gather gave the impression of intentions to set a strategy in motion. Whatever incursion they had in mind, Viola knew it would end bloody. Anything to prevent such an end was worth trying.

"I've set things up with Riva and a powerful defense attorney. If we can swing things Zane's way, not for the advantage of a win, but for the upper hand of a loss, he just might cooperate, stand down and let Angie go."

"Who's the attorney?"

"His name's Colin. Pat Travers is the DA that will probably be assigned to Zane's case once it's all over. Chief Reynolds is going to join me in front of the cameras. To try and sway him to end this."

"How did you manage to pull that?"

"Patricia."

Darrion nodded. Viola could tell by the look on his face, that answer didn't surprise him. "Yeah, she can do that." His expression changed then and he cast a doubtful look at her. "You really think that's going to work?"

"I don't know. But I hope so. Because if she doesn't make it, neither will your father, and…" Viola paused. Her eyes welled with tears. "God, Darrion, I can't lose him. I'm not ready to lose him."

Darrion pulled her into a hug and kissed her hair. "We're not going to lose him. That's not going to happen, Mom. Zane's not going to hurt her. We've got time for Pop's surgery. That's not a worry for you right now."

Viola pulled away from him and exhaled. She wiped a tear before she spoke. "Darrion, Luna's dead."

Darrion blinked at her. "How?"

"Devin found her. Covered in blood. Butchered! And I know it was that sick bastard that's stalking this family! I know it's him!"

Something went dark in his eyes then. Viola watched the jolt of it all pass through him like a slow shockwave. She had only seen that look once before. On the night Donald was beaten within an inch of his life by the police. Darrion was only eleven years old then.

When he stood in the living room, staring down as his uncle's battered face—both eyes swollen shut, a broken nose, both lips split open—Viola saw something in Darrion that scared her to pieces. A darkness crept into her son that changed him forever. Viola knew back then, in that moment he went from a child to a young man much too soon. That night he knew the grim meaning of racism and violence. That was the night he knew monsters truly did exist. Once realization that stark strikes, it can never be undone. It can never be unseen.

"I know how Zane wants this to end," she said. "But if there's any way I can convince him otherwise, it's worth a shot."

Darrion rubbed his eyes, exhaled and nodded. "Okay. We're going to hang back. As far out of sight as we can."

He walked off toward the back of the trailer.

"Where are you going to go?" Viola glanced at the mass of troops and the officers. "They've got every street covered from Larrabee to Oak to Sedgwick."

"Let us worry about that. We're working on a way in. The last thing we need is to be spotted on the news."

Viola followed him, pleading. "Darrion, I don't want you finding a way in. Or Taran or Casper or Turkell. That's what Zane wants. This is about you. Not Angie."

"A little girl got raped," Darrion said. "When Angie called the police, she broke the code of silence. Zane reacted. And yeah, we have some ugly history. I'm not saying that has nothing to do with it, but this is about covering up his blood trail and getting rid of any evidence that his sick ass brother had anything to do with it. And that means disposing of anyone who knows about it. This shit has to stop."

"Ms. DeGrate."

Viola turned in the directon of the voice and locked eyes on a uniformed officer swathed in police isignia.

"I'm Chief Reynolds."

Tall, dark skinned, with hard eyes, a solid glare, and a gut that protruded out from his service belt, he looked more like the standard Naval officer who'd let it all go to fat over the years than the Chief of Police.

"I understand Patty set up a camera spot for you to reach out to Zane. Unfortunately, that's not going to happen."

Viola smelled Derek behind that one. "Why not?"

"We've been informed that there's some negative history there. And we don't want to say or do anything to set him off."

"I see your Alderman is keeping you well up to speed."

The Chief nodded. "Both the Deputy Chief and the Mayor agree that it's best if you don't interfere."

"And he needs to stay the hell back," a stern voice interrupted.

Viola and Darrion watched the man approach. He did not look kind. An punitive face, loose dark hair, blue eyes, and the high cheekbones of an Anglo-Saxon. His badge flashed on the breast of his kevlar. As he neared, Viola glanced down at the 12-gauge pump action in his grip.

"This is detective Renfro," Reynolds said. "Usually he's a bit more... welcoming. But, given the circumstances."

"I want him gone," the detective said. "I wan't him out of this area, now. He can't be here."

"He has a fucking name," Darrion said. "I think you're well aware of what it is, how to spell it and how to use it in a sentence.

If you got something to say to me, talk at me not through me. I'm standing right here."

"And if you're still standing here in the next ten seconds, you'll be in cuffs in the back of a fucking squad car for interferring with police and breach of peace. How's that for talking at you?"

"Breach of peace for what? Being black, drawing breath or both?"

"How about a nigga with a brain?" T-Bone cut in, flashing gold teeth. "That's a breach of peace for your ass, huh?"

"Darrion," Viola warned, "Let's just go before we make things worse."

"He's armed, Chief," Renfro said. "All four of them are. They're the doctor's personal body guards. Employed by Executive Protection. The Alderman's private security company. This hostage situation has escalated to a full blown stand-off. This is now a police matter under military authority. The National Guard is here because this area is deemed a war zone. A civilian contractor has no jurisdiction in one. Any offensive force by a non-military person, who's not wearing a badge, will be tossed in a fucking cell and prosecuted. And if you think otherwise, does the term *unlawful combatant* mean anything to you? A nigga with a brain would already know that."

Viola watched her four boys cast equal looks of disdain.

She knew their glares of animosity would soon explode to a verbal assault that would lead to all of them getting arrested. She could have set the erruption with an egg timer. Like clockwork Darrion's brow furrowed to that Duke DeGrate angry 'V', his head cocked and he opened his mouth to retort. But before he let one fly, motherhood took hold. Viola gripped his arm and turned him around like an errant child who had just stepped out of line. "Come on," she said. "The further out of sight we are the better for Angie."

With that, Renfro turned and walked back towards the ranks of uniformed men.

Casper and Turkell turned and walked away. But, before Taran followed suit, he couldn't help himself. "Bitch."

Casper laughed. Turkell just shook his head.

The detective didn't seem bothered by the insult called at his back. He kept walking as if nothing had been said at all.

Unsure of how to end his own presence, the Chief still stood there. But his face bore a look of relief. Clearly thankful the confrontation had come to an end without turning physical.

♛

Viola, Darrion, Turkell, Taran, and Casper were escorted to the small trailor. Several police officers stood watch outside the door on orders from the detective. Making it clear the authorities would be taking no chances on unwanted intrusion.

Viola frowned.

One look about the dilapidated trailor brought thoughts of a tetnus shot.

"Whatever they're planning to do," Darrion said, "it's going to get her killed. We weren't expecting the roads to the tunnel to be blocked, but we've gotta find another way to get to it."

"Before they figure out they're sitting right on top of it," Casper added.

"I'll do whatever you need me to do," Viola said. "If you need a diversion, I'll give you a diversion."

Darrion shook his head. "I don't want you involved. We can handle it. Well figure something out. Right now the best thing you can do is go back to the hospital and see about Pop. He needs you there more than I need you here."

"Right now Duke is anything but alone. DaVita is there, so is Devin and Fang. And I'm sure Dutch and Donald are on the way if they're not there already. Making sure the surgeon who's supposed to save his life, makes it out this alive, is where I stand and I'm not leaving you, son."

Darrion nodded and looked out the window of the trailer. He could see the rooftop of Head Quarters in the distance. Viola knew his mind was reeling for a way to out fox Renfro and every cop assigned to keep watch.

"Leaving it to Derek's men," he said, "that was my fault. I should've put a stop to that before this shit happened. I knew they were going to get killed. Zane was just waiting for me look the wrong way."

Listening to Darrion's despair only brought forth her own foreboding and desperation. Their only chance seemed to be reaching out to the Harris' through the press and now even that was taken from her. Something needed to happen now and if Darrion refused her help, she had to make him realize he had no other choice.

"That's not the first time you were looking the wrong way, when they hurt her."

Darrion turned from the window, aghast. "What?" There was a composed look on his face and then it was gone and his voice took on a tone that bordered on anger. "What's that supposed to mean?"

Viola looked at him intently. Suddenly aware of what she was about to say and how it meant breaking her word to Angelique. In that moment keeping a secret no longer mattered. Viola knew then, inspite of wanting her son as far away from Cabrini as possible, Zane needed to be eliminated.

Nothing and no one got under his skin like Darrion. Maybe that self-absorbed menace was right. Maybe it was time to settle up with the family. Moreover, anything Zane felt the need to divulge to her son, any words he spoke against her about the past, Darrion would never believe him. A tyrant's tongue would never hold true against a mother's word. One thing Viola knew, she could lie faster than a Harris could kill. She'd lied before to protect Darrion. She could do it again. She could live with deception. In truth, lies are like armor. They only hurt when they fail to protect.

Time for you to die, Viola thought. *And my boys would be oblidged to do the honors.*

All she had to do was speak the words to mark his death warrant. "She made me swear not to say anything," Viola said. "And I gave her my word that I wouldn't."

Darrion looked taken aback. "She made you *swear* not to say what?"

"When she was attacked. She lied because she was afraid of what you and Derek might do. Her work in Cabrini is too important to her and she didn't want to have to quit."

By the stare in his eyes, Viola knew his patience had thinned. "She lied about what?"

"She wasn't robbed. They raped her, Darrion."

In rapid succession, emotions flashed over his face. Shock. Revulsion. Incredulity. Guilt. Disgust. Revulsion again. He let out an exasperated breath and cast his eyes to the window.

"Son, I don't want you think what happened to her was your fault. Angie wasn't just in the wrong place at the wrong time. I'm sure if Zane was being Zane, he had his soldiers watching every corner from every rooftop and every window. It could have happened to anyone he marked for it."

Turkell looked at her with incredulity. "Anyone impeding on a multi-million dollar drug ring."

What could Viola say to that?

"Derek doesn't know?" Darrion asked her.

Viola shook her head.

"Who does?"

"Ant and Calvin. Casper and Turkell. And now Taran. I made them promise not to say anything. For Angie's sake. It's like she's got this wreckless ambition to prove something."

"You noticed that too, huh?"

Viola looked to the door when it opened.

Derek Porter walked in.

An ice cold breeze wafted in behind him as the Alderman's eyes probed about the sparce furniture and settled on a stained, splintered folding table. Then his eyes set on Viola. He didn't speak a word of acknowledgement to Darrion.

Darrion didn't speak a byline to the Alderman either.

For that Viola was grateful. She'd had all the confrontation she could take in one day.

"I know you wanted to get in front of the cameras and speak on Angie's behalf. I appreciate that but, it might do more damage than we can risk."

Viola waved it off with a hand. "It's fine, Derek. I understand. Whatever is best for Angie. I don't want her to get hurt any more than you do."

"But, I'm set to give a speech in less than five minutes. If there's anything you want me to say…"

Derek left it open just like that.

Waiting for her to tell him whatever she wanted to say.

Viola decided then. Her silence was more useful than pleading with Muriel and her tyrants.

Again, the door opened. Thomas Prescott leaned his head in. He still looked the same. Well-groomed, well-dressed. Handsome, even with the hawked nose of an aristocrat. Blue eyes probed the trailer and fixed on Derek. "Are your ready? It's time. The film crew is ready to go and Riva is here."

Derek let out a breath and nodded.

"I know you don't have a speech prepared, but you want to make sure that you keep your voice calm yet firm and you want to make sure that the people understand everything is under control and the police and the Nationl Guard are doing everything they can to make sure the doctor comes out unharmed...And just so you know, Mayor Burns is here."

Derek nodded and walked to the window.

From where Viola stood, Prescott's presence seemed to trail off into nothingness for Derek. He seemed to be deep in thought. Every bit of his attention was locked on the highrise building. He looked up to the rooftop. Eyeing the busted out windows. Staring at every floor.

Like Viola, he was probably wondering which dilapidated, grimy apartment she was being held in and what they were doing to her.

"Derek!" Prescott called out. "Are you listening to me?"

The Councilman looked at him, blinking back to the now. "I heard you. Where's Garrett?"

Prescott leaned outside the doorway, looked around and said, "He's right there. Fifty paces away by the news van, Riva and the camera man. You want me to get him?"

Derek nodded. "Get Wendell. That kid can write me a speech in less than a minute and he can tweek it in half that."

Garrett nodded and took off towards the news van.

Then they heard it.

Gun shots rang out overhead, followed by screams.

TARAN

Taran Carter went to the window and shook his head. Watching Army troops line in formation and take aim at the building. Waiting for the command to open fire should they be fired upon.

"Zane is going to hurt her!" Derek shouted.

"That's not going to happen," Darrion said. "We'll get to him before he thinks of being that stupid."

"How?! Every way in is blocked."

Darrion crossed the trailer and stood next to Taran at the window. No bodies came flying through the mesh or from the roof. But Taran knew Darrion couldn't say with certainty no one else was killed.

Knowing the Cabrini he knew, someone had just lost their life. They looked to all of the tenants behind the baracade. No one was on the ground bleeding. None of the officers or the Army troops had been hit. It seemed the gunfire was internal within Head Quarters. Darrion must have assumed it was near wherever the good doctor was being held.

He cast a knowing look to Taran, turned to Derek and said, "There's a tunnel."

"What?"

"An underpass that runs under the projects, straight to Head Quarters."

"Where is it?"

"Before you get that answer, I'm gonna need something first."

"And that is?"

"Restraint. From you and your jurisdictive guard dogs." Derek gave him a hard look. But from Taran's take on the face off, Darrion couldn't have cared less. "And I'm not asking you to lie for me, I'm asking you to show some restraint for Angie's sake. The sooner you go running off at the mouth about that tunnel to the Chief, all hell is going to break loose. And if they're coming after me, I'm not getting to her. Their lead officer, this Renfro, made it clear he wants us to stay the hell back. He can't get to that tunnel before we do. If he does, it's all over."

Darrion turned to his mother. "And you're right. We need a diversion."

Viola stepped forward. Ready for anything. "What do you need me to do?"

Darrion turned his gaze to the guards posted just outside the window by the door. "Just be...Mom. Open the door, walk up to them and start some shit."

Viola shrugged and headed for the door. "No problem."

"Just enough to keep them busy not enough to make them arrest you."

"It's done." Viola pulled her wool coat closed and grabbed the door knob then paused.

"It won't be long before they notice you're gone."

"He's not leaving first," Taran said. He gave a nod to Turkell. "Me and T-Bone are going to slip out and find the tunnel. Then we'll come back for him."

"After that," Darrion said. "We're gone."

"Just give us a signal when it's okay to slip out of the trailor. Tap on the window pane or something."

Viola nodded and was out the door.

It didn't take long for Mrs. DeGrate to do what she did best. Taran, Derek, Turkell, Casper, and Darrion watched her from the window. She walked up to the officers. Moments later their voices raised in ire. From her defensive stance and the way her lips were moving, she raised hell well enough. When the officers were absorbed in their agrument, a tap came to the window.

"Alright," T-Bone said, drawing back. He tapped Taran on the shoulder. "That's it. Let's move. We'll be back, KD."

Darrion tossed him the car keys. "Stay live, man."

Turkell slowly opened the door and both men slipped out into the darkness.

♛

Turkell Scarbone and Taran Carter stayed low. Moving swiftly to Darrion's Mercedes. T-Bone popped the trunk and reached for his Kevlar.

Taran grabbed his own and did the same. He pulled the diamond cross from under his shirt and slipped it under the Kevlar. He was not a deeply religious man. But his uncle had given it to him with words that it once belonged to his father. Whenever battle was upon him, Taran kept it near.

"St. Dominic's right?"

Turkell pulled a rubber band off his wrist, swept his dreads into a low pony tail and nodded. "Yup."

"How far is Locust from here?"

"We on Locust. The church is less than a block."

Taran snatched a Remington 12-guage and two Browning double action pistols from the velcro of the trunk door. He slipped the pistols into the holsters of his vest, reached for a box of slugs and loaded the shotgun.

Turkell's steel of choice: The Beretta AR70, a Predator machete, and a Ruger P85 .45 ACP.

"From what Guesser said, there'll be four of Zane's soldiers on watch at the church entrance. That's two for me, two for you."

"There's only one problem with that."

Turkell's brow lifted. "What's the problem?"

"I don't know how long that tunnel is, but I'm guessing the two guarding the other end are going to hear the gunshots."

Turkell shrugged. "I'm a blades before bullets man anyway."

"In the projects, you don't bring a knife to a gun fight."

"Well I always do, Cause where I'm from. In Haiti, the bullets always run out. Sooner or later. Then, it's knives and knuckles, baby. Knives and knuckles. And I got a nagging suspicion, these niggas around here ain't shit without a gun."

♛

Turkell kept close to the church wall. Slowly moving toward the back entrance. Taran followed close behind. Careful not to step on broken glass or a firm twig.

St. Dominic's Roman Catholic Church often fed, clothed, and nutured the poorest of the neighborhood. It's massive size was built to serve a thousand devoted comfortably. Constructed of pressed brick and limestone trim, the architecture reminded all those that looked upon it of the Italian roots it stood to serve.

Taran surmised, somewhere along the line, the Archdioces chose to turn a blind eye and a deaf ear to Zane's subterranean ambitions. Whatever the arrangement was, money must have been exchanged to keep the police none the wiser.

After tonight, everyone with a television or eyes to read the paper would know.

Turkell came to the end of the building and peared around the corner to the back lawn.

Taran inched forward, waiting for Turkell to strike. His eyes probed the darkness restlessly. Despite the cold wind that swept over him, Taran was tensed for anything.

Just as Guesser had said, four men stood guard near the back door. Two looked tall and slim. Standing guard directly in front of the entrance. One looked short but thin and was off by a tree taking a piss. Their fourth looked young enough to be indebted to Zane, but not near the threat Taran had expected. His mass was all fat. Still, dressed all in black, they must have been familiar with murder, if not seasoned killers, because they were ordered to keep the underpass. Taran knew Zane would never assign a gun-shy soldier to such a task.

Other than the AK-47s they carried, none of them looked to be more than he could handle and none of them were looking their way when T-Bone moved in on them. He held up a fist, letting Taran know to stay back. This one was his.

What came next set the bar for carnage.

With both of the taller Disciples standing right next to one another, in the dark, their bordering view was all but blocked. They never had a chance to react.

Turkell unsheathed his machete, moved with the wrath of the devil's due and slashed their throats in a fury from left to right. Before they could scream, T-Bone spun the blade and jabbed the sternum of the first Disciple then pulled the steel from bone, and stabbed the skull of the second.

As they both dropped, the dull thud of their bodies hitting the ground made the fat one turn around. Stunned and wide eyed, he raised his AK and aimed to fire. T-Bone lunged forward, grabbed the assault rifle, pulled it toward him and used the close gain to chop off the hand that held a finger to the trigger.

Before fats could scream, T-Bone pushed the steel through his larynx, put a hand to his mouth to keep the blood spray from sputtering out and slowly lowered his mass to the grass.

Taran was agog.

Not just at the silence and swiftness of his kill, but at the Disciple who was still soaking the tree with urine. It seemed a strange thought at the moment. But Taran found it hard to believe the human bladder could hold that much fluid.

T-Bone rose to his feet, slowly walked toward the tree and flicked the blood off his steel. Splash from the urine soaking the bark masked the sound of red spraying the lawn.

Turkell didn't stand on ceremony.

Grabbing his head, he snatched it back and slid the sharp steel through the back of his skull. A wet, choking gurgle came from his mouth as the blade glided through his throat like the shearing of a melon.

Maybe it was morbid enthrallment.

Maybe it was the morose imprint Vietnam left on a man.

To watch his best friend murder like he was born to end lives, Taran had to smile.

ANGELIQUE

Angelique's eyes flew open when someone slapped her.

Not gently.

"Rise and shine, Doc."

A sharp pain arced through her skull like a thousand knives being jammed through her eyes. Then came the pounding. She could actually hear the blood rushing in her ears.

Her vision blurred for a few seconds and when it cleared, Zane's cruel glare came into view.

"I tried to avoid it coming down to this. But it is what it is. The code of silence, Doc. That's our law. You broke it. Here's the repercussions."

Zane moved aside and she locked eyes on Mr. Freeman.

From the looks of him, a harsh beating had been meted out.

Old dark blook coverd his face. His nose was malformed and crooked. One eye was swollen shut. He could barely stand.

"Where's the kid?" Zane asked her.

"I don't know."

Though it was not a lie, Zane took is as such.

With a nod of authority to Lefty, Freeman was hit with such force, two teeth went flying from his mouth. He went face down to the hardwood.

Angelique flinched at the sound of wet flesh hitting the floor.

"You can beat him to a pulp," she pleaded, "it won't change anything! I don't know where she is! When they came for me, she must have already been gone or you would have found her by now!"

"Who took her?" Muriel chimed in. "Them guards? Can't be cause they dead."

Angelique hadn't noticed the old woman sitting there until she spoke. Yet there she was. In all of her oxygen deprived, sickly glory. Grayed hair. Arms gone to flab. A sunken, kyphotic back. Muriel Harris wasn't long for this world and she knew it.

But clearly she meant to keep her grandsons in power before her head hit the grave.

"Who?" she repeated.

"I thid, bitch!" Mr. Freeman slurred. He groaned, rolled onto his back and spat blood. Tonguing the missing gap confirmed where his teeth had been. "And I ainth thalking, muthafucka!"

"Old Man Freeman," Muriel said, almost too calmly. "Always the brave one. Isn't he?"

Angelique just couldn't take her eyes off him. It was all her fault. If she had never set foot in Cabrini. If she hadn't pushed Derek into it for campaign advantage. None of this would have happened. Now, Cassius would live marred for the rest of his days because she couldn't see past her own blind impulses. But what could she do? Leave a little girl's life in the hands of the same hoods who clearly held no qualms in killing her. To Zane, Ophelia wasn't a life. She was a felony. A prison cell. A threat to his freedom. Nothing more.

Muriel reached between the couch pillows and pulled out a pistol. "One thing you never learned about the projects," she said to the old man. "In Cabrini, asking is a courtesy we don't have to extend." She cocked the steel, aimed at Cassius Freeman and fired.

Mr. Freeman's head flew sideways and blood sprayed the television screen. Instead of going limp from instantaneous death, his body began seizing.

Angelique wanted to throw up. Gastric juice rose up in her throat, but there was nothing in her stomach to give. In all of her years in the OR — all the blood. Sutures. Cracked open rib cages. Exposed beating hearts. Nothing in the operating room could prepare her mind for watching someone's head nearly blown wide open right infront of her.

It was easy to be jaded as a surgeon. To compartmentalize got the job done and saved lives. But to watch swift and brutal death come for someone she knew, it was more than traumatizing. It was mortifying.

Yet, she couldn't look away.

Despite the massive damage to his brain, his body was still convulsing. Followed by sporatic jerks. Then jerks slowed to a slight twitch until all that lay before her was a lifeless motionless body.

Angelique swallowed and tore her eyes away.

Staring down at nothing, she just shook her head."I don't know where she is."

"Don't matter," Muriel said. "She'll be found before it's all over with. I can promise you that."

She forced herself to look up at the old crow. "What happens now?"

"We wait for your boy to show," Zane said. "And he will. It's just a matter of time. And we he does, we're gonna get square. His demise is long overdue."

God, she had been hit that hard in the head. Darrion. He probably was on the way by now. And...

Now? When was now? How long had she been strapped to a chair? How many hours had it been? Did anyone know where she was? She gave a quick glance over to the window and saw nothing but darkness. It was nighttime. But how long ago had the sun faded?

She looked back at Zane. He had an expectant look in his eyes. Waiting for her to say something as if the mention of Darrion was supposed to spark some retort of defiance. She opened her mouth to speak but her throat was suddenly dry. An involuntary swallow was all that followed and it sounded like a gulp of fear. It probably was a gulp of fear.

A massive light flashed in her peripheral. She looked to the window and saw a military helicopter nearing the building. Its search light moved over the rooftop. Then shots rang out.

There was no telling how many squad cars were down there. But with military troops taking out snipers, she knew an officer engaging Cabrini solo was highly unlikely.

"The Army is here, Zane," she said. "There is no coming out of this alive unless you surrender. It's over."

"Oh, it's not over until your boy is in the fucking ground! And this little run in with Five-O ain't the first time. And it won't be the last. Let me give you a quick lesson on how it works when there's a raid about to go down. First, the Crown Vics show up, except this time, they can't sneak up the back because we got the doors welded. Which means they can only come at us from the front. Second, I sent my snipers to cover all the rooftops. Not just Head Quarters. They walk every adjacent building to the parking lot. No pig is safe on the ground. No chopper is safe in the air. And they know it. Why do you think they haven't stormed this motherfucker yet? Third, they'll try to block us off. PD got something they like to call the Black Wall. It's an automatic fence they roll up. Between the north tower and the south, so we can't use the Maze to take off on 'em and disappear. Then, when the mesh from the fence blocks any shots my snipers can take at 'em, they think they'll dart out from under their squad cars and raid the building. But I got news for their asses. It ain't going down like that, Doc. As soon as they step on to the Killing Fields, we lighting all their asses up."

A blaring noise seized the air then. It sounded like a fire alarm. Angelique hoped that was Darrion's doing.

DARRION

I found the tunnel!" T-Bone said as he burst through the door.

He sat two duffle bags on the folding table, unzipped them, tossed a Kevlar to Darrion and pulled out four gorilla smasks. "And I just copped a brick from one of the bodies at the entrance. SWAT is on the way to assist the troops. Aerial and ground units. ETA is three minutes. That's more choppers with snipers and if those searchlights start sweeping, they find the bodies. They find the bodies, they find the tunnel and it's game over. If we gonna do this we gotta do it right now!"

"Where's Lunch?" Darrion asked.

"Outside by the car, waiting with Taran."

Derek cursed.

Darrion turned around and followed the Alderman's gaze out the window. A mass of people were walking out of Head Quarters. None of them looked to be armed. Most of them were mothers walking with children in hand. A few elderly were among them.

Viola opened the door and stepped inside the trailor. "There's a hoard of people headed this way. I think they're from Head Quarters. What the hell is going on?"

"My guess," Darrion said, "it looks like somebody tripped the fire alarm."

"Zane?"

"Maybe?"

"That's a good thing," Viola said.

Darrion and Derek shook their heads.

"Not really," they both said.

"How's that?"

"If they're clearing house," Darrion said, "that only means one thing. If they have bricks they're listening in. They know SWAT's on the way and they're about to move in. It's about to go down. And they don't want a kid or a mother catching a bullet on national TV."

Viola cursed.

"KD," Turkell said. "We gotta go!"

Darrion reached in the duffle bag, pulled out his twin Colt holster and strapped it to the small of his back, then slipped on his Kevlar.

"Wait a minute," Derek said. "They're never going to believe I just let you walk out of here."

He thought on that for a few ticks then nodded in agreement. "You're right."

Darrion cracked his knuckles and punched him. Hard.

Derek hit the floor and landed flat on his back. He spat red, covered his bloodied lip with a hand and rolled onto his side. Groaning in pain.

Darrion stood over the Alderman. A devious look of reprisal gleamed in his eyes. "Tell them I hit you."

Derek slowly stood, moved his jaw and checked his lip.

Another shot rang out followed by screams.

Turkell sat the brick on the table and turned up the volume.

"They're coming, Zane!" a Disciple blared. "Get the Doc! Get the Doc! They're raiding the building!"

Every resident nearing the barricade scattered. Some protected their children with the their bodies. Some reacted in a panick and threw their children to the ground.

Derek went to the window and watched the mayhem as troops advanced towards the building. Using the adjacent structure of a liquor store for cover, they flanked the wall. Moving forward with tactical precision.

Every officer assigned to guard the trailer rushed to the crowd of panic-stricken residents. Helping them take cover. Shouting orders to keep them calm.

Darrion backed up towards the door.

"Go!" Viola said. "I'll handle the police. Blow through anybody that gets in your way!"

Viola slipped out and rushed torward the commotion.

With that Darrion and Turkell were gone.

Before Darrion cleared the trailer and slipped into the darkness, he glanced back once more.

Derek stepped out of the trailer, reached for the door knob and with a brute twist of his wrist, broke if off, tossed it to the pavement and walked towards the swarming media waiting to hear the Alderman speak.

♛

Darrion, Taran, Turkell, and Lunch slipped into the church and dashed passed the vacant pews. Strewn trash, empty crack viles and broken glass crunched beneath their every step as they moved passed the pulpit and into the only dim lit hall in the darkness.

It stretched out narrow. More like a dead gangway than a festooned corridor made for the high traffic of parishioners. They took a staircase leading them down to an unfinished cellar.

Darrion took in all of the fouled subterranean. Loose earth and stone made the walls. Frayed wires hung from the rafters. At the opposite end, the partially caved ceiling blocked broken stairs leading to nowhere. It looked like they were standing in a gateway to hell. With what they faced on the opposite end of the tunnel, technically that wasn't far from the truth.

Much to Darrion's surprise, the cellar was empty. Guesser had told him several men would be guarding the tunnel. Since they weren't physically in the tunnel, perhaps the self proclaimed king felt no need to have the cellar manned if both entry points were guarded at all times.

Before they got made by the soldiers guarding the exit to Head Quarters, Darrion thought where they stood was as good a place as any to plan a blitz.

T-Bone lifted the brick to his hear when a voice came through the speaker. "Renfro, the Black Gate is here. Where do you want it?"

"Copy that. What's your 20?"

"We're at the corner of Oak and Larrabee."

- 95 -

"That's far enough back from Head Quarters and sniper fire. Sit tight. I'm coming to you."

T-Bone lowered the brick and looked at Darrion. "A Black Gate? What is that?"

"It's a gate that has a vertical lift," Darrion explained. "It raises to block thru-traffic between the towers in high rise buildings. SWAT uses that shit during raids." He knelt down, picked up a twig and used it to draw in the dirt as he talked. "This is the layout we're up against when we exit this tunnel. We've got a small courtyard here. The front entrance to the breezeway here that's too exposed to shooters. And a small thruway to the left that goes around the courtyard to the otherside of Head Quarters where the door is bolted shut in the back." He picked up two small rocks and placed them on the dirt-map. "We want the back door, because it's unmanned. Zane won't send his soldiers where they're not needed. That's the easiest way in. We'll use a small shape charge to blow it off the fucking hinges. To get to that," he pointed to the rocks, "we're going to have to take out the soldiers posted up at the exit and the breezeway."

"What's that?" Lunch asked pointing to a piece of dark singed glass.

Darrion looked down at the burnt tube. He hadn't noticed it in his make-shift layout until then. There was no reason for it to be there other than the fact that it was just there. Left by some basehead. "That's a crack pipe, Lunch," he answered, knocking it away with the twig.

Casper pulled at the neck line of his Kevlar and gave them an abashed look. Conscious of his own unmindful ignorance. "A'ight then."

INTERVIEW

For some reason," Turkell said, "I guess, when it came to the Haitians, society decided to push us to the lowest of the low. So we decided, we wasn't gon' take that shit no more.

"Growing up in Little Haiti, that's something I wouldn't wish on nobody. You know, it was hard on us growing up. The culture was all the way different. Not speaking the language. I watched a lot of my friends struggle. I watched their parents struggle. Working two, sometimes three jobs, just to make less than minimum wage. Still can't put enough food on the table. Trying to pay the rent. Most of the time behind on rent. And if somebody gets sick, can't afford to take them to the doctor and even if you could, would you want to? Shit, I didn't trust 'em.

"And that was just the problems at home. Out on the streets, it was whole other nightmare. At school. With the police. Walking to or from church. We got hassled a lot. Especially on Fridays. They called it Haitian Fridays. That was the day of the week when, if you got caught by yourself, you got jumped by the blacks on the west side of Second Ave. They would beat you down for no reason at all. They had they own little gang. They was cliqued up. And they was coming to take some. That's the way it was growing up there. That's the way it is now, but it's not as bad as it was back in the 80's. The Majority of the population in the 90's today is almost seventy percent Haitian.

The rest is Hispanic, a few whites, and some Indians, Asians, and Samoans. Back then it was only about forty percent. The rest was Afro-Americans. And the war was brutal."

"Was it anything like what you experienced here in Chicago back then?" Zella Rice asked.

Turkell Scarbone went silent for a moment. Thinking.

"Yes and no," he finally said.

"How so?"

"Well, back then, in Chicago, we had our own Haitian community, but it wasn't as large as Little Haiti. And the wars I fought in with my brothers involved the Italians, the Asians and Hispanics and a few other black gangs. By and large in the Windy City that's what it was about. But back home, in Miami, it wasn't just about politics and bad blood. We was fighting for the right to just be. We was fighting for the right to exist. We didn't need nobody's pitty or hand-me-downs. You know what I'm saying? We just wanted to have our own. That's it. But to them, we wasn't just trying to have our own. We wanted theirs too. We wanted what they had and then some. That was the way they were looking at us. And they had no problem taking that conflict beyond words. So we had to fight. That's when the Zoe Lords was born."

"What year did you return back home?"

"From '85 through '86. I was in hiding for a little over a year."

"In hiding from what?"

"A job gone bad. It went real bad."

"You mean the bank robbery?"

Turkell nodded. "The task force closed in on us. After a while, we couldn't make no moves. The streets were too hot. Everywhere we went it was Feds."

DUKE

Duke DeGrate sat helpless in bed watching the news in his hospital room. Thinking about the blood in his kitchen. In his home. In the one place his family could always come to feel safe.

If Zosa was responsible, D'Amico would have to make good on his word to eliminated him and soon. Sending wolves to kill them at a hunting retreat last year was one thing. But to bring the blood to his doorstep, that was a blow Duke could not leave unanswered.

He looked up when the door opened.

A nurse walked in with IV tubing and a bag of saline in hand. Short blond curls. Smiling white teeth.

"Hello, Mr. DeGrate, my name is Connie. I'm going to be your nurse during your stay here at the hospital."

"What room am I in?"

"Your in room 415. On the cardiac-unit." She reached for the IV pole at his bedside and hung the saline. "You'll be here until we find a surgeon for you. Then you'll be transferred to Northbrook Heart Hospital for your surgery."

"What do you mean find a surgeon? I already have a surgeon."

Connie looked at him.

From the expression on her face, he could tell she knew something he didn't. Whatever it was, it was not good. A pang of worry turned his stomach and he instantly became nauseous.

"What is it?" he asked.

"Well…" she said. Then her mouth shut.

"Go on."

"I'm sorry to be the one to tell you this. But, Dr. James has been kidnapped. She's being held hostage in those housing projects by some awful drug lord. The police are doing everything they can to get her out, but right now it's…"

Her lips kept moving. But every word out of her mouth just slurred then. Muddling and distorting into inaudible speech as the room began to blur. Duke shut his eyes tight, exhaled, then sat up, threw back the sheets and put his feet down to stand.

"Mr. DeGrate, you can't get out of bed!" Connie rushed to his side to stop him. "You're in no condition to walk. With your dizziness, you're a fall risk and your heart can't take the stress."

"I need to call my son."

"Your son is in the lobby. I'll go get him." She raised his legs and helped him back in bed. "You just rest, Mr. DeGrate. I'll go get him right now."

Connie pulled the sheets up to his chest and tucked him in like a child. In that moment he felt like one. Incapacitated. Helpless. Bedridden with a taxing heart and no time. Every beat brought him closer to the grave than alive. There was never enough time to make all the wrongs right.

His nurse rushed out of the room.

In the sudden silence, Duke reached for the nightstand and grabbed the remote. He turned on the television and flipped to the news. He didn't have to find Fox 32 or any other local station. His worst fears were all over CNN. Stark and broadcasting live for the whole world to see.

Suddenly, the remote felt like lead in his hand. His arm dropped to his side and he just sat there. Watching his world crumble.

Moments later, the door opened.

Duke looked up. Expecting to see Darrion.

"Hi, dad," Devin said. "How are you feeling."

His heart sank. But he was glad to see his lastborn at his side. "I'm fine, son. Don't worry. You Pop's just fine." Duke looked to the door. "Where's your mother?"

"Oh, she's with Darrion. They're in Cabrini." Devin glanced up at the television. "I guess you found out about Derek's fiancé."

Duke turned his gaze back to the news. Oddly, his worry ran along side an encouraging wave of assurance. Knowing Darrion was there put his mind at ease. Duke knew he would do everything in his power to stop whatever Zander's sons had planned for the good doctor. "Don't worry," he said. "Your brother's going to bring her back."

Devin looked at him. His youthful face showed courage when he spoke. "I know."

"Good." Duke thought on how Devin had gotten to the hospital. Surely someone had brought him. "Who else is here?"

"Uncle Dutch and Uncle Donald. They're with DaVita in the cafeteria. I think they're getting coffee or something. Ronnie's here too. Fang was here, but he had to go back to Chinatown and take care of some business at the temple, so."

When the door opened once more Duke blinked in disbelief. Pastor Elbus Thurgood Troy.

His former minister still carried an apraised looked in his eyes. With a graying beard, wide jowls, closed trimmed hair, and a piercing gaze, he was the huge bulk of a man Duke remembered. Like some king of old, he still had that wisened way of looking at you. A way that made the person looking back at him want to be everything they had failed to be.

"Duke," he said in greeting. "How are you my old friend?"

"Pastor Elbus Troy. If they sent you to my bedside, I must have a seat in heaven or a cell in hell."

Pastor Troy laughed.

Duke didn't. "Which one is it?"

"I'm never at anyone's side to give them that answer. I'm there to help them face that fate head on when it's time. But it's never too late to ask for absolution. You know that."

"I've already rang that bell."

"And?"

"When it stops tolling I'll let you know."

The Pastor smiled at his humor. "The hospital didn't send me. Your wife did."

Duke couldn't feign surprise. Viola's worry forced that move. "Devin, I'm sure you don't remember him. You were just a baby the last time you saw him."

"But I remember you," Pastor Troy said to Devin. He held out his hand.

Devin shook it. "Hello, sir."

"The last time I saw you, you had a pamper on and a bottle in your mouth. How old are you now?"

"Seventeen, about to turn eighteen at the end of this month, sir."

The Pastor shook his head. "Where did the time go." He rubbed his chin, chuckled to himself then looked at Duke. "Looks like you raised a fine young man here, Duke."

"Yes I did."

Pastor Troy glanced up at the heart monitor and all of the IV tubing hanging from the pole. He exhaled. "So that heart finally gave out on you, hmm?"

Duke nodded.

"Who's your surgeon?"

Duke pointed to the television. "The doctor being held hostage by our dead foe's errant sons."

Pastor Troy looked at the television. Duke could tell by his silence, he was agog. His brow furrowed. He didn't speak right away. "May God have mercy."

"Help me up to the chair?" Duke asked. "Put it in front of the television."

Devin pushed the leather chair to the television. Pastor Troy carefully aided Duke out of bed.

When he sat, he leaned back and rested his hands on the wooden arms. "Son, will you ask that nurse to bring me some water."

"Sure."

Duke waited until Devin was gone and the door had closed before he spoke. "My son is there, Troy. Right now. In the one place he should not be. Trying to stop a thing we created. How could it fall on him? Our failures becoming his fate?"

Elbus went to Duke's side and put a hand on his shoulder.

"What do you need, Duke? Whatever it is, just ask."

Duke swallowed down the lump rising in his throat. He stared at the madness on the television. Inwardly asking for whatever strength heaven had left to give an old hood like him. "Pray for me," he finally said. "Pray for my family. Pray for my son. And pray for anyone to gets in his way."

An aerial view of several helicopters took over the screen. Hovering in position over a highrise building. Without warning an object was tossed from a window at one of the helicopters.

An explosion destoyed the tail rotor, sending the chopper spinning from the sky.

Duke exhaled and tight gripped the chair. It was all he could do not to lose his composure. His wife and son were in a war zone and there as nothing he could do to get them out.

An alarm sounded off on his monitor, but Duke didn't take his eyes off the chaos.

Devin returned with a cup of water and froze at the sight of bright red numbers flashing on the monitor screen. He blinked at the alarms with wide-eyed confusion.

Connie rushed into the room and pushed the silence button on the display unit.

"What is it?" Devin asked.

"Your father is V-tach."

"What does that mean?"

"He's stable, for now. But we've got to keep his heart rate below 120."

She slipped a needle into a small vial and drew out medication. "Mr. DeGrate," Connie interrupted, "I have some more lidocane for you to calm your heart rate down. We need to get you back in bed." She went to the bed, readied the sheets and glanced up at the television. All she saw was a massive crowd of people running in a panic and a helicopter exploding into flames as it crashed to the ground.

Connie gasped and covered her mouth. "Oh my God."

ANGELIQUE

I have to use the bathroom," Dr. James said.

Muriel's eyes darkened. "Do you now? How inconvenient for you and your bladder."

"I'm not lying. I really have to go. You can keep the door open if you want, but my bladder is about to explode."

Muriel just looked at her. From her hard gaze, Angelique could tell the old bird wasn't buying it. She'd push the ruse if she had to. If it came down to it, she would sit right there and piss on herself.

Muriel gave a nod to Lefty. "Untie her legs only and take her to the bathroom."

Lefty handed his shotgun to the Queen Bee and loosened the ropes from her ankles then led her down the hallway to the bathroom. It was close to the living room and a good line of sight for Muriel. To Angelique's surprise Lefty grabbed the knob to close the door.

"Make it quick. You got two minutes, bitch."

A wave of his foul breath assaulted her nostrils. She scowled at the odor. Either he'd been smoking the loudest weed on earth, or he had halitosis. "You might want to step in here with me and brush your teeth," she spat.

Lefty flipped her off and shut the door.

She looked around the bathroom for anything to help her escape. Of course there was no window. That would have been too much like right. She could have used one of the towels to break the mirror of the medicine cabinet. Then after Lefty came to get her, a quick slash with the glass would slit his throat. But then she would have to get past Muriel and the shotgun. There was always a chance she would have missed if she tried to shoot her. Grandma Harris was old. Unsteady on her feet. Just raising the steel to take aim would probably have thrown her off balance making a clear shot impossible. But Angelique knew she couldn't risk it. Muriel would probably aim true off of sheer hatred alone and blow a hole in her chest without a flinch.

Angelique looked down at the sink and noticed an empty porcelain water cup sitting by the faucet. She filled it with water, lifted up the toilet lid and slowly poured it. Making sure it sounded like she was taking a piss.

Then she opened the medicine cabinet in the hopes of finding a razor blade or a something she could use when the time was right. If she was lucky, when they weren't looking, she could work on cutting the ropes. A quick glance told her there wasn't one. On instinct she looked at the pill bottles. Three caught her eye. Two had labels, one was scribbled with chicken-scratch-hand-writing on a blank sticker in ink. Lisinopril, Diazepam, and Flunitrazepam. One was prescribed to Muriel O. Harris for her blood pressure. The Diazepam was prescribed to Zane E. Harris for his insomnia and probably other forms of psychosis Angelique didn't care to think about at the moment. The Flunitrazepam almost made her cringe inside. It had to be Zeno's hand writing on the label because it was never approved for use in the United States. It was ten times more potent than Valium. Those round little pills were odorless, tasteless, and dissolved undetected in liquid.

Brand name: Rohypnol, a.k.a.: The date rape drug.

As of yet, Rohypnol had not caught the eye of the DEA or the police department. But Angelique had seen enough women float through the ER with the drug in their system. In most cases, all of them required rape kits.

Angelique shuddered.

Fucking Zeno.

Sick, twisted, piece of shit.

Those three pill bottles were for three different people and purposed for three different afflictions, but they all had one thing in commom. They were round, little and white.

Angelique shut her eyes tight and breathed deep, then forced herself to act quickly. She flushed the toilet, turned up the faucet, then emptied out the Lisinopril and filled the bottle with Flunitrazepam. She dumped all of the old crow's blood pressure meds into Zeno's bottle, capped them and put them back in the medicine cabinet.

"I'm finished," she said.

Lefty opened the door.

When she stepped out, he patted her down. Making sure she had nothing on her. Then walked her back to the living room, sat her back infront of Muriel and tied her wrists — making sure the ropes were tight. Next he tied her ankles to the legs of the chair.

"Bring me an apple, baby," Muriel ordered. "There's a big red one in the fridge. And a plate. And my fruit knife."

Lefty nodded obedience and went to the kitchen.

Angelique looked around the living room, but saw no clock. Her own watch, that Darrion had given her, was covered with thick rope. It was too tight to move without hurting her wrists. She couldn't see the time or flip the face open to read the tracking device he'd had installed. Hopefully, he knew where she was and he was coming for her.

"May I ask what time it is?"

Muriel glanced to the wall clock in the kitchen. "A quarter past seven." She arched a gray brow at her. "Why? You got a bus to catch?"

It was just a matter of time.

She would have to take her evening dose of blood pressure medicine and soon. Dr. James had prescribed the Lysinopril twice a day for two months. Until her new valve healed and was functioning well without the stress of hypertension. She had not planned to reduce the dosage until the end of February. Angelique slowly exhaled. Keeping her nervous breath unnoticed. If she didn't egg it into motion, her plan could very well take all night. If they let her live that long. Dr. James knew Muriel was one of the stubborn types of patients. She wouldn't take her meds until someone reminded or fussed at her about the importance to.

Here goes nothing.

"You don't look so good," she lied.

"Well pardon fucking me. I left my stylist back in the Lows."

Lefty sat an apple and a fruit knife on the end table next to Muriel. She sliced the fruit and slid it in her mouth.

"Have you been taking your medication?"

"Why?"

"You look hypertensive to me. With a new valve, that could be potentially counteractive to healing and lethal."

"And I'm supposed to believe you so concerned for my welfare?"

Angelique didn't blink. Her eyes went cold, she looked at her dead on and said what needed to be said. "It just business. I called the police. I broke the code. You're doing what's necessary. It is what it is. You're the Queen Bee of Cabrini, but that doesn't change the fact that I'm a surgeon. Your oath to the Disciples holds you true to what needs to be done. My hipocratic oath binds me the same. You look at me and you see a snitch who has to be silenced. I look at you, I see a patient who's about to have a stroke. We're both detached in our own way I suppose. We can compartmentalize like that. Because we don't rise to the top of our worlds unless we do."

Muriel gave a harsh glance to Mr. Freeman's body.

"How do you compartemtalize that?"

Angelique didn't look at him. Because she couldn't. Not without breaking down into tears and Muriel knew it. She smiled a heinous smile and said, "Didn't think so." She slipped another cold slice of apple into her mouth. Chewed. Enjoying the crisp sweetness. Then said, "Let me tell you a thing or two about our world. Since you think you know every fucking thing." She pointed the knife at the corpse. "You see that?"

Dr. James refused to look.

"You look at him, you see a poor old man who deserved better than the death he got. I look at that body on my floor starting to rot...It's just another casualty of war. Killing is like eating an apple to me. You take a bite outta that, you want another one. And another. And that's feeding a belly that never has to get full. Pretty soon every time you wanna eat, you want a apple. Cause when it comes to murder no other fruit will do."

Dear God, Angelique thought to herself. *The devil walks.*

I'm staring at the fucking devil himself. Lucifer swathed in a dying old woman's body.

Muriel motioned to Lefty.

"Yes, ma'am."

"Hand me my blood pressure monitor off the dining room table." Lefty did as he was told and helped her slip the cuff on her arm.

Angelique's breath caught waiting for the damned monitor to give a reading.

Seconds later, she actually had to supress a wicked smile.

Systolic: 232
Diastolic: 149

With blood pressure that high, she was an aneurysm waiting to happen.

"You don't feel anything?"

"If I did I would've took care of it by now."

"No ringing in your ears. No blurred vision?"

"Naw."

"You need to take your blood pressure pills. Your valve can't take that much pressure. And your kidneys aren't liking it either. You could give yourself a stroke."

Muriel looked at Lefty. "Go in the bathroom and bring me my pills. It should say Lysinopril on the bottle."

Lefty went to the bathroom and returned less than minute later with a glass of water and her pill.

A voice came over his brick. "Lefty."

"This me."

"Zane wants you standing guard outside the apartment. Q-Ball got pulled to switch the stash."

"A'ight."

Dr. James watched him head towards the door. Reaching in his oversized denim, he pulled a pistol, cocked it and opened the door. "Queenie, I'mma be right outside this door. Let me know if you need anything else."

Muriel Harris took her pill, nodded and waved him off as he stepped out into the hall. She picked up the shotgun, aimed it at Angelique and sat there in silence. Staring murder.

♛

Muriel was starting to nod off.

It wouldn't take long now.

It had only been ten minutes and she was already starting to feel it. She had the 12-gauge nestled in her arms like a newborn infant. But every time her head dipped, she jerked back up straight and readjusted her grip on the steel.

Dr. James looked from the shotgun to Muriel. Back to the shotgun. Nervously waiting for the full potency to kick in.

Her head dipped again. This time she didn't jerk awake. For safe measure, Angelique waited until a line of drool spilled out of her mouth. Then she knew.

TKO, you decrepit old bitch.

Slowly, carefully she inched her chair forward.

It skidded on the hardwood. Muriel's head moved.

Angelique froze.

Slowly she lowered her head again and fell back asleep. Angelique did a double take when her dentures slid out of her mouth. She watched them plop into her lap like a wet chicken bone she'd gnawed all the meat off of.

She waited. Watching as Muriel's mouth sunk into her gums. Missing her teeth didn't seem to make her stir.

Again, Angelique inched the chair forward. It wasn't far enough to reach the shotgun across the coffee table, but the end table was within reach. Muriel's half eaten apple and the fruit knife was a grab away.

Angelique leaned the chair and quietly picked the knife up off the plate then went to work, cutting her hands free. Then she cut the ropes off her ankles.

She stood, rubbed the raw skin on her wrists, and looked down at the Queen Bee. For the first time in her life, thoughts of murder swam through her head.

For the first time, she could see how easy it was for Darrion to kill. Maybe Muriel was right.

Maybe killing was like eating an apple.

Now the gun.

Angelique leaned down and slowly worked the 12-gauge from Muriel's arthritic fingers. Then calmly sat across from her in the chair, aimed the steel at her and waited for Lefty to check in on grandma.

♛

A few mintues later, she heard the doorknob.

Lefty walked in. Froze at the sight of her holding the shotgun. Then reached for his pistol.

"Move and I'll blow her fucking head off!"

Lefty lowered his hand from the steel. "You don't got it in you, Doc! You take it there, you'll never make it out of this building alive. And Zane will take his fucking time in killing you."

Faster than she could register, Lefty pulled his gun and aimed it at her.

"I don't want to kill you," she warned. "Drop the gun."

"Fuck you!"

Lefty fired.

Dr. James ducked and kicked the couch over. Using it for cover, she fired back. Muriel went tumbling to the floor. Either it was the pill or the force of the blow when her head hit the hardwood that kept her unconscious, because she didn't wake. She didn't even stir from the fall.

Lefty fired again. Wood splintered off the couch frame.

Dr. James fired three slugs. Then she heard him holler and hit the floor followed by another shot. Blood sprayed from Muriel's skull. Dr. James froze for a split second and chanced a look around the couch. Grandma Harris' scalp was peeled like a grape.

When the Disciple hit the floor, he must have accidentally let a shot off.

Lefty screamed. "Queenie! Nooooooo! You fucking bitch!"

He let loose. Firing every round into the couch. All Dr. James could do was crouched low and hope his aim was as bad as his breath.

Nine shots later came that tell-tale click.

He was empty.

Dr. James was up in a flash. She moved around the couch. Aiming the shotgun at Lefty. Eyeing the carnage. His leg was blown clean off below the knee. He had dropped the gun and was gripping his leg. Hollering in pain. Trying in vain to stop the blood spray from his severed limb.

She pressed her finger to the trigger then stopped.

If she blew his head off, that would be one less round for whatever was waiting for her on the other side of the door.

One less slug to keep her alive.

"I would kill you," she seethed. "But you're set to bleed out regardless. So you're dead any-fucking-way. And I need the ammo."

She took her finger off the trigger, ran to the door and abandoned Lefty and the Queen Bee of Cabrini to their fate.

RENFRO

Renfro had the map of the projects laid out on the long table.

Of all the officers present, only three had the layout of the highrises and the lowrises already memorized. Campbell, Officer Sanchez, and himself. Commander Van Zant was vaguely familiar with public housing. He had joined the debriefing as well. For the members of the Task Force, the Chief, Deputy Chief, and Lieutenant Delgado, this would be a crude crash course.

Cabrini 101.

Renfro didn't understand why the Feds were hoping to find anything that would lead them to Zane's supplier. Here, it was futile. In all the years he worked Cabrini, not once had they ever confiscated enough product to lead them to a connect.

Zane's soldiers would just move their powder from one unit to another until the police gave up and left—which was often the wasted result—if they were actually even able to get past the ground floors to penetrate the buildings.

"Be advised," he began, "the King Disciples have taken control of more than fifty buildings in Cabrini Green. They run these projects. Some of that territory has been divided with the Almighty Renegade Disciples. A rogue clique that split off from the Kings during a street tax dispute. For now, they're still at a truce and they'll mob up and come at us if they have to. So we can expect resistance and violence from both. The second largest gang other than the Disciples is the King Cobras. But we don't have to worry about them, they're on the other side of the projects across Division Street in the Whites.

"All in all, the Disciples total more than four thousand members. About 800 or so are in their fourties and fifties. They're considered O.G.'s. They mostly run the narcotics. Very seldom are they involved in guns and they rarely participate in shootings." He looked at Agent Stahl. "When you go in, you want the O.G.'s because that's where the drugs are. We want the units their girlfriends and family members of live in because they usually hide the guns. And don't forget the elderlies. When our undercover hit the fire alarm, most of them evacuated, but there are some who are probably still there."

"And what makes you think we're going to find anything?" Agent Stahl asked. "The second the troops stormed in, they started moving their product from one unit to another. It's like a crap shoot. There's no telling what apartments their stash is in."

At least she was thinking. Renfro had to give her credit for that.

"Because the only ones who stayed behind have something to lose. Those are the units we want. We hit the breezeways and start kicking in doors. The second we see the white of someone's eyes, we put their asses on the ground, cuff 'em and start pulling sofa cushions, flipping matresses and gutting closets.

"Bishop went to escort the officers bringing the Black Gate. Hopefully, that fallen helicopter won't be in his way. When we move into Head Quarters for the doctor, the Gate should be in place. We'll raise it to keep the Discples from slipping into the Maze and disappearing from one tower to another. Now, here you'll find the Lows." He moved a finger over to the lowrise buildings, then moved a finger to the wider structers that took up more acreage. "Here's the corner of Hudson and Oak. The building where the doctor is being held is here. That's a problem because the Lows are right across the street and the building is surrounded by Hudson Mob, Camp Ball, and 2 Bill. You want to watch the Lows because the trees make it easy for them to disappear. You want to watch the highrises because the rooftops of every adjacent building are still covered by whatever snipers aerial couldn't take out."

"What about this Maze," Agent Lomax cut in. "What is that?"

"The top floors of all of the highrises have man-sized holes knocked in the walls. All the lights are knocked out. So once you're in there, there's no sence of direction. Turn after turn, every room leads to another, which leads to another knocked out wall or door, which somehow leads to the next building over. It's a fucking labyrinth."

"And every Disciple up there has it memorized," Campbell cut in. "By the time you get from the bottom floor up to the Maze, they'll be long gone."

"So what's the point of going in there?" Agent Cohen asked.

"You don't. You'll never catch them in there. So don't try it. When the raid goes down, your best bet is to make as many arrests as we can from the ground up, before they can slip into the Maze. That's what the Black Gate is for. The highrises are divided into two towers. But they can jump through a small space in the Maze which is over the courtyard. Once they hit that, they're home free. Ghost. The Black Gate can rise up between the two towers and block that escape."

Officer Sanchez cut in. "How are we supposed to make any arrests when they still have snipers on every roof? Even if you have another way in, as soon as they see us they're gonna open fire." She looked at Renfro. "I'm sure you remember the last time we tried that. It got real bloody, real quick. And an officer lost his life."

"SWAT is flying in as aerial backup to the Army choppers. When we move, they'll take out as many as they can. They have night vision so, they'll have better eyes up there than we will. Let's just hope their aim is as deadly as the guns their up against."

"Who's waiting for the go?" Agent Stahl asked.

"The SWAT team leader, McGunner. As soon as we give the word, they're inbound, weapons hot."

Stahl nodded. "Okay."

"If there's no objection from the Chief or the Deputy. We'll be keeping our word to Zane in the meantime. Once all of his soldiers in the adjacent buildings are disarmed and detained, then we can go after the doctor and get his grandmother out safely. Until then, every other building is fair game."

"He's just going to give up his mole," Campbell said. "Just like that? For what?"

"Immunity for his grandmother and protection."

"You and I both know there is no protection or immunity in the streets. He should have negotiated a bit smarter than that."

"It's gonna be a bad day for his minions," Sanchez added.

"Zane doesn't give a shit about his minions. He made that clear when he bartered with me. All he cares about is his brother and the old Queen Bee."

Sanchez folded her arms across her chest. "And you think you can protect them from the blowback of thousands of Disciples? All of them pissed cause he flipped?"

"Once he gives up his mole, I don't give a damn what they do to him to be honest with you. He wanted to make a deal, we made a deal. Other than that, unforeseen events...Shit happens." He looked at Agent Stahl. "As far as I'm concerned, when this is all over, he's your man. He's your problem."

"We should be going after the Harris brothers first," Van Zant said. "Our target is Zane and Zeno Harris. Our objective is to get the doctor out safely and without any further harm coming to her. You're dealing with a force ready and willing to defend their empire with jealous interest. What makes you think the second we storm that building, they won't kill her?"

"We can't come at them head on through the front entrance. I've tried it in the past. It doesn't work. And you have a point, Commander. A lot of potential fuck ups. This isn't the most ideal training ground for a bunch of rookies. Even SWAT won't go any where near those towers without aerial. But this is the only tactical solution we have that keeps our fellow officers from getting killed. If you've got a better plan that spares the lives of our men, let's hear it. I'm all ears."

"I don't want to put a badge in jeopardy any more than you do. But Cabrini is a lot of ground to cover and we need the man power focused in the right direction. You said it yourself, Renfro. Based on the intel from your informant, we don't even know what unit she's in. And there's a missing little girl that's yet to be accounted for."

"We'll be on the look out for her. But in the meantime, this is it. This is our only shot to take some and put an end to the Harris Organization." He looked around the command center at all of them. "Does anybody have any questions?"

Agent Lomax raised a hand. "Where's the Mayor?"

"With the Alderman, addressing the public."

"You mind briefing her on what's going on?" the Chief said to the Deputy Chief. "She needs to be kept up to speed on what we're doing here."

Riles nodded.

"Any other questions? Now's the time to ask?"

Heads shook no. No one said a word.

"Okay, when everyone's ready to move, SWAT goes to work. Let's keep all of our bricks on the same channel. Stay frosty. We're about to be in some heavy shit."

Everyone filed out of the bus. Leaving Renfro alone with his thoughts. Moments later a knock came at the door.

"Come in."

A uniformed officer stepped inside and held the door open. "We got a couple of people who want to speak with you."

Renfro motioned a hand to let them in.

A young black woman with a bruised, battered face stepped in. Her hair was uncombed. Swathed in an Adidas suit, sneakers and huge gold bamboo earrings, she looked no older than twenty. But she could have been sixteen for all Renfro knew. He didn't recognize her. But the young hooligan who came in after her, sparked quite a memory.

Calvin 'Punchy' Forte.

That young shit had made quite a name for himself in the projects. When he was younger, he used to be a loud mouthed, lookout-stick-up-kid. Now he just ran dope for Zane.

"Calvin Forte," Renfro said. "What can I do for you?"

"I can't do this," the woman said. "They'll kill me."

"Look at your face!" Calvin spat. "I'm sick of this shit! And if you won't put a stop to it I will." He looked at Renfro. "You want Zane and Zeno, we might be able to help you out with that."

"In exchange for?" Renfro asked.

"Get her cleaned up. And get her the fuck out of here. Another city or some place."

Renfro looked at her. Whoever did that to her face meant to mame. From the cuts on her cheek alone, he knew everytime she looked in the mirror, the menace who did it would come to mind. A beating like that would never be forgotten.

"What's your name?"

"Keisha," she said, meekly.

Renfro motioned to the officer standing by the window.

"This officer here is going to escort you to a nearby ambulance. The EMT's are going to get you cleaned up and comfortable. Then we'll talk about getting you some place safe."

She looked at Calvin. Unsure of whether or not to believe him. Then she looked back at Renfro. "I don't have go come back here? Ever again?"

"We'll find you a place to stay. Even if it's a shelter. You won't come back here. You have my word."

"A'ight," Calvin said. "Tell him."

She let out a breath. "Ya'll probably looking for guns right?"

Renfro nodded.

"Well, they have a number system. Everytime there's a raid, they move 'em from the odd numbered apartments to the even numbered apartments. But from the even numbered floors to the odd numbered floors."

"So they move from, say, 201 to 302?"

Keisha shook her head. "Never below the fourth floor."

"Why not below the fourth?"

"One, so the customers can't rob 'em. The lines for serving always go up to the fourth floor. And two, if a raid goes down, they can move 'em before you have enough time to get up them stairs. That's why they shut the elevators down when ya'll come. By the time you make it up from the first to the fourth floor, they already made the switch. All the guns and the ammo is moved."

"So they're moving right now, from 401 to 502?"

"Yup, that's it. That's how they do it."

Renfro nodded. "Thank you, Keisha. I'm gonna make good on my word to you. Don't worry."

He motioned to the officer. "Make sure she's watched at all times and get her something to eat."

The officer nodded and lead the Kiesha out the door.

Calvin folded his arms across his chest.

"I want that in writing."

Renfro didn't flinch. "Oh I intend to. What do you think? I keep my informants happy and coming back for more with a smile and a fucking shiatsu? Pull up a chair and sit down."

Calvin grabbed a chair and sat across from Renfro at the table.

"So? We good then? You got what you needed?"

"No. She's good. She gave me what I needed from her. You want the same protection, you gotta give me something, Calvin."

Punchy scoffed at him. "I ain't got nothing for you, baby. Sorry."

"Oh, but I think you do."

"And what's that? Product? Them bricks ain't no where you can get at 'em."

"I know. But that's where you come in, Forte. Rumor has it, there's a tunnel. Running under Cabrini. A tunnel that leads right to Head Quarters and to your boss Zane."

Punchy gave a nonchalant rub of his stomach and said, "You sho' was quick to offer Keisha something to eat. But you know, damn I'm hungry, too. And I mean my belly is in my back. But seeing as the block's on lockdown, I just don't know what I'm gonna do about that. When I don't eat, my mind goes. I start misremembering shit and I just can't seem to think on a empty stomach. Know what I mean?"

Renfro let out a breath. He was losing patience with the hoodlum. "What do you want?"

"Hmmm...I'm thinking Ruth's Chris. Yeah. A nice thick sized porterhouse. And nice sized baked potatoe with butter. And some crab cakes. And a grape pop. Extra cold with no ice."

Renfro cursed and stood. "I'll be back. Stay your ass here. And I mean you better be here when I get back. If I have to come find you, deal's off."

"Medium rare," Punchy called after him. "I like my meat bleeding!"

Renfro mumbled a few other choice words under his breath as he walked out the door.

When the cold nigh air hit his face, he took in a breath. It was a good burn to his lungs. Now he thought on how he could hustle up a meal from one of the busiest establishments in the city.

He could grab the soda from a liquor store. No problem. But he didn't have the cash for a steak and crab cake meal from a restaurant like Ruth's Chris. Nor did he have the clout to get it thrown on the grill at a moment's notice. But he knew someone who did.

He walked towards the crowd of bystanders, officers, and reporters and waited for the Alderman to begin his speech. When the Mayor finished addressing the cameras and stepped down from the podium, Renfro introduced himself.

She swept a lock of graying blonde hair from her face and looked up at him. "What can I do for you detective?"

"I'm in a tight spot. I've got an informant who's willing to give up some useful information, but he's playing hard ball. He's demanding a steak dinner from Ruth's Chris. To be honest with you, ma'am, I don't know anybody who has enough pull to make that happen with a phone call, but you."

Mayor Jayne Burns smiled. Crows feet and green eyes gleaming up at him. She was a small boned, short woman. High cheek bones rouged with a hint of blush. Her narrow lips carried the lines of a smoker. She gave him a pat on the arm and said, "Then I'm your woman, detective. And I'll be sure to throw in one for you as well." She reached in the pocket of her trench coat and pulled out a pair of leather gloves. Then hooked her arm in his. "My car phone is in the sedan. Would you care to escort a lady to her car?"

"Absolutely, Mayor."

DARRION

Darrion, Turkell, Taran, and Casper crouched low behind the bushes of the dividing courtyard.

Watching six foot patrol and four SWAT officers set up the Black Gate.

Taran cursed.

This was not good.

If they moved now to stop it, they'd be arrested. Even as fast as Turkell and Taran were, they'd never get a shot off before they were killed.

If they waited, the gate would raise, stopping them from reaching the Maze. They raised the gate six feet. Testing it. Then lowered, raised and lowered it again.

Casper spoke on it first. "What do we do?"

"We wait," Darrion answered. "And we pay close attention. If we watch them setting it up, we know how to work it when we need to. As soon they raise that gate, we take it over."

"How?"

Darrion shook his head. "I don't fucking know."

"That's too many cops, man," Turkell said.

"That's not just cops," Lunch added. "That's SWAT. Them niggas don't play."

"We need another distraction," Taran said.

"Like what?"

"Something to make it two to four, instead of ten to four."

"Somebody would have to put the chase on 'em for that."

"SWAT are pitbulls," Darrion said. "And to pits everything looks like a bone."

"All they need is a reason to chase it," Taran added.

Casper looked around. Under the dim street light, his brown eyes reflecting through the holes of his gorilla mask. "With that much heat," he said, "who the hell is crazy enough to do that?"

Darrion, Taran, and Turkell looked at him.

Casper 'Lunch' Phoenix cursed. "Why it always gotta be me?"

"Cause," Turkell said. "You're...you."

"Don't flatter. I hate that shit." He exhaled. "Ya'll owe me for this!"

"Stay live, baby," Taran said.

Lunch put down his Remington pump action, pulled off his mask, rubbed dirt all over his face, leather jacket and blue denim, then leapt out of the bushes and skipped up to the officers like a little girl getting in line for double-dutch. He said nothing. He just stood there, looking wide eyed and spooked at a tall, black mountain of a SWAT officer guarding the gate.

"Step back," Mountain said. "You don't need to be here."

Lunch moved to the gate. "Can I climb this tree? My...My cat's up there! I gotta get my cat!" He started climbing up the gate. "Hitler! It's okay!" He feigned his best Arnold Swartzenegger voice. "Arnold the Swartz-zen-nigger will save you from the 3rd Reich!"

"Get the hell down here before I put you down!"

"Hold on Hitler! I, Arnold, am coming for you!"

"I said get down now!"

Lunch looked down at him, still in full on Swartz-zen-nigger mode. "Arnold is speaking! If I wanted to hear from an asshole, I'd fart!"

Mountain blinked shock up at him and screamed, "I'm gonna come up there and—"

"You want Arnold!" Lunch yelled, spit flying through his teeth. "You want me, I come!" With fury in his eyes, he leaned back, spun, then jumped off the fence and swan dived, belly down, six feet to the ground. His entire body rim-rod straight, he hit the grass like a statue. Skidding five feet to a stop. He just stayed there. Unmoving. Face planted in the dirt. Legs straight. Arms locked at his sides. Stiff as a board. It was like watching a blonde haired black mannequin get kicked over at the mall and no one bothered to catch it.

"What the fuck is this hype smoking!"

Another SWAT officer approached him and gave him a kick. Hard as a mummy, Lunch didn't move.

"Get up!"

Nothing.

"Aye! I said get up!"

Not a wince of life.

The SWAT officer exhaled and rolled his eyes. "Goddamnit! Help me pick this crack head up and get him out of here!"

Darrion watched the other two SWAT officers move to hoist him off the ground.

"You want one of us to go with you?" one of the foot patrols asked.

Mountain cursed again. "Well, we can't carry this ass-clown and open the meat wagon too, so yeah."

Another SWAT pulled a key chain from around his neck and handed it to the foot officer. "If we're carrying we can't shoot, so we need one of you to hold the key, two for back-up. One at the head and one at the feet."

Darrion was agog.

Lunch you beauty.

Turkell smiled.

"I hope he didn't crack his skull again," Taran said.

"If he did," Darrion said, "he'll just stutter, twitch and repeat shit like last time until it heals. Viola knows the drill."

They waited until Lunch's pallbearers were gone and all that remained were three cops. Two against three would have been better. But with three against three, atleast the odds were even.

"No shots," Turkell said. "We need the ammo."

Darrion adjusted his mask and gave the nod. "Let's move."

They dashed out from the bushes and issued a brute force attack. Moving to disarm them, Turkell slashed at their service belts with his machete.

Caught off guard, all three officers fought like Darrion knew they would. Service trained. Like proper boxers. They were fast. More agile and flexible than Darrion expected. But fighting with such a rule-bound style, they were practically cripples throwing punches in a wheel chair.

Fang's training took hold.

Darrion, Turkell, and Taran wove in among the punches. Blocking them aside, weaving in, falling back with timed precision. Using their shotguns to block kicks and deflect more blows.

Darrion kept moving, waiting for the right time to put one of them on the ground. Surprisingly a roundhouse kick came at his face. It was a move he didn't see coming, but he turned astonishment into advantage. Ducking low, he used the butt of his 12-gauge to sweep the cop off his feet. Then aimed the barrel at his face before the could even think about getting back up.

Darrion didn't take his eyes off the man, but by the sound of things, Turkell and Taran had the other two cops bested the same. "I don't want to kill you," he breathed. "But try me and you'll be a closed casket funeral."

"You can be a live bitch or a dead badge," Turkell added. "Pick one."

It didn't take them long to decide their immediate futures. Within seconds, the three officers scrambled to their feet and ran away.

Taran, Turkell, and Darrion kept their shotguns aimed at them until they were out of sight. Then they went to the gate.

"How high does this thing go?" Taran asked.

"All the way up to the nineteenth floor."

"That'll block like the wall of China."

"Okay," Turkell said. "Let's shut this thing down."

"Wait," Darrion said. "When I move, I'll have company. Zane's soldiers, cops, they'll be on me. Maybe that wall of China is what we need."

They went quiet and the three men looked at each other.

"Let's do it," Taran said.

"Okay," Darrion said, "I'm going after Angie."

"Wait," Taran said. "You're gonna need one of us with you."

"If you're with me, who's keeping an eye on the gate and who's backing you up when I'm gone?"

"Who's backing you up nineteen stories in the air?"

"That gate if we use it right." Darrion waited for them to catch his meaning. "If I take to the roof...You thinking what I'm thinking?"

Taran cursed. "Unfortunately." He powered down the gate and hit the 'STAND BY' switch. "Okay, we'll stay here."

"We'll stay on the bricks too," Turkell said, looking at the walkie-talkies on the slashed service belts. "Keep you informed."

"Watch you back up there, man. And your front."

Darrion nodded and was off.

RENFRO

Damn, Casper," Punchy said to Renfro, chewing as he licked the greasy fat off his fingers. "It only took 20 minutes to deliver me a sizzling hot porterhouse. On a Sunday! Ain't that some shit?! But any other day, let a body catch a bullet around here, y'all don't show for all the flat-assed, snow bunnies in Jackson Park." He belched. "Man, this steak is so fire!"

Bishop entered the command center bus.

"We've got the Black Gate set up and ready to roll when we move in."

Renfro nodded. "This is Calvin Forte."

"Yeah I know who he is."

His partner's tone was less than enthusiastic.

"And he's going to tell us how to find that tunnel," Renfro added. Bishop walked around to Renfro's side of the table and leaned against the map wall.

Renfro's brick beeped.

"Detective Renfro," a voice said.

"This is Renfro. Go ahead."

"Uh, this is officer Moorehouse. Uh, we got a problem."

"What problem?"

"DeGrate's missing. His boys too."

Renfro cursed and shook his head. "I asked you to do one thing! Don't let DeGrate out of your sight! That's all I asked you to do!"

"In all of the madness, crowd control, most of the officers were gearing up to raid the buildings. Then, with the helicopter crash, we had to get these people to safety to avoid shrapnel from the explosion. It was a lot going on. So maybe we took our eyes off the trailor for a minute or two. I guess that was all the time he needed to slip away."

Renfro exhaled. "Yeah, I guess so."

"You want me to set up a small group of officers to search for him."

"No. I've already got a good idea of where he's headed."

Renfro sat the brick on the table and turned down the volume. He looked at Forte. "I know there's a way in that's not in the blueprints."

"Maybe there is, maybe there isn't," the Disciple said with a cocky shrug as he forked another piece of steak.

"Oh, we know there is."

"Maybe you wouldn't mind telling us about it?" Bishop pressed.

"If you know it's there," Forte said, "you don't need to know nothing from me. So what you asking me about it for?"

"Is it manned?" Renfro asked.

"If so, how many?" Bishop added.

"What kind of guns are they armed with?"

"Grenades? Smoke bombs? What?"

Punchy leaned back in the chair and kept chewing. Then said, "How about them new Nike Cortez at Foot Locker? I been peeping them for a long ass minute."

"It's damn near eight o'clock at night," Renfro spat. "On a Sunday! They're closed!"

"Then so's my mouth!"

"I don't have time for this shit!" Renfro slapped the styrofoam container off of the table, sending the perfectly seared steak crashing to the floor along with Punchy's crab cakes, snatched him up by his collar, yanked him out of the chair, and slammed him up against the map wall. Bishop had to jump out of the way. "You don't give up that entrance, that porterhouse won't be the only dead ass piece of meat on the floor leaking blood. And I will deem you a compromised informant for failure to cooperate. The protection I had set up for you and your girlfriend will be gone and when word gets out that you're a rat, you'll be dead in a day. You're king will see to that, if DeGrate doesn't kill him first."

"DeGrate kill Zane?! Oh, I'm counting on it, Casper. And he's not my fucking king!"

Renfro threw him in the chair, reached for a pen on the table and rammed it down Punchy's throat until every tender morsel of that steak came spewing out like Linda Blair's Exorcist.

Calvin coughed. His stomach lurching up the remains until nothing but gastric juice splashed all over his sneakers. He sucked in a deep breath, coughed again and looked at the vomit all over everthing with wide-eyed revulsion.

"You motherfucker!" he yelled.

"When I make you eat it up, you're gonna see how much of a motherfucker I can be." Renfro kicked the chair out from under him and pushed Punchy's face down until his nose was inches from his own puke. "Where is it?!"

Calvin shut his eyes tight and turned his head away. "Okay! Okay! I'll tell you where it is, just let me up, fuck!"

♛

Renfro and Bishop approached the church with caution.

Both men kept their weapons drawn. Staying close to the wall as they moved toward the back entrance. Five foot officers followed close behind.

They rounded the corner and locked eyes on four dead gang members. They weren't shot. They were sliced up like someone went to work on them with brutal intent.

Bishop looked at Renfro. "DeGrate's work?"

He shook his head. "Don't know. I always took him for a bullets man. Not blades. But maybe they didn't want to make noise. So I wouldn't doubt it."

"Ready to see what's on the other side?"

"Let's do it."

Bishop motioned for the backing foot officers to flank the doors. Then the detectives moved in swiftly, pointing their weapons in all directions. Expecting more warring Disciples. But the church was empty.

Bishop tapped Renfro on the shoulder and motioned to a dim-lit hallway. They jogged passed the pews, down the hall, and paused at a flight of stairs.

"Looks like the gateway leads down," Bishop said.

"Let's wait for the officers to catch up with us."

A few seconds later, the foot officers were coming down the hall.

"Where does this lead," one of them asked.

Renfro shook his head. "We were told it leads to a cellar. Looks like we're about to find out."

They took the stairs one by one.

As Calvin Forte had said, they were indeed standing in an unfinshed, dark cellar. There was only one way out, straight ahead.

They ran though the church tunnel, jumping over bullet-ridden bodies in their path. More of DeGrate's work, Renfro assumed. They neared what appeared to be a solid cement wall ahead. But as they jogged on, it became a sharp left turn with no thruway in sight.

As they neared the turn, they flew back to the wall when shots rang out, shredding the concrete within inches of their faces.

Renfro didn't know if it was Zane's soldiers or Regengades, one of DeGrate's crew or any other gang that felt the tunnel was theirs. But he knew if they turned the corner they were dead.

"I'm guessing that's the exit," Bishop spat.

"You guess correctly."

"You got any smoke bombs on you?"

"Come on now, who are you talking to?" Bishop reached in the pocket of his Kevlar and pulled out an M18.

Renfro smiled, snatched the pull-ring igniter and rolled it down the remaining length of the tunnel.

"What the fuck are we supposed to use for masks?" another officer asked.

"It's for concealment," Renfro said. "We're not talking chemical warfare here. You'll be fine."

When the exit filled with white smoke and he heard gangsters running away, Renfro gave the signal to move forward down the tunnel.

Campbell's voice came on Renfro's brick.

"Stop DeGrate! I'm gonna beat your ass for making me run! I said stop, goddamnit!"

"Campbell, this is Renfro. What the hell are you doing on DeGrate? You're supposed to be working one of the adjacent towers with Sanchez!"

"We got ambushed, like Van Zant said we would. I sent Sanchez your way."

"This is SWAT. McGunner on aerial. We got Darrion DeGrate on the roof, coming up from the south east tower and he is triple timing it. He's hauling ass!"

"This is Campbell on foot! Seven officers in pursuit through the south east tower. Hold your fire! We're on the roof. I repeat, hold your fire!"

"We have DeGrate in our sights. He is on the roof. We are in position to take the shot. I repeat, aerial is in position, waiting for the green light to take the shot."

"Officers are on the fucking roof! You are facing the pursuit. You do not have a side shot! Do not give a green light for a straight shot!"

McGunner cursed.

"This is Renfro, aerial stay in position. Keep a 20 on DeGrate! Do not loose him!"

"Copy that. SWAT still has him in our sights headed for the south west tower."

Renfro heaved deep breaths through the smoke. "Let's move!" They jogged down the final stretch of tunnel. Weapons aimed and watched a mass of Disciples running out of the exit.

"Officer Campbell," he breathed. "I need you to direct your men to split up. Three of the fastest break left and head towards the Black Gate. It's positioned at the dividing courtyard, between the north and south towers. It's in the middle of the Maze. I'm headed to hit the switch and raise the gate."

"Negative, if we split up we'll loose him."

"Not if I raise the gate first. Then it won't fucking matter where he is because he'll have no choice but to come back your way or come back down here to me!"

"We'll catch him! We're gaining on him!"

"He wants you to think you're gaining on him, Campbell! When he makes that last right at the south west corner, he'll break full speed and he will smoke you! You have to raise the goddamn gate!"

Renfro exited the tunnel and looked skyward, checking the rooftop for snipers.

"We'll run him down," Campbell said. "We're already in pursuit."

DeGrate's former track star days flashed in Renfro's mind. No way could a foot officer, with twenty pounds of equipment on a service belt, match him.

"No! You can't catch him on foot! Goddamnit!" He lowered the brick and motioned to Bishop. "We have to get to the switch and cut him off before he gets past the gate!"

Renfro, Bishop, and the officers took off toward the dividing courtyard. All they saw were gansters running every which way. Through the main courtyard. In and out of apartments. Up and down stairs.

They were moving their stash. Renfro knew.

They were on every Disciple they could catch. Throwing them to the ground. Kicking their weapons away. Zipping their wrists behind their backs with plasticuffs.

Through the darkness, Renfro looked up and saw officer Sanchez. She had her gun trained on a Disciple resisting arrest.

"Sanchez, come over here and help me detain this mess!"

ANGELIQUE

Dr . James flew down the stairs to the third floor.

Her eyes searched every door as she ran down the breezeway. She wasn't sure which unit Sammy lived in and there was no telling where Mr. Freeman took Ophelia.

She had to assume he placed her where she could be found should something happen to him. Much to her surprise, several apartments had no door. A quick glance as she blew past them revealed no furniture and no occupants inside.

The fourth to the last unit was the only apartment that appeared worth checking. Dr. James stopped, tightened her grip on the 12-gauge and raised a fist to pound on the door. Then she paused.

There was a chance Sammy could answer the door.

There was an even higher chance she'd been staring down the barrel of a gun when a Disciple answered the door. She looked down the breezeway making sure she wasn't followed.

Here goes.

When she raised a fist to knock, the door opened.

She raised the shot-gun.

A feeble old man was staring back at her.

He didn't flinch. He didn't draw back from the gun.

He just stood there. Cane in hand. Every unkempt hair on his head had gone to gray. By the staid look in his eyes, it was clear that wasn't the first time he had a gun in his face.

She let out a breath of relief and lowered the steel.

"I'm sorry, I'm — "

"You looking for little girl," he whispered.

She nodded. "Yes."

"Next door. Sammy's. And you better hurry. She don't look too good."

She'd guessed right. Sammy's was the one place Ophelia would actually be safe. For a little boy, he was a brave one.

Dr. James thanked the elderly man, went to Sammy's door and knocked. Her breath caught when the lock unbolted and the door opened.

Instead of a small child with big brown eyes, Angelique was staring at a stout, wide-hipped woman with loud, red flaired hair and large eyes. One glance and she knew the woman was Sammy's mother. They shared the same smooth brown skin and small perfect nose.

"It's the doctor, mama," Sammy said. "You can let her in."

Sammy's mother quickly ushered her inside.

Dr. James found Ophelia on the couch. Wrapped in a quilt.

"I put my grandmama's quilt on her," Sammy's mother said. "She looked a little cold to me. Wouldn't stop shaking."

Dr. James leaned the shotgun against the couch and carefully sat down to inspect her.

Much to her surprise the little girl tried to open her eyes when she lowered the quilt the get a better look at her swollen face. But the instant her lids parted, she whimpered and closed them.

Dr. James didn't know exactly what had been used to blind her, but she knew if Ophelia didn't get to a hospital and soon, the loss of vision would be permanent.

"I need a clean towel," she said.

Sammy's mother rushed to the back room and returned in seconds with a wash cloth.

Dr. James motioned to the kitchen. "Warm water please. Thank you."

Sammy ran to the kitchen, leaned over the sink and turned on the faucet.

His mother wet the towel and brought it Dr. James.

"Name's Capricia," she said.

Angelique carefully pressed the towel to Ophelia's eyes.

As expected she reached a hand up and tried to push it away. Every touch must have burned like hell. But something had to be done to try and remove as much septicity as possible.

"What happened to her eyes?"

"I don't know." Dr. James wiped away a trickle of blood and gently pushed on some of the swelling. More discharge oozed out. Ophelia let out a cry. That was enough. Anymore would be too much pain and Dr. James had no sedative on hand to give. "I think it's roach poison." She glanced up and locked eyes on the television.

At the first sight of a man in a black shirt and slacks, being chased by police, she stood and stepped closer to the screen.

If it wasn't happening right before her eyes, she never would have believed it.

It was Darrion.

Bolting across a rooftop in a near full sprint.

He was coming for her.

She checked her watch, flipped up the face, and pulled out the dial. A display screen lit up:

500 FEET / 0.152 KILOMETERS

And closing.

If she made it to the Maze, he'd find her.

She crossed the living room and carefully scooped up Ophelia in her arms.

"I know how much much you're risking, keeping her here. I owe you one. Thank you."

Capricia nodded. "You're welcome."

Angelique reached for the shotgun, but Sammy had it on the floor. With a box of shells at his knees. Reloading it. Capricia must have been no stranger to weapons. He handed it to Dr. James, went to the door and held it open like the perfect gentleman. "I hope she's okay," he said.

"Where you gonna go?" Capricia asked. "You can't go down stairs. There's a capture-kill on you. There ain't no where Zane can't find you."

"There's one place," Angelique said.

With that, she stepped into the darkness of the hallway and made for the Maze.

♕

She climbed the stairs as fast as she could. Though she carried a child, it didn't take long before Ophelia's weight was heavy in her arms.

"Where you going, Doc?" a voice called.

Angelique paused mid-step and looked down.

A Disciple was looking dead at her with a squint in his eyes. As if he was trying too hard to seem...friendly. From where she stood, he was high on something. Gut instinct told her he was not there to help her escape.

"You need some help?" he said. Inching closer. "Why don't you come down here and let me help you."

Just the fact that he thought she was that slow, pissed her off.

"Cover your ears, honey," she said to Ophelia.

Angelique waited until the little girl did so, then aimed the shotgun down at him and fired.

He ducked to the side and slammed into the wall.

She cocked the shotgun, got a tighter grip on Ophelia and dashed up the stairs.

She must have missed, because the Disciple gave chase. "I got the Doc! I'm on the bitch! I got her! She just moved past the fifth floor! I got the Doc!"

To her horror, she looked up and saw a horde of Disciples coming down the stairs at her. She the flew up the stairs to the sixth floor and dashed down the breezeway.

Cut off from the Maze on that side of the building, she had no choice but to take the stairs of the other tower and work her way up to the Maze from there.

She made it to the other side, looked up on instinct and no surprise. More Disciples were coming down the stairs at her like roaches running down a wall.

She dashed down the stairs to the first floor and out into the main courtyard.

A rock flew past her face.

She spun around.

Anton Smith was staring at her through a first floor window.

"Quick this way!"

She ran to the window and handed Ophelia to Anton, then climbled through, careful not to drop the shotgun.

"She's got some injuries, give her to me. I know how to carry her without making them worse."

Anton handed the little girl off and placed a board over the window. Sealing them in the dark of an abandoned room, he motioned her to follow him. "This way."

"Where are you going?"

"To Bank Roll. Zane's got every Disciple looking for you."

"I noticed."

"You and the little girl will be safe at my place."

"How do you know that?"

"Because I'm a Disciple and he thinks I'm trying to kill you."

RENFRO

He just made the south west corner, Renfro!" McGunner said. "Aerial still has him in our sights."

"Christ, he's fast," Bishop said. "When we get to the top floor, we'll be closer to the Maze than he will. We'll be ahead of him but only for a few seconds. You and Sanchez break left for the lever. I'll head for the roof and try to stop him. We can leave backup here until more officers arrive."

"Take them with you," Renfro said with a glance to the foot officers. "All five of them. I don't want you going up to that roof alone. You'll never get past the fourth floor without backup."

"You sure?"

"I got Sanchez here, we'll be alright. Hopefully more backup will be on the way. If not, these fuckers aren't going anywhere."

Bishop nodded and motioned the five officers to follow him.

Renfro watched them take off into the main entrance. They dashed through the breezeway and up the stairs.

Renfro called over the brick. "This is Renfro requesting more officers. We got fifteen Disciples cuffed on the ground. We need them escorted out of the main courtyard."

"This is Delgado. Which courtyard?"

"Head Quarters."

"There's no way we can send backup there. They're all at adjacent buildings on narcotics shake-downs and weapon's recovery and taking fire in the process."

"We have to detain them somehow and take them back to the station."

"On what charge?"

"They shot at us!"

"Are you hit?"

"No."

"Did Bishop or any of the other officers take one in the vest?"

"No."

"Then it's big fish or little fish. You can set to catching the little fish on the ground or you can set to catching the shark that's trying to kill the big fish. And that shark's flying over your head as we speak. It's Zane's soldiers or DeGrate. It's your call."

"Well what the hell am I supposed to do with them, Lieutenant?"

"The only thing you can do. Strip 'em of any weapons or paraphernalia, cut 'em loose, give them a kick in the ass and let 'em go."

Renfro cursed.

"What do we cut them with?" Sanchez asked him. Staring at the plasticuffs.

Renfro looked at her. "This your first time using these?"

She nodded.

He looked at her young face. Olive skin. Brown eyes. High cheekbones. Sleek dark hair pulled into a high pony tail. She looked a fledgling at best. A rookie. He remembered now.

"Ideally," Renfro said, "a flexi-cutter. But since I didn't bring one with me, and I'm assuming since you've never used one before, you don't have one on your service belt, a knife will have to do."

Other than a couple of dime bags and eight pistols, they had nothing. Renfro kicked the weapons away and pulled a switch blade from his Kevlar. Sanchez pulled a knife from her service belt and they went to work. Cutting the Disciples loose.

Zane's soldiers took off the moment they were set free. As soon as they were out of sight, they shouted insults and threats back at them. One of them threw a trash can.

Renfro dodged it and aimed his shotgun. "Throw something again! Do it again!"

He waited until no one was in sight, then lowered the steel.

"Alright, Sanchez. Let's get this fucking gate up."

They took off toward the dividing courtyard.

TARAN

Taran Carter looked up when the wind shifted suddenly.

A shadow moved forward.

Before he could react, he was staring up the barrel of a shotgun.

"Move," detective Renfro said, "and I will blow you out of your socks!"

Turkell looked at the female officer.

She had her weapon trained on him. "Toss the machete, the pistol and the shotgun! Step away from the gate and put your hands where I can see them! Now!"

Turkell tossed his weapons and held up his hands.

Crouching low to keep an eye on the motor was a mistake. They couldn't see anyone moving through the bushes. Leaving them vulnerable to an ambush. Taran knew.

Now that it was too late.

"Up...slow," Renfro commanded. "Keep those hands up. Nothing slick, nothing stupid. Nice and slow."

Renfro motioned at Taran to do the same.

There was nothing they could do but abandon the gate. That was the art of surprise. As much as he didn't want to let Darrion down, he didn't want to get shot either.

Taran moved away from the Gate and stood next to Turkell.

"Down," she ordered. "On your knees. Hands over your heads."

They did it.

To Taran's surprise, he watched the detective turn off the 'STAND BY' switch and flip the motor it to 'ON'.

Instantly the Gate began to rise.

Taran and Turkell looked at each other. Renfro had no idea what he had just done. In that moment, he helped their cause more than he intended.

When she moved toward them, Taran looked at her nametag.

He usually remembered most cops who had the blind fortune or skill to creep up on him in the dark. But her, he didn't recognize.

She cuffed them then stood them up.

Renfro spoke into his brick. "Moorehouse."

"This is Moorehouse. Go ahead."

"This is detective Renfro. What's your 20?"

"I'm on SUSIE."

"Good, step out of the command center for a minute and make it down here to the Black Gate. We got two detainees for you and Sanchez."

"Copy that. On the way."

Taran looked up to the black sky. Then at the roof of the building. He hoped Darrion was still on the move. Shots rang out in the distance. He didn't know if it was Disciples shooting first and cops shooting back or the other way around or a little bit of both, but from the sound of the conflict, the war in Cabrini was far from over.

On his knees he waited for whatever came next.

He didn't know how many minutes had gone by when he looked up and saw Renfro speaking to a small, lanky officer with glasses. A wide nose, big eyes, and pointy chin, his Adam's Apple protruded like he was still waiting for his testicles to drop. He looked like his service belt weighed more than him.

"Moorehouse," Renfro said, "Collect their weapons." He looked at Sanchez. "You think you can handle the both of them?"

She nodded.

"Lock them up in the command cage. Let either my Lieutenant or Van Zant know you're on the way."

Sanchez nodded then pulled both of their gorilla masks off. She glanced over Turkell's Haitian features and dreadlocks. But she seemed taken aback by Taran.

She glanced over his face, looked down at his diamond necklace and back up at him again.

Taran said nothing. He just stared right back.

"Are they Disciples?" Sanchez asked. "They're not dressed like them."

Renfro shook his head. "No. They're with DeGrate." He looked at Moorehouse. "Make sure you don't let them out of your sight this time."

"Copy that, detective," Moorehouse said.

As the detective ran off into the building, Taran felt not one ounce of pity for his folly.

"Get up," Moorehouse said. He stood Taran up by an arm. "Let's go."

Sanchez followed with T-Bone in tow.

When they reached the edge of the courtyard, Moorehouse paused and looked both ways down the sidewalk as if unsure of which way to go. It took all of Taran's resolve not to roll his eyes. In Cabrini, the only thing worse than a cop was a rookie cop. This tadpole was going to get them all killed.

"If we cut through the building," Sanchez said, "we'll come out at the back parking lot. We should be able to see the squad cars from there. Command post shouldn't be too far off."

"Alright." Moorehouse walked Taran back through the courtyard and into the building. Sanchez followed, keeping a firm grip on Turkell. A few steps down the breezeway Moorehouse stopped again, unsure of which way would lead them to the back of the building. He gave a nod to Sanchez. "Lead the way."

Sanchez moved to pull Turkell infront of Taran and took the lead.

RENFRO

Renfro froze at the top of the escape ladder and looked to his right just in time to see Bishop stop running, crouch low and take aim. Renfro ran further for a few seconds just to get closer and realized DeGrate was coming at Bishop too fast.

He wasn't going to have a shot in time. Neither would the foot officers with him.

Renfro watched DeGrate fly past his partner. Ten seconds too late, Campbell and several foot officers passed over as well. If he wanted a clean shot, he had no choice but to break left and keep moving to cut DeGrate off. If he moved fast enough, he could get between DeGrate and the Black Gate.

He climbed down the latter onto the breezeway of the 19th floor, kicked in the first door he saw, and found himself sprinting through another apartment abandoned from the fire alarms. Renfro knew the only way to the roof, without going back into the main hall, was through the living room window and out onto the outside walk way, then he could take the fire escape around the corner to his right, make it to the roof and put a stop to DeGrate. He sprinted to the window, threw up the glass, and climbed out onto the walk way. He could hear the officers radioing to the helicopter on the brick. They were less than 20 paces behind.

Renfro broke into another sprint toward the fire escape and as he neared the corner, on instinct Renfro looked to his left and caught a Cubs jacket, an arm raising and a gun waiting to meet him. Renfro pulled his Glock, aimed center mass and fired.

He didn't even wait for the Disciple to drop.

He moved passed the wounded thug and took the fire escape to the roof.

"He's headed north," McGunner reported. "He is headed north and he is gaining speed."

"Six still in pursuit," Campbell radioed.

Renfro made it to the far end of roof just in time to see DeGrate pull a balisong and slice several clothes lines. A strong gust of wind turned them into floating blindfolds. Campbell didn't slow. He ducked the sheets and kept moving, but the officer behind him ran smack into them.

"Uhhpp," McGunner said. "Five in pursuit."

Renfro watched another officer slow like an invisible brick wall dropped down before him. He projectile vomited and slipped on his own spew.

"Four."

Renfro crouched low and took aim at DeGrate.

He lined up his sights. Tracked through the interferring roof vents and smoke. He took steady aim as best as he could in the night with only a floating aerial spotlight to guide his vision.

Closer. Closer.

Renfro waited. Watching DeGrate come nearer, faster. His aim cut across more intrusive structures as he tracked his mark.

Closer. Closer. Now.

He fired at the black swathed blur that came sprinting by and heard the buckshot resound off of something steel with a loud metallic chime. He probably would have hit more if he aimed at the moon. DeGrate didn't stop.

Son of a bitch didn't even slow.

ZANE

Zane was furious.

Hot tears streamed down his cheeks at the sight of his grandmother. Bleeding her last blood. Lying helplessly on the hardwood floor. He was so jarred, he didn't even stir when the door opened behind him.

Zeno walked in and froze when he looked upon Muriel and Lefty's mutilated bodies. He didn't seem to notice when his pistol slipped from his hand and hit the floor with a hard thud.

Zane knelt by Muriel's side and held her in his arms.

He looked at Lefty's corpse then looked up at his brother.

"That doctor bitch is dead. I want her dead!"

She had slipped away, but not for long. They'd find her. There was nowhere in Cabrini she could hide. When Zeno found her, Zane knew he would bleed her slow.

Q-Ball's voice came over the brick. "Zane, we getting hit left and right, man! All the stash spots are getting hit!

"How are all of them getting hit?" Zeno radioed back. "We got more than a hundred stash-spots in these projects! Make sure you get to 'em first to move the steel. It's simple. Don't freeze up! They ain't stopping, so you don't stop! You keep it moving!"

"We already moved what we could. They still got damn near everything. The zoo-zoo's, wham-whams, the ammo! Everything! They didn't leave us shit! That's what I'm trying to tell you! It's like they knew exactly where to go! They're flooding the towers and we don't have time to move shit without getting arrested!"

Zane shut is eyes and cursed. Then, "What about the powder?"

"They looking but they haven't found that yet."

"Haul ass to Bank Roll. Page Anton and all the old heads holding our stash to give 'em a heads up. When you get there, move the product to new spots. When you call me back I better be captivated, nigga. I mean awe-struck by you abililly to get shit done. You feel me?"

"Got it," Q-Ball said. "And just so you know, DeGrate's on the way. He's running the rooftops. Headed for the Doc."

Zane lowered Muriel carefully to the floor, stood and walked over to Zeno. He picked up his brother's gun off the hardwood, handed it to him and said, "It's time to end this."

He reached in the pocket of his baggy denim and pulled out a small shape charge bomb. Zane placed it in Zeno's hand and said, "I want you to find the Doc and DeGrate. When you do, take 'em off this planet."

Zeno didn't look at him. He didn't even blink.

He stared down at his helpless grandmother. At the pool of blood encircling her red soaked, gray hair. Zane recognized that daze. That far away look when the darkness took over.

In his pain, Zane almost wanted to smile then.

When the dark took him, nothing and no one was safe.

Zeno would stalk that bitch doctor from hell to heaven, walk right up to the pearly gates and bust Saint Peter right in the teeth if he got in his way.

"Zeno!"

His brother tore his eyes away from Muriel and looked at him.

"I know what you're feeling. But we got work to do. We can make this right. And there's only one way to do it." Zane clapped him on the shoulder. "Make sure the Doc and DeGrate don't get out alive."

Zeno nodded obedience and with the bearings of a trained legionnaire, he took off out the door. Off to war.

Zane went back to his grandmother.

When he leaned down to kiss a farewell to her forehead, a wet cough parted her lips.

A sickly gasp escaped her lungs. Filling the silence of the room. Zane put a finger to her neck and checked for a pulse.

Muriel Harris was alive.

TARAN

M oorehouse walked Taran to the door of the command center bus, unlocked it, led him in and spoke into his shoulder mic. "Lieutenant Delgado or Commander Van Zant, this is Officer Moorehouse. I have two KA's. Taran Carter and Turkell Scarbone. Known associates of Darrion DeGrate. They've been detained for tampering with the barrier gate. I'm brining them in." After a few seconds of silence, Moorehouse called in the notification again. Still nothing.

"You can't raise them?" Sanchez asked him.

Moorehouse shook his head, reached for a large lock box and placed their confiscated weapons inside.

Sanchez grabbed a smaller lock box and sat it next to Taran on the long table.

"I'm removing your jewelry and placing it in this box. When you get to the station, you can fill out a belongings form, after you're printed and processed. Understand?"

"Whatever," Taran said.

Officer Sanchez removed his watch and necklace, placed them in the box, a sat it aside. "Okay, let's lock them in the cage for now and try to raise the lieutenant and Van Zant again in a few minutes."

She tried to unlock the cage but found the lock was a strange fit for the key. She gave it several tries before giving up, then grabbed a T-chain from the wall locker and chained Taran and T-Bone to the metal siding of the command post long table. She slipped the keys back on her service belt and joined Officer Moorehouse at the window. Taran was on edge. It was quiet. Too quiet. With all of the officers raiding the buildings there was no one in sight. He looked up at Head Quarters in the distance.

"So far it looks like everything's under control," Moorehouse said.

Sanchez shook her head. "I'm not so sure."

"Why is that?"

"Where's the Commander? He was here when you radioed in?"

He shook his head.

"You think something happened to him?"

"I don't know. Maybe he had something more important to take care of. Like placating the Councilman. Porter is occupied with keeping the Mayor satisfied. If the Chief and the Lieutenant slid out of that one, Van Zant's probably stuck with it and caught up in politics. We should be alright until they get back."

S.U.S.I.E. shook then.

A hard rocking sent papers flying, chairs toppled sideways. Coffee cups spilled over. Shouts billowed through the window. Death threats sounded through the glass. Comparing officers' faces to unsightly animal parts. Vivid descriptions of ways to torture the human body. Colorful, punishing vernacular. As they rocked side to side, Taran braced his sway with a foot to the wall. T-Bone did the same.

Sanchez crouched low by the door and snatched Moorehouse down. "Get away from the window!"

"Maybe we can bargain with them," Moorehouse said.

"Bargain?" T-Bone spat. "Do you know where the fuck you at?!"

A shot rang out and instantly the door blew open. Moorehouse missled back and slammed into the wall. Eyes wide, he coughed and sucked in a ragged breath through traumatized lungs. He sat there stunned. Blinking in horror at the force of the gun blast. His shirt was shredded, but there was no blood.

Taran hated cops, but for the kid's sake he hoped he was wearing a Kevlar. A buckshot could shred flesh like an iron mincer. Before Sanchez could think to check him, gittering steel flew past past her head and she locked eyes on a machete scewered in Moorehouse's chest. She screamed, pulled her Glock and fired through the doorway. When the chamber clicked empty she slammed the door shut and pulled the slide bolt, locking them in.

She crouched low next to the door, reloaded the Glock and waited for the Disciples to return gunfire. Then, just as quick as they raised, the shouts and threats died out, the trailer stopped rocking, and nothing but silence hung in the air. A strange scraping noise sounded out. Like steel on steel. Suddenly Taran recognized who made the sound. It came to his ears as familiar as a song. Then that familiar voice crooned through the door. "One, two Freddie's coming for you."

Sanchez blinked through the jarring reality when she looked at the door. That sound of sliding razor sharp steel drew closer.

"Oh shit," T-Bone said.

"What?!"Sanchez said, blinking horror. "Who's that?"

"Freddie Machete."

"Freddie who?"

Turkell glared at the door.

"I'm guessing he carries a machete?" Sanchez asked.

"You guessed correctly," T-Bone said.

"Threeee, four better lock your door," Machete crooned on. His voice much closer than before.

She looked at Taran. "Friend of yours?"

"I don't keep company with madness."

"Why do I find that hard to believe?"

"When this is over, I want my necklace back."

"Fiiiive, six grab your crucifix."

"Unlock me," Taran said.

Sanchez drew back from the door and shot a quick glance to his cuffs. "No."

"If you want to live unlock me."

"I can't just cut you loose," Sanchez said. "If he wants a fight, I can handle myself."

"Freddie will fight you just because it's cloudy outside. He doesn't need a reason to kick your ass, so he didn't come here for a brawl. He came for murder. He will break every bone in your body, rape you bloody, and kill you. And not in that order. You get dead, he gets my diamonds. That's not happening. Unlock me!"

Sanchez glanced at the box on the table.

"I know how cops get down with personal effects going missing. When this is over, I'll be getting that back."

"Seveeeen, eight don't stay up late," Freddie sang.

"If Freddie doesn't get it after he kills you," T-Bone added.

Officer Sanchez reached for the box, opened it, slipped the watch in her pocket and tucked the necklace into ther Kevlar. She took another step back when a loud bang resonated off the walls of the trailer. Freddie must have taken a foot to the door because a screw blew of the hinge and skidded across the floor to the corpse.

"Niiiine, ten never sleep again."

He kept striking the door. Each pounding shook metal. Sending every piece of tactical equipment on the walls to a clatter. One thunderous boom after another. Sanchez flinched and drew back.

T-Bone cursed. "Unlock us!"

Sanchez hesitated, then caved and removed their cuffs.

"Where's the key to the gun cage?" T-Bone asked.

"I don't have it." Sanchez said. "Only the lead has it. Our commander. Van Zant."

"Take off, T-Bone," Taran said. "I got him."

"You stay we stay," T-Bone said.

"He's not here for you. He's here for me." Taran looked down at the floor and spotted a steel hatch door. "Take off. Find Lunch. I got it."

Turkell threw open the floor hatch.

Just as he slipped through, the slide bolt busted and the door blew off its hinges landing on the hatch door. Slamming it shut. Freddie Machete and several thugs rushed through the doorway. Taran expected the worst then. But Freddie threw his arms out. Stopping all of his henchmen from pouring in after him. As if they were suddenly infringing on his moment, they backed away. He shooed them off with quick nod, then stepped forward with a calm easy stride like he owned the bus and everything in it.

His men stepped out of the doorway and stood outside in the cold of night. Watching whatever was about to unfold. Taran looked at that drooping eye and missing ear — the ear Fang took from him. Whatever offense caused Freddie to lose the appendage was never spoken of and Taran knew far better than to ask the old Ainu about it. Just to look on it now, reminded him that Freddie never forgot his reprimand whenever he looked in the mirror.

"Taran Carter," Freddie said in greeting. He reached down to the corpse and retrieved his weapon from its chest. Easing it out from severed ribs with a long, long, slow pull. He stood, then spun the machete in his hand like the flipping of a switch blade, flicking blood over the map wall.

Taran did the only thing he could do. He turned back to Sanchez. "Get in the cage, lock yourself in," he told her. "Fuck off, Freddie."

One look in the Disciple's crazed eyes as he drew nearer was all it took. Without another word of protest, Sanchez snatched the key from her service belt, scrambled under the table and crawled over Moorehouse's corpse towards the cage. Taran turned around to face Freddie as he stalked closer.

"Yeah," Machete said. "Get in the cage, bitch. Cause me and this nigga, we got unfinished business."

Sanchez slipped inside the cage, pulled the bars shut, and stepped back to the wall. Taran grabbed a chair and pinned it between the cage lock and the bars, blocking a hand from reaching the lever or sliding the bars open.

"I sent the guns away," Machete went on. "When I heard you were here...I had to." He stalked closer, sliding his machete across the cage bars as he walked.

"Some years ago, your master and I had a conversation. It was a conversation, I will never forget. I was invited that day to Fang's tea house over in Chinatown. And I was sitting there, with this loud, rude, obnoxious, cracker motherfucker. And he says to me, after watching me win a match against an opponent, *'You were good. You were fast. Quick hands. But I know somebody faster than you.'* And of course I said, *'Nobody's faster than me. I've been trained by the fastest hands in the world.'* Then he said, *'Then you are mistaken youngblood. Because the fastest hands that I've seen were trained by him as well.'* Then he looked at Fang with a slick smirk on his face." Freddie threw the machete down blade first. It shared through the floor with a loud metallic chime. "So I had to know. And I asked Fang, *'Who?'*" Freddie undid the clasp of his gold watch, slipped it off and put it in the pocket of his denim. "Fang didn't answer. But his obnoxious friend did. *'Taran,'* he taunted. *'I saw a match unlike anything I have ever seen. Just last weekend. Shadow Hands they call him. They say he's even faster than DeGrate. No sword play though. But his hands...nothing shy of deadly.'* I looked at my master and I said, *'Fang, he can't be better than me.'* And you know what he said then?"

Taran just looked at him.

"Nothing," Freddie spat. "Not a fucking thing. He didn't utter one word to correct that rude, fat fuck. So I said, *'He's not faster than me,'* and Fang said, *'There's only one way to find out.'* Those words stuck in my head for years. Day and night. Day and night. Like a fucking itch I just can't scratch. And then it dawned on me." Freddie slipped his shirt off and cracked his neck. "He was right."

Freddie came at him hard and fast.

Taran expected nothing less.

He dodged a palm strike to his throat, dodged more and jumped on the table for height advantage.

Freddie walked forward calmly. Surging with strength. Ready to deliver more. He kicked the table legs out from under Taran and set to delivering a barrage of kicks.

Taran went down hard, spun on the ground and blocked every blow with fists and feet. Then flowed into a floor sweep and knocked Machete on his ass.

My turn motherfucker.

Taran backed off of him and stood.

"Get your ass up! Get up!"

Freddie stood in a flash and came at him with the rage of a cut crook. Deflecting Taran's blows and dodging more. Ducking kicks and side-stepping chairs, Taran stayed with him. Taking and giving the salvo. Waiting for the right moment to execute a death blow. With lightening fast speed, Freddie threw two more blows to distract Taran's hands and landed a hard kick to his chest. Taran hit the steel flooring and flew back to the gun cage.

That hurt.

A stinging sharp pain, arced up his back. Burning his lungs. He actually had to concentrate to breath. He rolled on his side, teeth clenched and sucked in a breath.

Get up Taran, he thought to himself. *Get up...*

He stood, cracked his neck, and the instant he turned, Freddie was on him, throwing more palm strikes.

Taran caught his arm, locked his wrist, and threw a strike to his armpit. He heard the pop when Freddie's shoulder gave and Taran gave no mercy to let the pain set in. He kicked him dead in his chest and sent Machete flying clear across the bus.

He slammed into the corpse he'd made and gripped his shoulder. Groaning, he let out a weak cough. But he didn't get up.

With Freddie put down, Taran turned and locked eyes on Sanchez. He reached for the chair, blocking the lock, then he heard a pop. Not a mechanical one. More like the muscular-skeletal one bones give. He blinked at Sanchez. Instead of Latin brown eyes filled with relief staring back at him, they were wide with dread.

"Behind you!" she screamed.

Taran turned just in time to dodge the blade.

Freddie's machete flew past him and skewered into the map wall.

Cheating bitch.

He never could keep it with fists. Sooner or later, when he was tired of getting the shit beat out of him, he'd pick up a rock or a brick or something. Anything just to win. That was part of the reason Fang never qualified him as a top protégé in his temple and he knew it.

Taran blinked in shock at the steel in the wall and how accurate a throw it was. In a matter of seconds, Freddie had popped his shoulder back in place and launched a blade with enough force to cleave a wild boar.

Clearly, he'd earned his namesake.

Taran was perfectly set to keeping the duel with hands. But if Freddie wanted to take it there, so be it.

Time to end this shit.

Taran pulled the machete from the wall and lunged forward. Slicing at Freddie with all the speed he could conjure. Dodging, ducking, spinning, Fang's errant former student whirled around the sharp steel as if shielded by some invisible force that kept it at bay.

Sanchez reached a leg through the bars of the holding cage and kicked the chair at his back.

It rolled right behind his knees and Freddie stumbled backwards. Landing on the floor.

Undaunted, he spun quickly and recovered. Blocking the steel as he stood. He pulled a night stick from the service belt of the corpse and used it to counter the blade. Delivering blows to Taran's arms and shoulders, he blocked more slashes and jabbed the night stick into Taran's stomach, then swung it at his head.

Too slow.

Taran ducked, dropped low, and with a slash of the blade, chopped his leg off clean below the knee. Freddie screamed, hit the floor and dropped the night stick.

Arterial blood sprayed everything near him.

Taran lunged forward, spun the blade, turned at him and slammed the machete into this skull, then wrenched it free to let the red spew.

Freddie looked up at him. Wordless. Unblinking. Holding the leg that drained the last of him.

Both men stared in silence.

Taran watching Freddie die.

Freddie watching Taran live.

When the last breath was gone, Freddie keeled over to the cold flooring. Taran watched until his eyes went unseeing.

Satisfied at the corpse he'd made, Taran turned away and locked eyes on a crowd of Disciples at the door.

They'd been watching the whole time.

Taran knew the look of murder when he saw it. This wasn't it. Not only did they look paused. They were cowed.

Not one of them made a move to attack him.

He inwardly thanked God for it. Because if they stormed the bus, he didn't have the strength to fight them all. If they came at him, they'd kill him.

Taran's only advantage was they didn't know it.

He stared them down. Unflinching and said the only thing he could. "We cool?"

"Yeah, man," a Disciple said. He threw a hand to the men at his side, backing them up from the doorway. "We good."

DARRION

Darrion ran, but fear and doubt ran faster.

A cop called at his back. "Stop, goddamnit!"

Darrion kept running, rounded another exhaust fan and slowed to a stop.

He flipped up the face of his watch, pulled out the dial and checked it.

1500 FEET / 0.457 KILOMETERS

If he had the breath to spare he would have cursed. If Angie was that far away, she wasn't in Head Quarters anymore. He mentally mapped the distance in kilometeres. There were only two buildings she could've been in from that far away. Bank Roll or 2 Bill. Hudson Mob was too close.

More calls and threats came at his back. Darrion took off once more and kept leading them through and around the air vents and piping like a pacer on the track at Nascar. Keeping a steady speed, not yet ready for a full sprint.

Coach Nokes came to his bones.

Guiding him. Telling him to keep it smooth until it was time to bolt. Less than fifty paces away the Black Gate came into view. Rising. Slowly ascending above the roof. If he didn't make the Gate, it was all over.

He looked to his left and saw a helicopter rising. When it set level to the roof, the door slid open. Several SWAT officers and three German Shepherds leapt out and set after him.

Oh...fuck.

Darrion burst into a full sprint. Chest heaving. Pushing his muscles to the limit. Kicking it out with everything he had.

Barking at his heels grew closer, but he didn't slow.

Using the piping as a lift, he jumped, pushed off the top of the Black Gate and felt the sickening sensation of flying into space. He hit the ground and rolled just as the dogs slowed and pawed the fence.

Before he could think of how close he came to be mauled, Darrion was up on his feet. Running until he made it to the fire escape.

He climbed down and slipped into the window of the 19th floor, and dashed down the breezeway.

Out of nowhere a Disciple came at him with a baseball bat.

Darrion pulled a balisong from his Kevlar, flipped it open, sprinted toward the thug and slashed his throat in a fury as he blew past him.

He flew down the stairs, floor after floor, until he reached the courtyard. As soon as he hit the grass more Disciples came at him. He turned to make for the bushes and saw foot patrol coming his way.

For a moment he hesitated. Then he spotted a trash can. He ran to it, quickly sifted through the garbage and spotted a discarded Raid can. He poked a hole in the bottom of the roach killer with is balisong, waded up discarded newspaper, stuffed it in the hole, then pulled his lighter and lit it. He picked the trash can up, sat it on top of the flames and ran back into the breezeway.

Seconds later, the can blew. It was a bang so loud, every gangster flooding the courtyard mistook it for gunfire and started shooting. Darrion dashed back up the stairs, letting the Disciples and foot patrol shoot it out.

He stopped at the 2nd floor, ran through the breezeway to the other side if the building, then dashed down the stairs and ran for Bank Roll.

As he neared the building, he could see a large crowd gathered outside. Either the police evacuated the building because they raided it, or somebody hit the fire alarm.

His luck, probably both.

Just paces away from the main entrance, he saw foot patrol coming his way. It didn't take long before he was spotted. As soon as he neared the courtyard they gave chase.

"Stop right there, DeGrate!"

Darrion had had it. He picked up a trash can and hurled it at them. "Fuck you!"

He dashed into the main entrance, through the breezeway and up the stairs. He could hear a badge on his shoulder mic. Calling it in.

"We got DeGrate, he's headed up the stairs in the highrise on West Oak Street! I repeat we have DeGrate, Renfro. He's headed up the stairs in Bank Roll. Five officers on foot in pursuit!"

As he flew up the stairs, every muscle in his legs burned for him to stop, but he didn't slow.

He ran all the way up to the top floor.

Darrion felt his stamina starting to wane. Another minute of running, maybe two, and he was finished. But there was no Black Gate to stop him this time and he knew just how to lose them.

Calling on memory from his childhood, he dashed into the Maze.

♛

A few rights, a few lefts, and a few more swift rights and lefts through the man-sized holes was all it took and he was gone. All he heard behind him was curses followed by frustrated words of separation and desertion.

Every cop on him, got lost like a knat in the dark.

Even with the authorities out of the way, he was still at a disadvantage. This high up was a problem. Going back down without running in to more Disciples, or cops raiding the building, was slim to none. He didn't know how far Angelique was from him or what floor she was on.

He checked his watch again.

142 FEET / 0.0432 KILOMETERS

Darrion let out a sigh of relief. He was close. But now he had no other choice but to leave the safety of the Maze and go back to the war on the ground. His best chance was to use the pandemonium to his advantage and hope to find Angelique in the crowd.

He jogged up to the wire mesh covering the façade of the building and looked down. Spying for a white medical coat among on the horde of people gathered in the courtyard.

He couldn't spot her.

She wasn't there.

ANGELIQUE

Angelique followed Anton.

It came as no surprise he knew more about navigating the breezeways and abandoned units of Head Quarters than she did. When they walked the distance to his highrise and neared Bank Roll, Anton froze and cursed.

"What?" she asked.

"We must be getting hit! Everybody's spilling out of the building! It's probably cops everywhere!" He looked around and spotted a passed out drunk in the nearby bushes. Anton ran over to him and snatched off his black hooded coat. "Here, put this on. Throw the hood over your head."

She handed Ophelia to him and gave the coat a sniff.

It was worse than repugnant.

Not even the stench of pestiside on the little girl made her nose deaf enough to block out the sheer reek. A dank smell of old urine and unwashed body took over her nostrils.

"Christ," she said, scowling as she slipped it on.

"What?" Anton asked.

"This coat smells like feet and ass."

He handed Ophelia back to her and shrugged. "Welcome to Cabrini."

"What now?" she asked.

Anton looked around. Deciding which way to go.

"We'll move through the crowd in the courtyard. Separately but together. Keep close enough not to lose me but far enough not to look like we're together."

"Okay."

"Let's go."

He carefully guided her through the crowd of the courtyard.

"Anton!" a voice called at his back.

He froze.

Angelique's breath caught. Not wanting to let whoever it was know she was with him, she kept walking.

"Where the hell you been, man?" the gangster asked. "We been paging you."

"Q-Ball," Anton said. "What's up?"

"What you mean what's up? We getting hit! Head up to the fifth floor and start switching the stash, man! That's on orders from Zane. Let's go!"

She blinked through the shock of realizing their plan had just gone to hell. Anton had no choice but to answer to his Disciples.

Like that he was gone and she was alone.

♛

If Bank Roll was being raided, her only hope was to make it through the crowd without being spotted by a Disciple and flag down the first cop she saw.

Dr. James shouldered through the tenants. Looking every which way for a badge. Nearly fifty paces away she saw an officer. Tall. Caucasian. She couldn't spot his nametag from that distance. He must have been watching the ground for Zane's soldiers. She kept moving toward him until he turned in her direction.

She took the hood off and threw up a hand. Waving at him. Hoping he recognized her as the doctor on TV.

His eyes seemed to take on something like recognition. Or maybe it was just his response to a citizen flagging him for help.

He took a step towards her.

A shot rang out.

With impossible speed the cop was hurled back to the ground.

She saw the blood spray from his skull.

Everyone scattered. Running in all directions like a bomb went off.

On instinct, Angelique turned and locked eyes on hell.

Zeno Harris. Staring murder at her from across the courtyard.

He fired two more shots.

Angelique felt the fabric tug as a bullet when through the hood of the coat. It was a miracle Ophelia wasn't shot in the head. She ducked and took off. Running towards the entrance, she turned and fired the 12-gauge at Zeno. But, with a one-armed trigger pull it was bad shot.

He didn't flinch. She cocked it and pulled the trigger again, but it didn't fire. It didn't even click. It was jammed. She tossed the gun and moved as fast as her legs could carry. Climbing the stairs two at a time. She looked down and saw Zeno flying up the stairs after her.

Darrion had once told her all of the building's top floors had a Maze. Dr. James' only chance was to make it to the 19th floor and try to lose him.

She ran up to the 4th floor and dashed into an abandoned apartment. She knew she wasn't going to make it to the Maze before Zeno caught her.

With no other option, Angelique ran into the empty kitchen and placed Ophelia in the cabinet underneath the sink.

Tiny arms reached for her in a panic. "Don't leave me!"

"Shhhh, I'll be back honey, I promise! Shhhh, just stay here!"

"Please! Don't!"

Angelique picked her back up, shut the cabinet and took off back up the stairs.

DARRION

Darrion had spotted Angelique in the courtyard the instant he heard the gunshots. She was moving up the stairs on the north tower. Zeno right on her heels.

He ran down the south tower stairs and when he hit the 9th floor another shot rang out. Darrion pulled a Colt from his back holster, spun on the stairs and fired at the first thing moving.

A Disciple fired two more shots and ducked into an empty apartment. Darrion almost fired through the unit's window, hoping to hit him, until he realized the soldier wasn't shooting at him. Darrion looked in the direction of the gangster's aim and blinked in shock.

It was too late.

Chicago PD had flooded the building and the raid was on in full effect.

Cops were kicking in doors, yelling threats. Throwing gangsters on the ground without pity. Pressing shotguns to their heads and knees into their backs. Disciples that weren't caught, were running wild in all directions. In and out of doors. Dashing through the breezeways. Jumping in and out of windows. They all had kilos of cocaine in hand or arms full of guns.

Those who weren't moving product or getting arrested were coming up Darrion's way. Headed for the Maze.

In the midst of the mayhem, he had two choices, he could either fight his way through them, only to get arrested when a cop caught him, or he could run back up to the Maze and try to lose them.

On the up side, if Zane's soldiers were busy switching their stash and going for self, they didn't have time to kill him.

Darrion quickly looked down the breezeway at the stairs of the adjacent tower for Angie. From the south tower where he stood, he could still see her coming up the north tower. On the 6th for and climbing. But with a child in her arms, she'd never make it. Zeno was gaining on her.

Darrion ran to the end of the breezeway, aimed true and fired two warning shots at Zeno. He watched the sick twist duck back against the wall.

Angie crouched and covered Ophelia.

"Angie!" Darrion yelled.

She looked up. Eyes wide.

"Keep coming!" He fired more shots giving her time to flee. She moved up the stairs, past the 7th floor, making it up to the 8th.

Zeno fired back until the gun was empty. Sending bullets ricocheting off the brick inches from Darrion's head.

For a one-eyed psyco, he was a damned good shot.

Darrion fired back until his Colt clicked empty. He holstered it, pulled the second Colt and fired two more shots. By then, Angie was passing the 9th floor. "Get to the Maze, Angie! I'm coming for you!" All he could spot was a slither of Zeno's dreadlocs moving up the stairs. "I'm coming for you too, motherfucker!"

Darrion ran for the Maze, just as a crowd of Disciples rushed at his back. He jumped the stairs two at a time. Keeping an eye on Angie. Making sure Zeno didn't catch up to her.

He made it to the 19th floor and into the Maze along with every hoodlum behind him.

In the dark of that catacomb, it was the devil's mansion. All that came to mind was the rhyme that helped navigate the walls in Bank Roll. Every Disciple knew it. *'Bank to the right, Roll to the left. Right 'til it's nothing but turns to the left. Bank Roll up, Bank Roll down, fly down the steps 'til your kicks hits the ground."*

He moved to memory, all the while checking for Angie. He flew through the walls. Taking all the turns. Then he flew through another wall and skidded to a halt when he locked eyes on a tall, ill-fitted suit standing next to a foot patrol cop.

In the dark, the suit looked high ranking. They both had their guns trained on him.

Darrion didn't know how many Discples flew to his back. But they all froze the same as he did.

He cut his eyes to the right when he spotted Angie. She flew through a wall, locked eyes on the suit, then Darrion, then drew back in horror when Zeno came flying through the opposite wall.

They all stood there in the empty room.

Frozen in time. Staring each other down.

"Don't fucking move!" the patrol cop yelled.

They all broke wide like a pack of zebras.

Running every which way.

Every leap cleared a hole. Every turn was madness. Every hood breaking left got passed up by a hood breaking right. Darrion was running and leaping past so many people, the confusion was nothing shy of sheer chaos.

He escaped the Maze and found himself in the hall. Watching other Disciples spill out from several walls and doorless units.

He turned when he heard the scream.

Zeno had a woman by a fistful of hair at the far end of the hall. A knife to her throat.

Darrion aimed his Colt. "Don't!"

Zeno smiled the devil's smile. It made a menace of his red glittering false eye. He gave two quick jabs at the woman's neck and backed up. Keeping her pulled to his chest.

Darrion saw the red run down her neck from where he stood. He stepped forward. Keeping his aim.

"You want me, Zeno, I'm right here. Don't do this! Let her go!"

Darrion took another step forward. Then another. Just a few more steps, even in the dark, and he would've had a shot sure enough to blow Zeno's head off.

Darrion took one more step.

Zeno spun the woman away from him, threw her down the stairs, flipped the switch blade closed and just stood there. Glaring evil.

Darrion heard the woman scream, followed by a loud crash when she hit whatever broke her fall.

Then silence.

Then ticking.

Darrion blinked at Zeno. He could've sworn he had a gun. Unless he was out of clips...

Why the hell aren't you shooting at me?

On instinct the ticking sound drew his attention to the fire extinguisher in the wall...And the bomb strapped to it.

Darrion turned and ran as fast as he could.

Then the world tore open.

He didn't register the explosion until his back hit the wall and his face met the concrete flooring with a crunch. His Colt left him. Spinning off into obscurity. Shattered glass ripped the palms of his hands when they smacked the cement. Everything flashed white.

He stayed there. Unmoving. But he didn't pass out.

A ringing came to his ears and his vision blurred. A cloud of smoke so thick took the air, he could barely see infront of his face.

Get up Darrion, he said to himself. *You're not dead. Get up.*

His whole body stiffened when he stood. His hands throbbed and his back burned from the force of the blow.

Gritting through the pain, he cracked his neck, arched his back and looked around. A large portion of the Maze wall was gone. Part of the roofing was missing.

He shook off a dizzy spell and saw mouths open in a scream. Inaudible words from those still alive. But no sound came to him. Both ears were deafened.

He should have been dead. Every Disciple near him should have been dead. Zeno's bomb must have been a half-detonation. Not a full blast. Something was wrong with the timer. Darrion wasn't a science major, but he and Taran had built enough shape charge bombs to know, a timing discrepancy of just one microsecond, when building an explosive, was enough to create a partial dud.

Then again, Zeno didn't run when he knew the bomb was about to go off.

Darrion knew then. It wasn't meant to kill a room full of people.

Just him.

Just her.

Angelique flashed in his mind. Had she been killed by the blast? Was she bleeding? Was she in once piece? Fear hit like a sledgehammer. Getting to her was all that mattered.

Darrion walked towards the remains of the Maze. Before he could blink about it, out of the smoke, Zeno slammed into him like a battering ram. Knocking the wind from his lungs.

As Darrion hit the ground, every sound came rushing back to his ears like a switch had been tripped.

He looked up at the roofless sky and saw a police helicopter, the night and Zeno's fist beating down on him with the wrath of an angry God.

Darrion blocked the blows with his forearms until Zeno stood and aimed to kick him in the chest. His foot barely slowed by the brick Darrion picked up to block it.

He tossed the brick, pulled Zeno's leg until he nearly fell, then gripped his jacket, put a foot to his chest and hurled him clear over his head.

Zeno flew in the air and landed through a massive shard of glass, head first. His lanky body smacked against a pile of concrete rubble.

It was all the time Darrion needed to get to his feet.

He was up in an instant. Ready for anything. Adrenaline was a marvelous thing. Zane rolled off the broken concrete, shook off the blow, stood, and came at him like the warrior Darrion knew so well.

Strength met strength. Rage met rage. Speed met speed.

Zeno launched into a blistering attack so fierce and fast, it should have been impossible.

Darrion moved back. Blocking blows and stepping backward to dodge more. In keeping pace with Zeno, something about fighting with his style of hand to hand combat, calmed him.

Zeno Harris studied Tae-Kwon-Do.

Fang despised it because it relied too much on striking with heavy emphasis on kicks. Worse over, though it was a disciplined martial art, it was only one martial art.

As he so eloquently put it, *'A master of one is a master of none.'*

Zeno's fighting skills were focused on offensive moves. Darrion, through his master's grueling tutelage, learned to adapt to his opponent through defensive moves.

He kept retreating. Back. Back. Waiting for it. Sooner or later, those hands would tire and Zeno would lead with a kick.

Like clockwork, a leg came at him.

Darrion dropped back and lashed out with a foot to Zeno's leading knee. Thrown off balance, Zeno dropped to the ground but recovered with a floor sweep, knocking Darrion to the concrete.

Before Darrion could stand, Zeno was up with a brick in hand. All he could do was roll sideways and avoid the slab raining down on him.

When it struck stone, Darrion grabbed a steel pipe and jammed it down into Zeno's foot.

He let out a scream and dropped the brick.

Darrion swung the pipe and hit Zeno dead in the chest. Knocking him back into the rubble. He came at him and swung again, but Zeno grabbed the pole, snatched it free from Darrion's grip, tossed it aside and lunged for him.

Both men went crashing up against a wrecked wall. Zeno had his arms around his waist in a death grip. Darrion pounded on his back with a fist, kneed his face and delivered more kidney shots until Zeno reared back and lifted him clean off the ground.

Refusing to be body slammed, Darrion outstretched both legs and let Zeno turn a throw into an unexpected man carry. He planted both feet on the wall, gripped Zeno's dreads, used him as a pole vault and flipped over his head.

Darrion spun, both fists still locked in his dreads, slammed Zeno's face into the concrete and rammed his head through a window. Then snatched him up, reared back and hurled him as hard as he could, sending Zeno flying through a hole in the flooring.

Darrion walked over to the edge of the hole and stood here. Chest heaving. Looking down on Zeno's unmoving frame.

"Rest in piss, motherfucker."

Satisfied he was dead, Darrion cracked his neck and ran for Angelique.

♛

A quick search of the remaining rubble revealed she wasn't there. But if she was still in Bank Roll, there was only one place she could have gone. Anton was the only Disciple she trusted.

Watching for cops, Darrion ran down to Ant's apartment and beat on the door. When it opened, he quickly stepped in.

One look from Darrion's ravaged clothes to his swollen fists and Anton's eyes went wide with shock. Darrion didn't have a mirror, but he must have looked like he'd been through a mortar.

"Damn, KD," Anton said. "You alright?"

"Just making friends the Zeno way. Where's Angie?"

Angelique stepped out of the living room and into the hallway. The little girl still clutched in her arms.

"I'm right here."

His heart was so light then, he would have smiled if his entire face wasn't throbbing.

"Are you alright?" she asked.

Darrion nodded. "Yeah. Let's go."

He turned and the door blew open so fast it flew off the hinges. Zeno came at him like a mad bull.

He rammed into him sending them both hurling down the hall and into the living room.

Darrion threw him off, but only half stood before Zeno picked him up and slammed him down on the coffee table. Glass shattered, wood splintered and the entire frame collapsed under Darrion's weight.

Fucking Zeno just won't fucking die.

Zeno picked up a thick brass candle holder and swung it at him. Up on one knee, Darrion caught it pulled it forward, yanking Zeno well within arm's reached, and used the first two fingers of his free hand to gouge out Zeno's good eye.

Darrion jabbed so hard and fast, he could've sworn he pushed all the way to his brain. Blinded, Zeno screamed an earsplitting, deafening scream. It was unlike anything Darrion had ever heard. It was blood-curdling. Horrific.

It was beautiful.

He dislodged his fingers with a hard kick to Zeno's chest. Anton jumped out of the way and watched him fly back into the bathroom. Zeno hit the tub with a hard thud and flopped around like an eyeless fish.

Darrion rushed into the bathroom, snatched a towel off the wall rack and wapped it around Zeno's neck. In air-deprived desperation, he reached up. Clawing for something. Anything.

Darrion slaped his hands away and pulled the towel even harder. Pushing on Zeno's shoulders with his with both feet until he felt both collar bones break. Another pop sent Zeno's jeweled eye flying out. It rolled down the porcelain of the tub. Hitting the drain stopper.

Darrion gritted his teeth, choking Zeno Harris with all the rage he had left in him, until the notorious henchman's arms fell slack at his sides.

Darrion exhaled, released the towel and slumped back in the tub. Exasperated. Fatigued. He laid there motionless. His head against the wall. With Zeno Harris' lifeless body cradled on his chest.

♛

Darrion ushered the good doctor and the little girl through the crowd toward the ambulance. Minutes later, Ophelia was carefully loaded onto a gurney and taken away. Knowing she would be mended and healed meant nothing. Cabrini scarred youth like no other. He knew she would never be whole.

Darrion looked to the building. A horde of officers were flooding the breezeways. Shouting commands. Rushing up the stairs towards the remains of the blast.

"We gotta go."

Angelique blinked up at him. "Where's Zane?"

"I don't know."

"He's not dead is he?"

Darrion shook his head. "No."

"So what happens now?"

"We get the hell out of here." Darrion turned and looked at the good doctor. "And you save my father's life."

EPILOGUE

R enfro entered the apartment of Anton Smith with caution.

As he quietly stepped forward, a strong breeze turned the hall into a wind tunnel. It seemed too hard a gust to be coming from a window.

Renfro chambered a round and followed the cold to the sound of a helicopter. As he stepped into what had formerly been a living room, a hard search light swept over the room. Illuminating the remains of whatever mayhem took place.

Signs of a lethal struggle filled his vision.

Broken glass. A busted coffee table. Splintered wood lay in pieces all over the floor. Shattered tableware.

An infant's noise drew him to the far end of the room.

Anton Smith and Taniesha Berry were standing in the doorway of the bathroom. Staring at a very dead Zeno Harris.

Renfro had seen more dead bodies than any undertaker could boast. But this one would sear into his memory for years to come.

Rigor mortis had yet to set in.

DeGrate's kill lay in the bathtub, dreads in a wild state. Salivary stains on his face. One eye gouged out of his head and his infamous bejewled eye was missing. Leaving a red meaty hole filled with blood from what Renfro assumed were ruptured

Before he could open his mouth to ask what was witnessed the Disciple threw a hand up to stop him.

"Don't even ask me cause I ain't saying shit!"

With that he walked right passed him and out the door.

Taniesha said nothing. She didn't look at him or give one inkling of acknowledgement. She simply cut her eyes away and followed Anton. Adjusting the weight of her baby on her hip as she stepped around Renfro like he was a coat rack in her way.

♛

We have to bring him in while we have a good reason," Renfro said.

Everyone in the room just looked at him.

Chief Reynolds. Deputy Chief Riles. Lieutenant Delgado. Agent Stahl and her two loyals, Cowen and Lomax. This was going nowhere. For the last thirty minutes, Renfro sat in the booking room, trying to explain why DeGrate needed to be brought in for questioning. All he had gotten in return so far was differing questions that begged more questions, because every answer he gave didn't seem to satisfy them. Bishop was in the report room. Up to his elbows in preliminaries and complaint sheets. He had to miss this little pow-wow with the Chief and the task-force frontrunner.

Lucky bastard.

"What's the charge?" Chief Reynolds asked.

"Obstruction of justice and murder," he answered. "You were standing right there, Chief. He was specifically told to stay back out of the way and let PD and the National Guard handle the hostage situation. Both you and nearly two dozen uniformed officers were there when I said it. Both him and his henchmen were told to wait in the trailor and we would keep them informed. Next thing I know, I'm arresting Taran Carter and Turkell Scarbone for tampering with the barrier gate."

"But what did DeGrate do to warrant an obstruction charge?"

"He ran Cabrini, led dozens of officers on a wild goose chase in the dark, and killed Zeno Harris."

"Do you have any proof?" Deputy Chief Riles asked.

"No," Renfro said. "I didn't exactly see him kill Zeno. But I know he was in the apartment."

"What apartment?"

"Where the fight took place."

"Who's apartment?"

"Anton Smith. He's one of Zane's soldiers. Or…he was."

"Did Anton say DeGrate killed him?"

"No. But he wanted Zeno dead just as much as everybody else in those towers."

"And how do you know that?"

"Everybody knows. Most of the Disciples in the city wanted him dead."

"Did Anton tell you that?"

"He won't talk. Taniesha Berry was there too. She won't say shit either."

"Who's Taniesha Berry?"

"The mother of his nephew."

"So you got blood on DeGrate's hands then?"

"No."

"Any prints you can lift off the bathroom that don't belong to Anton or Taniesha?"

"DeGrate's not that sloppy," Agent Stahl cut in. "And even if he was, it just puts him in the home of an acquaintance. That doesn't mean he's a killer."

"So you've go no blood from DeGrate," Riles said, "No prints on him that's anything other than substantial in a courtroom. And no witnesses willing to come forward. And Zane, you're informant, is on the lam."

Renfro gave a slow, defeated nod.

"So murder is a stretch. And to force a confession, you plan to bring DeGrate down to the station on an obstruction charge?"

"An obstruction that was caught all over the fucking news!"

"Wrong detective," the Chief corrected. "A black man running the rooftops in the dark was all over the fucking news. Hundreds of them were all over that building. Running like roaches from a Raid can. At least that's what his lawyer will say when this bullshit winds up in court. You think any facial features, tattoos, or scars are going to show up on any of that footage with those choppers flying around in the fucking dark with the wind blowing? Even SWAT probably couldn't identify

"Campbell was on him. With five other officers in pursuit."

"Until they lost him in the Maze."

"His speed alone is enough to make it stick! I've never seen anybody run that fast! He was a track star for Near North High for fuck sake! He still holds division records!"

Chief Reynolds leaned against the steel table and folded his arms across his chest. Everyone in the room stared back at him with the same look of reproach.

Renfro knew he was not going to win this one.

But he earned his say. Regardless of what they thought of his position on the matter, more than two hundred guns recovered and more than fifty arrests had earned him the right to speak his piece.

"He's the good doctor's personal body guard," Renfro added. "He works for Councilman Porter's private security company. Makes it easy to legally carry a concealed."

"Did he use his weapon on Zeno?" the Chief asked.

"No."

"So how did he kill him?"

"With his bare hands. Had to be. I could see the asphyxiation marks on his neck. You should've saw the poor fuck. It looked like somebody put his head on a hydrogen tank and tried to blow it up like a balloon. And his infamous eye was missing."

"You think DeGrate took it? As what? A keep sake?"

"Don't know...maybe."

"Or maybe it just rolled down the fucking drain? But you're willing to take a whole bunch of no's, I-don't-know's, and maybe's and haul his ass in on an obstruction charge that may or may not stick — depending on how it all plays out in court after he lawyers-up and makes a fool out of you — all so you can get a bite on a bank robbery that happened up in Northbrook last year?"

Renfro could tell he was pissed.

Reynolds cast a hard glare at him. "I don't know what kind of shit you're used to pulling down at Robbery/Homicide, but in my neck of the woods, if *you* have an informant, that means *we* have an informant. That means we stick to whatever it takes within the law to draw Zane out of hiding. Since you claim DeGrate is on his shit list for deep-sixing his brother, waiting for that rat to lead us to the cheese is top priority.

"In other words, you can do shit the old way and bring DeGrate up on charges if you want. And if by chance you actually get a win in court, then he'll do...what? Short time in county. Because it's his first offense since his juvy record was expunged. So, he'll be out in six months, except this time, he'll know you're on his ass. And he'll make it twice as difficult for you to catch him again. Or...you let this one go. We watch and we wait. We do real police work. Not this small-time-conviction bullshit. If you really think DeGrate is tied into those bank robberies and the killings in Cabrini, it's going to take more than an anonymous undercover, a missing informant, and an obstruction charge to put him away."

Renfro thought on that long and hard. He wanted DeGrate so bad he could taste the gunpowder through his fingers. But he knew the Chief was right.

"If you put up a red flag that no criminal is stupid enough to ignore," Riles added, "that's on you. I'm leaving it up to you, it's your call. But I'd let this one go. We made dozens of arrests. Thanks to you and Bishop we seized hundreds of guns and the Harris Oganization is finished. The Queen Bee of Cabrini will be a vegetable if she survives, so she won't be a threat to anyone and we cleaned house in the those projects enough to shut Burns and the Councilman up for a long while. That's result. That's a win for everyone. And that shit breeds budget funding. And a bigger budget means more overtime and more recon work for this task force. Again, it's your call. But my advice? Don't put ripples in the water when the sharks are too far away to even give a shit."

♛

Renfro walked out to the parking garage to think.

A cold, January wind brought the thick smells of exhaust and motor oil to this nostrils. Of all the places a cop could go to for a silent one, the sound of car doors opening and closing and Crown Vics pulling in and out of the station was the only thing that eased his mind.

They were out there.

Scouring every edge of the city for all the dregs of society.

One duty-dilemma that would never fade always rang true to an officer. To serve one is to serve none. Duty to all meant duty to none. That right to reject any greater obligation to others individually. Which meant, no enforced duty of care stood except the enforced duty owed to the public at large.

It put Renfro at ease knowing most the men in his station undertood that in taking on such enforced duty meant service to every indivudual who felt oppressed by the evils of society. So the task force going after an entire drug organization meant serving those who lived in fear of them individually.

Any cop worth his badge knew to serve all is to serve one.

"Still mulling over DeGrate?" Bishop said.

Renfro hadn't heard him approach. Car engines and the sounds of winter drowned out everything. Maybe that's why he preferred the chill and darkness of the garage over the break room or the archives where the rookies liked to nap. All the traffic just drowned out the world.

"We could look into which banks have similar surveillance and security measures to Northbrook," he added. "Usually they like to hit the same institution with the same alarm system."

"No," Renfro said. "We won't catch them that way. By the time we figure out what bank they're going to hit next, whatever sloppy ass rent-a-thug they send to do their dirty work for them will already be robbing it. By then, we won't be able to catch our Machiavelli Crew. By the time we respond, the second they see our cars pull up, they'll pull out, use whatever Houdini they have set up to disappear, and then vamonos. They are gone. They'll lay low for months, maybe even years before they make a move on their next take and all we'll have to show for our man hours is a bunch of half-retarded bandits who were set up to fail anyway. That's not how we're going to catch our boys. They're too smart for that. If we can't catch them after they send in the bait squad to rob the next bank, we'll have to catch them before they set the bait."

"How are we gonna do that?"

"Well...Think about it. Where would they get a crew desperate enough to rob a bank with all of this heat we're putting out on the city? Every bank owner in Illinois is scared shitless behind all of these robberies. So their security is being upgraded as we speak. But regardless of the upgrades, regardless of the risk, who would still be desperate enough to try it?"

Bishop stood silent. Thinking. "Junkies."

"Think more dependable than that, Bishop. Dope fiends will bleed you faster than a knife fight in a phone booth if you pay 'em to. So they're no stranger to violence. But can they think on the fly? Or is their mind clouded by their next fix? If their exit is threatened, can they hold the gun steady enough to make the kill? Or is their aim too shaky because they haven't smoked or shot up yet that morning? Junkies under stress are no good. Because they always crack. Their bodies are weak, their minds are even weaker, so their reaction under pressure is shit. Especially when they're staring down the barrel of a gun and all they hear is sirens in the distance getting closer by the second. Our Machiavelli Boys would never put millions of dollars on a bunch of crack heads or spikers."

Bishop shook his head. "No, I can't see them risking that on a bunch of base heads."

"Addicts don't think about their families. They think about themselves. But who would think about mouths to feed? Rent to pay? Petro and paying for the car to put it in?"

"The average, underpaid working man."

"How about the below average, non-paid umemployed man?"

Bishop's eyes took on a sudden comprehension. "Ex-cons."

"Not your newly paroled first timer. The careful cons who only got one conviction. They don't fuck up to get locked up for life. They do nothing but eat, lift weights, and think about their futures. Not them. But the cons who've already been locked up before, they've already found out how bleak their future is. And they're hungry. And they know what's coming. Ex-con, don't even think about applying for a 9 to 5 in this city. Five, six months out. Still can't get a job. So they got two choices. Dealing or stealing. We need to talk to the puppets in county. See what they remember."

"But how are we supposed to find out who they're going to use next? DeGrate and his crew can't know every prisoner and is, all we have to do is wait. We'll wait until after they hit their next bank. And as soon as our Machiavelli Boys arrive to intercept that cash, we'll be on their asses like dots on dice."

INTERVIEW WITH THE AUTHOR

Tell us a little bit about yourself.

Well, I'm a fictioin writer currently living in Los Angeles, California—though I was born and raised in Chicago, Illinois. Since the age of 9, I always knew I wanted to be a writer of crime, action, and science fiction novels. I spent many years mulling over it before actually taking the plunge. To reach that pivotal point of having a completed novel, I've made many mistakes along the way. But it has only made me more determined to get inspired, get better, get heard and get published.

So how do you pull inspiration for your writing?

Many of my novel ideas, dialogue and characters often come to me in dreams. I don't know why, I swear. They just do. One morning I woke up in a panic because I had this amazing idea about my hometown and I didn't have a pad or a pen on my night stand. I flew out of bed and took down as many notes as I could remember from my crazy dream. I knew then I wanted to tell a story about my birthplace, what it meant be apart of Chicago, and how a part of recent history and the failure of the public housing system shaped so many lives. I also wanted to employ all of the things that I love about Italian and Asian culture in the story as well. More than 300 pages later, Cabrini Green Volume One: Return Of The Prince was completed. It was ˌˌˌˌˌˌˌˌˌˌˌˌˌˌˌˌˌˌˌˌˌˌ Near North Magnificent Mile Series.

Tell us a little bit about your interests when you're not writing.

Well, I'm an avid gun lover. I was introduced to guns at the age of 18 and never looked back...I've been such a gun whore ever since. Serving six years active duty in the Air Force—from 1996 to 2002—sparked my love of weapons. During my time in service I also learned extensive knowledge about the medical field—specifically surgical procedures. And it's all over my novels. I spent two years of my time in service stationed in Okinawa, Japan and fell in love with their culture and the art of the Katana sword. But I didn't seek to learn the language. I could have, but I wanted to pursue other passions instead. Afterwards, in 2003, I was honorably discharged and moved to Kansas City, Missouri where I studied creative writing at the University of Missouri Kansas City. Four years later in 2007, I moved to California. Since then, I have several novel series in mind. Two of them are in progress.

Are you married or single? Kids? No kids?

I've never been married and as of now, I have no children. I'm currently single, my child is my lap top, and my hubby is my career. I could make time for a relationship, but I'm just not looking for it. I'm not trying to get wifed-up to anyone right now. I'm much too selfish these days. When I'm more accomplished maybe that'll change. But for now, selfish is good.

And who is Warwick Shackleford-Masters?

Ah yes. I do have an alter ego who has earned a mention. Warwick keeps me from sliding too far into the feminine side when it comes to my writing. I think a lot of women try to write dark, fast paced action. But they fail, beause they don't know how to think like a man when it comes to getting raw and gritty. I do believe Warwick helps me do that well. He and I will have a long lasting, otherworldly relationship. I guess you could say I'm married to him!

HERE'S YOUR
SNEAK PEEK
AT THE SCI-FANTASY
NOVEL

STARFALL: THE LOST APOCALYPSE

PROLOGUE

Our sun is dying," Dr. Langston-Hughes began.

She cleared her throat and continued.

"Today, while using the VL Telescope, we spotted something very disturbing. A massive solar flare caused an extreme radiation burst. The spike was proven though Carbon-14 testing in the tree rings of our lab cedars. This caused a solar storm similar to the Quebec incident of 1989. It knocked out all of our power for nearly twelve hours. I can't imagine what cities across the planet are going through. We're just barely coming back on line. As you can see behind me, everyone is fussing about the lab trying to bring all of our systems back on line. Not only was it devastating to our technology, but my Neutron Monitoring Site in Antarctica recorded the largest neutron output since 1859. This solar flare was astronomical. It caused a burst of charged particles from the sun to break off and travel towards our planet at 7 million miles per hour. This was an S4-Level radiation storm. Coronal rain on the sun, two massive coronal mass ejection waves and strong G4-Level geomagnetic aftermaths here on earth were the end result.

"I think my passengers and crew were safe here on the ship, but no doubt, any pilots and airline passengers and personnel were at risk from solar radiation poisoning. When we aimed the VL Telescope at the sun, we spotted a massive hole that covered more than a fourth of its surface. Record temperatures are being recorded all over Siberia as we speak. We don't know how this opening happened. But we do know what it means.

"Though the sun seems quite large compared to earth, it's actually one of the smaller stars in outer space. When larger stars meet their demise, a spectacular supernova explosion takes place and all that's left of them is a cluster of neutron stars and black holes. However with mid-sized stars like our sun, they meet their end with a far more gradual transformation that destroys everything in its path. When a star suffers core hydrogen exhaustion, there's nothing left to burn but helium. When this happens, the sun will burn at an accelerated rate, unable to keep it's shape. This will cause it to swell to a Red Giant. It's predicted that while Mercury and Venus would be burned to a cinder, Mars would remain safely out of reach. I agree with this theory because similations have shown the Red Giant will swell to 250 times its original size. With the gradual temperature increase on Earth, carbon dioxide levels would rise to a point where photosynthesis would no longer be possible. When that occurs, plants will cease to give off oxygen, the air will become extremely hot and toxic, then all living things will die out.

"There was once the theory that our blue planet would escape annihilation. When the sun looses its gravitational pull, Earth would drift outward, away from the swelling star. However based on the research from my scientists our descendants won't be that lucky. Though our planet will infact drift, it won't drift far enough to be outside of the sun's heat atmosphere. If that outer atmosphere has enough density to cause some gravitational pull, it would be more than enough to cause the planet to drift toward the sun and not away. By this time, the earth would become a global desert.

"So far, there are only three alternatives to certain destruction. Gravitational maniuplation from a captured asteroid, erecting a planetary-based orbital city, or the discovery of another inhabitable planet similar to our own.

"Though this impending annihilation won't happen anywhere near our lifetime, five thousand years is a lot sooner than the predicted five billion. I will be talking to my helio-sizemologists to discuss this further. I truly hope that these later the video on the flat screens displayed the military confidentiality warning:

GOVERNMENT PROPERTY
CHAD COMMAND
OPERATION STARFALL
CIVILIAN FOOTAGE
ZENITH RESEARCH VESSEL

"Jesus Christ," the President said. "We have a cruise ship at the bottom of the sea, an AWOL Marine pilot, and a raging disease that's nothing shy of a global pandemic because the survivors all went to the largest hospital in Miami and the CDC couldn't do their damn job." He looked at his Secretary of Defense, Charles Burdt. "This is the worst Maritime disaster in history. Worse than the Titanic."

"In order for something like this to happen," Burdt said, "there had to be a massive and rapid chain of events followed immediately by a rapid chain of failures. What happened? Or I think a better question for the President is, what happened to the crew and the passengers? Something turned them into...whatever the hell caused them to start eating each other. And I doubt it was because someone ate a bad burger."

"Why don't we start from the beginning," General Garrison said. "From the time the first passenger was infected."

Martyr skimmed forward through the civilian footage.

"Do we know who this footage belongs to?"

"Eugene Puckman," Martyr answered. "He's one of Dr. Hughes' top researchers."

"And where is he?" The President asked.

"Missing as well."

Martyr stopped the footage and pressed play. "This is at 1745 hours. Port time. What you're seeing now is a wide shot from an upper tier in the grand ball room of the cruise ship. And all of the footage you'll be seeing today is from several different passengers. But Puckman's is the most valuable because he stayed close to Roberts, Mahr, Harmon, and our interplanetary visitor. And good thing it came from his camcorder, because he was using the most advanced piece of hand held recording equipment on the planet. If you notice, as he skims over the dance floor, the motion is extremely smooth. No matter where he moves with it, even if he coughs or hiccups, there's no blur and the image doesn't bounce."

"What kind of camera is it?" General Garrison asked.

"A Sony 360 Spider Action. Like an arachnid, it has six eyes or lenses. Each one capable of capturing different angles at the same time. It has three main features that make it top of the line. One, it was designed by NASA to have the same RCC surface material used on the nose of their space shuttles. The material has an atmospheric re-entry temperature of 2,300 degees fahrenheit. Second, it's waterproof for up to 250 feet. And lastly, it never allows for any motion to disturb and distort the image being filmed. And it never tips over. No matter where it lands, it always rights itself."

"Won't all that material make it heavy?" President Fitzgerald Carter asked.

"It wasn't designed to be a light carry. It was made for durability in harsh environments during space missions."

"How much does it weigh?"

"About ten ounces."

"How much does it cost?"

"About a hundred grand." Martyr aimed the remote control at the nine plasma televisions, pressed play, then aimed his laser pointer to the far back right corner of the ball room footage. "Look right there," he expounded. "See all that commotion, Mr.

speakers. Van Leuwin cursed. Burdt and Garrison sat shock-still. Engrossed in the chaos on the flat screens.

Celebration turned to savagery in a flash. Violins screeched to a halt. Musicians stopped playing. Melodious, soaring octaves of a woman drowned under the shrill of screams. Seconds later, the microphone amplified her cries of terror.

People running. Men slipping on blood. Women slipping on blood. Slipping on their ball gowns. Teeth tearing flesh. One bit another. Another bit another.

Then the eating began.

Then the hunger chose no favors.

"It just took them over," Martyr said. "Like a wave of murder." He looked back to the screens. Puckman's panicked shouts thundered through the speakers. Ordering everyone to run for the exits. His 360 Spider Cam was on the exit. Puckman was running. Screaming for the people in front of him to keep going. "Don't look back! Just run! Run!"

He was heaving breaths. Cursing. Calling out to God in between every expletive that flew out of his mouth.

Maximoff Martyr stopped the footage and the screen went black. He pressed the power button on the corner of the table and waited. Rosewood center leaves slid parted. A silent whir sounded and the virtual display screen rose and came to life. Martyr touched the screen and accessed the Automatic Information System for the Zenith vessel. He aimed a laser pointer as he talked. "This is what our investigation of the cruise ship disaster has yielded so far. When we found it, she was on her side. Nearly at a list of more than 80 degrees. Before the catastrophe, at the time of the ballroom celebration, the ship was traveling at roughly 15 knots. That's a relatively safe speed for a vessel that was farther from land. Unfortunately, when the crew was rendered hostile, no one was able to lower the speed to keep it from crashing ashore. That's when I sent in my Blitzkreig in a submarine to breach the hull and sink the Zenith before it could reach dry land—"

Martyr paused when Burdt, lifted a finger to interrupt. "Exactly what is this Zenith supposed to be?" he asked. "First I'm hearing it's a research vessel then I'm hearing it's a cruise ship. Which is it?"

"Actually it's both, Mr. Secretary. Dr. Hughes owns three vessels on her Hienburg Cruise Line. They were named after her father, Harold Heinburg. He was one of the most gifted astrophysicists of the 20th century. And when he wanted to break away from Harvard and fund his own research, he thought the best way to do it was to combine the two things he loved most. The sea and the stars above it. He built three cruise ships. The Zenith, the Starlight, and the Orion. While the passengers are living the high life and enjoying stargazing exhibitions, they're funding his research lab below decks."

"That's ingenious."

"He was quite the nonconformist. A very unorthodox man. His idea worked and he generated millions annually. He never needed funding. When he died, Dr. Hughes inherited it."

"How many people were aboard the vessel when the madness took them?"

"According to the passenger manifest, four thousand and twenty people."

"How many survivors?"

"We honestly don't know. All of the bodies have yet to be recovered. But we do know twelve uninfected made it off that ship."

"Do you have the names?"

"We'll start with Hybrid-1. Dr. Denarii Harmon, born April 19, 1980. Graduated from the University of Chicago with a Masters in Astronomy. Her father was the assistant to famed archaeologist Hanz Ruper. He was killed in an accident on site at one of their excavation digs. Her mother died in childbirth. Early testing indicated an elevated inclination towards science and mathematics. Her foster parents were advised to ᴬ enrichment activities towards science. Tᴸ somewhere along the line, all iᴺ Since the age of fourteen, she for petty theft, five for assault, conduct, and a partridge in a ⎰

"That's only sixteen," Burdₐ

"Yes, well, the last one stem with aerial hostile attackers on the ⹁

"What were the charges?"

Martyr exited the vessel footage. ⹁ listing several video files appeared. He selected:

GOVERNMENT PROPERTY
CHAD COMMAND
OPERATION STARFALL
INTERSTATE FOOTAGE
HOSTILES VS. HYBRID-1/ATLANTIS
PRIMORIDAL

"Violating CHAD protocol, not to mention a National Security breach, credit card fraud, skyjacking a military aircraft, grand theft auto, kidnapping, wreckless driving, wreckless endangerment, attempted murder, and lastly...for pissing me off."

Martyr pressed play and the interstate footage came to life. He watched his most valued Mach Menace Combat vehicle screaming down the Dan Ryan Expressway. Being steered by Hybrid-1 with the Atlantis Primordial in the passenger seat decapitating a rival extraterrestrial with his sword. The attack vessel veered out of control. It's headless unhuman driver spraying the windshield with blood as it slumped forward. Vehicles in nearby lanes crashed into one another. Metal grinding against metal. Several cars skidded out of control to avoid the flames igniting from the attack vessel. An eighteen-wheeler hit the median and flipped over. An explosion flooded the speakers of the conference room.

Martry pressed pause on the playback. "Both Hybrid-1 and her brother were being detained aboard the vessel until she slipped our Primoridal past security and decided to catch a red eye to Chicago. The incident was hardly possible to contain as our sentient friend got made on national television which went global within minutes. Our only advantage right now is the media is making up their own stories. But we all know that's not going to keep."

"And we have no idea as to his whereabouts at this point?" Presidnet Carter asked.

Martyr shook his head.

"So that's two missing," the Secretary said. "The other ten?"

Martyr pulled up a profile database.

Several headshots appeared on the table screen. One was a candid photo of Hybrid-2.

"We'll start with Hybrid-2, Harmon's brother, Angelo Roberts. He was born to the same parents on August 9th, 1978. After their death, he was adopted and took on their last name of Roberts. He spent the last 15 years in the Navy as a SEAL. He was thought dead after a failed recon mission in Iraq, until this footage aboard the vessel revealed his identity."

"Who identified him?"

"One of my own Blitzkrieg," Martyr answered. "A former SEAL. He did two tours with him in Iraq. After the recon went bad, I guess Roberts didn't feel deemed to inform the Casualty Office that he was still very much alive. His name was not on the passenger manifest. It's obvious he was a stowaway. Harbored on the Zenith by Harmon."

With a finger, Martyr slid Robert's profile aside on the table screen and pulled up the next missing person. "David Roachiere. One of Hybrid-1's research associates. He wasn't aboard the Zenith. But Harmon made contact with him shortly after she and our Primordial touched down in Chicago and traveled to the Naval Station in Great Lakes. He attended CIT in Pasadena and has a Masters in Quantum Computing. He also specializes in Quantum Mechanics. Ergo was the head of my Quantum Research team. He's also the one who removed the tracking chip from my Mach Menace ." Martyr closed his file and pulled up the next one. "Calvin Teixiere. He served with Roberts, also as a Marine pilot for 12 years. As far as combat goes in the 21st Century, he's seen it all. India, Palistine, Lybia, and Iraq. He volunteered for Special Forces training and joined the ranks of Marine Expeditionary Force for Operation Iraqi Freedom. Roberts made contact with him to commandere a helicopter in an attempt to be rescued from the Zenith when she began to sink."

He pulled up the next file. "This one here is of particular interest. Victor Mahr. You are looking at one of the most notorious war merchants out in force today. Knows almost every warlord and dictator on this planet by nickname basis. He's known on the Blackmarket as the Sandman. He was aboard the Zenith conducting business. Supposedly, unbeknownst to Dr. Hughes. At least that what she said."

"Do you believe her?" General Garrison asked.

"She passed the lie detector test. So that's proof enough. Until proven otherwise. However, I do know from intercepted phone conversations, the Captain and four of his crew members were in on it. They're whearabouts are unknown as well."

"You mean a war merchant was aboard that ship selling guns?" General Patton asked.

"He was the sole reason they had a fighting chance of coming out alive. He's also the sole reason six of my soldiers are dead. When we checked the wreckage for surviors, we found an aresnal of weapons. Most semi-auto with special modification. A few cases of assault rifles, and few bazookas. Anything else was used and discarded by Puckman, Mahr, our two hybrids and our Prime. It wasn't a massive load of artillery, but more than enough to kill my men and sink the Zenith a lot faster than she should have went down." He pulled up the next file. "Which brings us to his daughter, Kelisa Mahr. Looks to be the age of nine give or take a year or two. She was also on Puckman's footage though Victor wasn't. We don't know if he drowned or if he escaped from the ship with the others. So he's deemed as missing until proven otherwise."

"Good God," the President spat. "You couldn't pay somebody enough to make this shit up."

"At this time, you have no idea as to the whereabouts of our sentient being?" General Garrison asked.

"We have a search team tracking the surveillance radar stations for any sign of his aerial vessel. So far we've only picked up a few signals which were imprecise scrambles of interference given off by the vessel's radar deflection mechanism."

"So basically he's ducking you?"

"Not for long."

"Okay," Garrison cut in, "Let's concentrate on what we do have at the moment. How did the ship become infected? It couldn't have just been some wave of ecoli that took every passenger over."

"We don't know," Martyr answered honestly. "What we do know is we intercepted the SOS call made by Hybrid-2 at 2100 hours. Roberts reported the missing Captain had already abandoned ship. The vessel had left the coast of New Zealand just two hours prior at 1900 hours. At this time, she was already nearly a mile off shore and out to sea. With no power to the ship, wind began to push her even further starbord. Once we had access to the ship's surveillance feed, and we were able to see realtime what was happening to all of the passengers, I immediately contacted NORAD. Operation Blackstorm was put into effect immediately."

"Operation Blackstorm?"

"Yes, General. My secondary objective was the rescue and quarantine of any surviving passenger or crew, and irradication of any hostiles who proved to be neither."

"And your primary?" President Carter asked.

"My primary directive was to contain the infection, minimize the risk of transmission to the public, and secure the location of the contagion. To put it plainly, Mr. President, we sunk the ship. We had no other choice. Quaratine was top priority. Kill thousands, save millions. The choice was not a hard one."

"And how exactly did you go about doing that?"

"I sent in a mini-sub which came in close enough contact with the Zenith to breach her hull. With the ship only being a mile off shore at the time, the damage to the hull was made to look as if she came in contact with a rock bed on the sea floor— should Maritime investigators look into it. Without engine power, as predicted, the Zenith's speed began to decrease until she was dead in the water.

"We anticipated that the crew would contact harbour authorities and we intercepted those calls so no true Maritime SOS was ever made. I sent four mini-subs with twenty blitzkreig to erradicate and evacuate. During the six-hour mission, the ship lost all power, propulsion, and she began to list from side to side as the engine room took on water. When the lower decks were flooded, the Zenith capsized portside. With the ship on her side, all seventeen decks began to flood simultaneously. By then, any of the infected still onboard went down with the ship."

"What is this infection?"

"At this time, we honestly don't know. Right now, what we do know is that it appears to be contact only. Not airborn and it attacks the amygdala, the ventromedial hypothalamus, and the entire frontal lobe."

"Which means...what?"

"Well, we don't want to think zombies. But when one has seen what you've seen...Hell, you think zombies."

"And you think our visitor brought that virus here?"

"More than likely. Based on the information Hybrid-1 provided us, our Atlantis Prime has enemies. Enemies who have traveled a long way to make sure he never makes it home. That virus was not just meant for us. It was meant to kill him and anyone giving aid to him. Unfortunately it spreads like hellfire."

"And you actually think you can contain it?"

"I don't know," Martyr said. "The sea was doing that for us. Until it hit Australia."

"And what about the bodies floating in the Tasman Sea, Commander? Their water supply? Can they contract it from that?"

"They don't consume sea water. The majority of urban New Zealand citizens receive their water from more than 130 treatment plants that pull water from underground aquifers and lakes. In no small part, thanks to the New Zealand population being relatively low, the water in those reservoirs and lakes are more than enough to supply and recycle the water used for decades to come."

"And what about our dying sun?" the President asked. "How can we preserve that for decades to come?"

"Something is draining it much faster than Dr. Hughes predicted. Her solar model was set in years. Not days."

"Days?" General Garrison interrupted.

"What she predicted wasn't even close. Her estimate was five thousand years. Which is alarming enough. According to our new solar model, we have less than one year before our closest star is depleted."

"What then?"

"Our visitor has given the human race a chance for survival. He just doesn't know it yet."

"How is that?"

"We discovered a series of star coordinates in the navigational system of his vessel. Leading us right to the planet of Solarus. His home world. Based on the bio-studies we have on him, that tells us all we need to know about his planet. Oxygen, a thriving sun, and more than enough plant and mammal life to support mankind for eons."

"That's promising," Van Leuwin said. "But seeing the destination is one thing. Reaching it it another. How are we supposed to get there?"

"There must be a way of travel that we haven't discovered yet. And I emphasize yet. There is an interstellar device. And I belive it's here on earth."

"How do you know that," President Carter asked.

"Our visitor didn't just crash-land out of nowhere, Mr. President. Something brought him here. And it's that same means of interstellar travel that'll bring him home. We just have to find it."

"Well, when you do find it, I hope we can find a way to make it work. We still haven't even fully deciphered his language, let alone operate a device which we've never even seen."

"My team of linguists are working on that as we speak."

"Okay." President Carter leaned back in his chair. "And when you do fully decifer the language and you do find this means of *interstellar travel,* what makes you think our race will be welcomed to a foreign world? Have you even discussed this with our sentient subject? If not, we might want to run that by him the next time we see him. You've seen the carnage of that highway footage probably a thousand times since it happened. You've seen how violent he is. We show up on his planet uninvited, his indigenous could just blow us all to hell. Then what?"

"And more importantly, Commander," Burdt added, "is deciding who gets to go and who remains." Every head in the conference room turned his way. Martyr could tell Burdt felt the eyes of scrutiny piercing through him. The Secretary of Defense was quick to defend himself. "That sounds cruel and it sounds malicious as hell, but," he looked at President Carter, "you said it yourself, Mr. President. Just last week after that press conference went sour, you said if you could blast off into outerspace you would. And you would take only right wing registered voters with you."

"That was hyperboli, Burdt," Garrison spat.

"But that doesn't mean that he was wrong for thinking it or inappropriate for saying it. Look at our society today. We've got cities, states, and countries full of criminals. Murderers, rapists, thieves, vicious warlords, ruthless dictators. All scum. And you mean to tell me if you had the chance to weed out the righteous from the wicked, you'd be taking the dregs of society along with you to the new world, General? I don't think so. The herd needs thinning." Burdt looked back to the President. "We now have a sun that's withering like a shrinking violet as we speak. When this turns into a World War III shit fight for survival, and it will, you are the most powerful man in the free world, Mr. President. It will be you who has to make the hard and severe choices for the existence of the human race. That is not cruel. It's not malicious. That is just matter of fact."

"Actually," Martyr cut in, "it is cruel and it is malicious. But you're right nonetheless."

"Okay," Garrison said, "before this dog day begins, how are you going to find our alien friend? If we can in fact call him that."

"I don't have to, General. We don't need to find him. We need to find what he can't." He fingered another file. A virtual image emerged before them. "This is what we're looking for. The Solarians know it as the Arcanum Confinium. Arcani means bridge. Astranum means stars. Confinium means to an end. A travel of limits. I call this interstellar device the Starbridge or the Allstar. And when our sentient friend discovers that we've found it, he'll come to us. And when he does, Harmon will come with him."

SIGN UP FOR
THE N & M NEWSLETTER
AND LOOK OUT FOR DETAILS
ON HOW TO ENTER FOR CHAVOHN NAKIA'S
'FREE FOR LIFE' CONTEST.

THE WINNER WILL RECEIVE NAKIA'S LATEST
PUBLISHED NOVEL FOR FREE...FOR LIFE!

For a sneak peak at all things Cabrini Green visit:

chavohnnakia.com

facebook.com/cabrinigreen

or visit The Non-Blog for posts, events,

give aways and more at:

starfallseries.com/thenonblog

(be patient while it loads)

and follow Nakia & Masters at:

twitter.com/nakiamasters

twitter.com/chavohnnakia

instagram.com/nakiamasters

CPSIA information can be obtained
at www.ICGtesting.com
Printed in the USA
BVHW04s0220250418
514384BV00001B/8/P